Joe Treasure was born in Cheltenham and
studied English at Oxford. He has lived in
California and in Wales, and is a graduate of
Royal Holloway's Creative Writing MA.
His first novel, *The Male Gaze*, was
published by Picador in 2007.

Also by Joe Treasure

THE MALE GAZE

JOE TREASURE

BESOTTED

PICADOR

First published 2010 by Picador

This edition first published 2011 by Picador
an imprint of Pan Macmillan, a division of Macmillan Publishers Ltd
Pan Macmillan, 20 New Wharf Road, London N1 9RR
Basingstoke and Oxford
Associated companies throughout the world
www.panmacmillan.com

ISBN 978-0-330-44898-7

9 8 7 6 5 4 3 2 1

A CIP catalogue record for this book is available from
the British Library.

Printed in the UK by CPI Mackays, Chatham ME5 8TD

Visit **www.picador.com** to read more about all our books
and to buy them. You will also find features, author interviews and
news of any author events, and you can sign up for e-newsletters
so that you're always first to hear about our new releases.

For Rita Looney

AUGUST 1982 KILROSS

To kill time, Michael followed the old Cork Road from the town square over the bridge towards the fields. The heat was oppressive, but it was some relief to walk. When there was no distraction, the anxiety was a solid thing that pressed on him so that his breath was tight in his throat. He'd left his mother back at the house, trying to get through to the school office, but there was something wrong with his gran's phone, so maybe they wouldn't find out how badly he'd fucked up until they were all back in England.

There was a squat row of cottages, then the cattle market. He turned into the yard and walked between the pens where cows scuffed and snorted. A bull startled him, clattering down the ramp of a cattle truck. Inside the shed he was assaulted by the smothering warmth and the smell of livestock. He thought he might be challenged, but if the men took notice of him it was to mumble words of greeting with a wink or a nod.

A young priest asked him was he home for good and would he be staying above at Keilly's. Michael shrugged and said he didn't know any Keilly. 'No offence,' the priest said. 'I took you for someone else.' And he stood with the dust staining the skirts of his cassock, twisting his hands in embarrassment.

In the saleroom, a window in the corrugated-iron roof let in more light. A raked circle of benches faced the auctioneer's box across the ring. The farmers sat with their knees splayed, gripping their thighs, shirts dark with sweat. Michael slid onto the end of a seat and edged his way along to get a better view. He had his sketchbook in his pocket but wasn't going to draw where people might look over his shoulder. Five heifers jostled for space in the ring, splattering their dung on the concrete. A sixth hung back in the gate. A shrivelled man in a brown coat gave the straggler a thwack on the rump and she joined the others.

'You're from England.' The young priest was sliding onto the bench beside him.

'Yes.'

'So you're visiting like me.'

'Just for a week or so. We leave the day after tomorrow.'

'Saturday. Me too.'

'But you're not from England.'

'No, Dublin. I'm leaving for Dublin.' The conversation stumbled. The eyes of the priest flared and darkened and in his lap his long fingers twisted awkwardly.

Michael wondered if he was really a priest. There was no clerical collar. He might almost be an altar boy who had come from morning Mass, leaving his surplice in the vestry.

'I'm Fergal Noonan, by the way.' He offered Michael his hand. 'I'm sorry about before. I thought you were someone else entirely.'

Michael shrugged. 'So are you here to bless the cows, then, or what?'

'Oh no!' Fergal Noonan's laughter went on for longer than necessary. 'The cows don't need any blessing from me.

My uncle thinks if I'm to minister to regular people I should learn more about their lives, and educate myself about commerce. It's my uncle I'm staying with in Kilross. I have studying to do, but here I am anyhow to see how cattle are bought and sold. I'll be sent to England, I should think, and will be in a city among factory workers, so . . .' He trailed off, turning bashfully to watch the progress of the auction.

It was more than the cassock that set him apart. He sat with an upright posture. His face was studious but not pale, and not reddened either like the farmers around him, but with a strong earthy colour. He was older, Michael guessed, than his awkwardness made him seem.

The auctioneer banged his gavel, and the heifers crowded towards the exit, the shrunken man prodding them with his stick. An arthritic hand fell on Fergal Noonan's shoulder, and he turned to greet the old farmer who sat behind him.

'So, was it you bought my heifers, Father?'

Fergal laughed to show that he knew he was being teased, to show that he didn't mind. 'Oh now, Mr Crottie, you know I'm not yet ordained.'

'And how long before the learner plates come off?'

'A while yet, I'd say, Mr Crottie.'

'And would this be Moira Doyle's boy?'

'Doyle?' Fergal turned back to Michael, his face animated. 'You're a Doyle?'

'Well, Cartwright, actually. Michael Cartwright. But my mother's name used to be Doyle.'

'Good day to you, so,' the old man said. His voice sounded squeezed, leaking air at the edges. 'You can tell old man Doyle that Sprinter says hello and I'll maybe see him below at Docherty's for a jar.' He rose stiffly, supporting himself with a stick, and moved towards the cattle pens.

'So you're a Doyle,' Fergal said. 'That makes us second or third cousins, I think. Do you know Dennis O'Connor at all?'

'I'm not sure.'

'He sells suits and jackets. Away beyond the church in Freemantle Street. He's my uncle. I think maybe your gran's an O'Connor.'

Michael shrugged. 'Maybe.' He'd never thought much about family names.

'And you came by yourself?'

'With my parents, and Kieran and the girls.'

'Kieran?'

'My brother.'

'Older or younger?'

'Younger, but only by seven minutes.'

'You're twins. So next time I see you it might be him I'm seeing and not you at all.'

'We're not identical. People expect us to act alike and be good at the same things, but we're just brothers really.'

'It must be grand, even so, to have a twin.'

The voice of the auctioneer rose above the mumbled conversations and the animal noises, the rhythm changing at the nods of the bidders. The strange music of it reminded him of his gran saying the rosary, the way she would cut in each time with the next Hail Mary before the rest of them had finished the response. They'd knelt among the living-room furniture, the first night of their Kilross holiday, fractious and disgruntled after the cramped car journey and the ferry crossing. As soon as they'd finished, before they could get to their feet, his mother had launched into the Litany of the Virgin – *Holy Mary, mother of God, virgin of virgins, mother of Christ, mother of the Church*. She'd done this to please her own mother, perhaps, or to punish the rest of them with more kneeling. *Mother most pure, mother most chaste, mirror of justice, seat of wisdom, mystical rose, tower of ivory, gate of heaven, morning star* . . . And in his head, Michael had started improvising a nonsense litany of his own to the Blessed Virgin Mam – *queen of martyrs, tower of dishes, mangler of language, thrower of wobblies, door of the larder, Evening Gazette* . . . When he was bored with that he had started on his father.

He winced now in anticipation of his father's anger.

'Something troubling you, Michael?'

Over Fergal's shoulder, he saw little Emily silhouetted between cattle pens. She moved towards him and light from a high window caught her face. Her eyes were solemn under her fringe. He felt his stomach lurch.

Fergal turned to see where he was looking.

'I'm wanted,' Michael told him.

'You're leaving already?'

'I'd better.' The school must have called back with his results. He squeezed past Fergal's legs and climbed down onto the concrete.

'Well, I'll maybe see you again.'

'I don't know,' Michael said. 'I don't know what I'll be doing.' He followed Emily into the yard. She was frowning as though ready to deliver a lecture – she was earnest for an eleven-year-old. The certainty of failure gathered inside him and for a moment he had difficulty breathing.

It occurred to him to pray but he rejected the thought at once. What could he ask for short of a miracle?

The front room was stuffy and smelled of soot. There was a clatter of saucepans from the kitchen and a sound of sawing in the back garden. Michael's twin brother sat at the table by the window with a book.

'You did OK, then?' Michael asked him.

'Yeah, I did OK.'

'More than OK, I bet.'

'I got a B in French.' Kieran spoke defensively, as though the bond between them might be re-established by this small lapse.

Katherine had appeared at the foot of the stairs. Her face was crumpled. She was thirteen and newly alive to life's tragic possibilities. 'Mikey,' she said, running towards him. 'I'm so sorry.' She threw her arms round his waist. 'Stupid O-level people. What do they know?'

'A lot, actually,' Emily said. 'They know about every subject there is.'

The back door swung open and their father stood watching them. 'I've got a job for you, Michael, if you've got nothing to do but mooch about.' He moved out of sight. After a moment they heard the handsaw again.

'They've been waiting for you,' Kieran said.

Michael disentangled himself from Katherine. 'Yes, I know.' *Tower of scaffolding,* he thought, beginning his litany, *reader of pamphlets, scourge of the clergy, bane of the council, drowner of kittens, prick of self-righteousness.* For some reason it wasn't as funny to him as his mother's.

Gran came out of the kitchen, a slight figure dressed from her shoes to her collar in black. Half a cigarette dangled from her lower lip and fluttered up and down as she breathed. 'Ah, here now,' she said, as though these words were heavy with meaning. Looking up at Michael, she took his hand in hers. Her eyes were piercing and full of sadness. 'You're a good boy.' With skeletal fingers she pushed a coin into his palm, closing his hand around it. 'Take your girl out,' she said and limped on towards the front door. Michael looked at the coin. It was an old threepenny bit, darkened by use.

He found his father sawing. He'd removed the door from the outside toilet and was taking half an inch off its bottom edge. There was a wild look in his eyes as though the door was getting what it deserved. Every now and then, with a quick move of his left hand, he swept back a strand of grey hair from his forehead. He was older than other people's fathers and understood nothing, but there was this energy in him that made him dangerous. Behind him in the whitewashed wall, the doorway buzzed with flies.

Michael looked down the garden towards the river and thought he would like to wade across it and keep walking and not stop until he dropped to the ground with exhaustion.

The loose strip at the bottom of the door began to flap.

'Hold it steady, would you,' his father said.

With two clean strokes of the saw the loose piece came free and Michael was left holding it.

'Well, it looks as though you've made a mess of things.'

Michael stared down at the flaking surface of the door.

'I'm not going to waste my breath reproaching you.

7

You're not cut out for school work and that's all there is to it.'

'What did I get?'

'What are you going to do to justify your upkeep, that's the question? I was giving my parents a wage packet every Friday by the time I was your age.'

'Michael!' His mother had appeared at the back door. There was a sob in her voice. She held a scrap of paper in her hand. 'How could you? And Kieran doing so well.'

'I hate that school, Mam. You don't know what it's like.'

'Oh, Michael, if it hadn't been for me they'd have thrown you out years ago. Will I ever forget that third-form parents' evening, and it was Father Brendan who said, *If the boy turns over a new leaf, Mrs Cartwright, I'll stand behind him all the way*. And there was me promising him you had it in you, and now you throw this in my face.' She flapped the piece of paper at him.

'Michael's a dreamer, that's all there is to it.' His father rattled through tools in search of something. 'And he won't wake up until he has to earn his own living.'

'What did I get in art?'

'Art? Never mind about art. It's always the line of least resistance with you, isn't it – whatever comes easy. You won't earn your living with art.'

'And you could have passed science,' his mother said, 'if you'd put your mind to it. Look at Kieran. Nine months you had together in my womb. You might have learned something from him. And what about Christopher? He sailed through all his exams. Even Eileen passed biology, though she couldn't abide it, and had that hoyden Sister

Patrick teaching her. Poor Eileen! Light a candle for me this afternoon, she said to me once, for I have a rat to dissect.'

Christopher, who could do anything he turned his hand to, and Eileen the slogger, and Matt who was in everyone's bad books since he'd dropped out of teacher training to live in a squat – they'd all left home, lucky bastards, but here they all were still, cluttering everyone's heads, crowding the air from the backyard.

Emily wandered out. 'I think you'll find it's time for lunch,' she said.

'You, put the Hoover round and be quick about it or you'll feel the back of my hand. Jack, talk to this boy.'

When they were alone, his father said, 'It seems to me you've got a lot of thinking to do.'

Together they put the door in place. Michael held the hinges against the doorjamb. His father drove the screws with rhythmic twists of his hand, the tendons in his forearm tightening and relaxing, his rolled sleeve flapping at the elbow.

When he was done, he dropped the screwdriver into his tool bag and stooped to pick up the saw. 'And that's not an excuse for you to hang about all day. I'm sick of the sight of you doing nothing.' He turned in the doorway. 'Come to me if you need something to do.'

Out in the river, two men in waders cast their lines upstream and the green water tumbled around their legs. One of them raised his hand in greeting. Michael imitated the gesture, imagining himself the autonomous being for whom the fisherman had mistaken him, an adult who might raise a hand in greeting to another adult. The man drew his rod back behind him. As the line whipped forward, Michael caught a glint of blue, high against the trees. He breathed in slowly and the air felt hot and sluggish in his mouth.

Vaulting the wall, he followed the river downstream, behind the houses on Strand Street, past the church and out into the fields where cows huddled in the shade of trees and hedges, too dazed by the heat to move.

He took his sketchbook from his pocket and settled against a trunk. For a while, he did what he could to capture the shapes of things, scoring the shadows into the paper and leaving space to suggest the light, but the dizzying haze was beyond his skill. He pulled out a paperback and tried to read, but the words made as much sense as the insects buzzing on the riverbank.

He was thinking about things that had come to an end sooner than he'd expected – art lessons in the cloisters and down by the playing field with a stool and a drawing board, RI with Father Kenton, orchestra practice. And he thought about Salema who came down from the convent every week with the other girls and sat by the accompanist to turn the pages and sometimes, when the accompanist wasn't there, played the piano herself. He wondered what her O-level results were like. Perfect, probably, like her piano-playing, like everything about her. Even her name was delicate and mysterious. Salema Nikolaidis. It sounded Greek, but someone had said she was Indian and she looked as though she might be. From his seat among the trombones he'd heard the timpanist call her Saliva Knickers and the other brass players had laughed, and he'd allowed himself to smirk and felt immediately a pang of guilt at this small betrayal. One fumbled attempt to ask her out was as close as he'd got. And now he might never see her again.

It was dusk when he returned, coming in the back way among low whitewashed cottages with tin roofs. Beyond the trees, the sky was losing its colour. There was a prickle of moisture in the air as though the stifling weather might be about to break. He pushed against the back door and found it locked. He rested for a moment with his head against the wood. A breeze had begun to agitate the trees along the riverbank, ruffling the runner beans and the fuchsia by the kitchen window.

From an upper room came a sound of keening. Unsettled, he picked up his father's sawhorse and positioned it at the end of the outhouse, on the uneven ground next to the compost heap. Raising a foot to the top of the garden wall, he scrabbled up onto the slates. He hugged the roof while his heartbeat slowed. The sound came again, familiar after all – a long, low note on a violin. He stood, balancing on the slope. Through the window he saw his brother, head tilted, bowing arm rising towards the wardrobe.

Kieran had set up his music stand beside the iron bed. His eyes met Michael's but showed no reaction. His attention was on the sound he was pulling from the instrument with his elbow and his bent wrist and the bow drawn across his body. Michael raised his arms in mirror image, miming the action of a left-handed violinist. What must it be like to be Kieran, he wondered, to have your impulses so conveniently aligned with adult expectations, to be driven today to do what tomorrow you would be glad to have done?

He tipped his head towards his right shoulder and tried to intercept Kieran's gaze. He was invisible, he realized, standing on the dark side of the glass. If Kieran could see anything other than the colour of the note he was playing, it was his own reflection.

Michael tapped with his fingers on the glass. Startled, Kieran peered into the darkness, then crossed the room to open the window. 'Where *were* you?' he said, his mouth wide with the pleasure of seeing his brother.

'I don't know. Wandering around. There's nothing out there for miles.'

'What were you doing?'

'Nothing much. I drew a bit. I tried to draw some donkeys but they kept moving.'

'Can I see?'

'No, it's crap. I can't draw.' He climbed over the sill into the bedroom.

'You got an A.'

'An A. Big deal. Doesn't mean I can draw. Where's everyone gone?'

'Mam went with Gran to bingo. Dad took the girls out for a walk.'

'What did you have for tea?'

'Boiled ham and carrots. Haven't you eaten?'

'Not recently.'

'There's probably some leftovers in the fridge.'

Michael sank onto the bed. He thought about boiled ham, the thick salty smell of it. He'd missed lunch as well as tea. 'Maybe in a minute,' he said.

With the violin cradled on his chest, Kieran had begun moving his fingers across the strings. He was looking at

Michael, then at nothing in particular, his head leaning towards the instrument. He played a slow phrase, feeling his way from note to note.

'Sounds nice,' Michael said as the sound faded.

'As a dirge, maybe, but these are semiquavers, look.' He pointed with the tip of his bow, tapping the music. Perched on their stalks, the notes fluttered above the stave.

'It looks difficult.'

'The chromatic bit's not so hard. It's this jump here . . .' He played the sequence again, pausing at the awkward interval. 'When I do it up to speed, it's a mess.' He played it faster, fumbling the same two notes. Groaning with exasperation, he dropped the violin onto the bed and began adjusting the tension in his bow.

'Were they worried about me, then – while I was gone?'

Kieran shrugged. 'They were going on about your results.'

'Still?'

'What do you mean, still? Don't you think it's important?'

'Don't you start.'

'I'm not starting anything, I'm just saying. They were arguing about it.'

'About what?'

'Mam thinks they should ask the school to let you back. Dad said he wasn't going cap in hand to Father Brendan, tugging his forelock, etc. Then he went up on the roof to a fix a leak.'

'What leak?'

'Search me! A leak, that's what he said.'

'There is no leak. How would he know there's a leak? It hasn't rained since we've been here.'

'Well, he went up on the roof anyway.'

'I would've thought they'd celebrate your results with me out of the way. You might have all drunk champagne or something.'

'Well, we bloody didn't, all right. They just had a fight about you.'

'So what was the point of you doing all that work, then?'

'I don't do it to keep them happy, if that's what you mean.'

'No, you do it because you're a creep.'

Kieran scowled, and the bow moved in his hand as though he might do something violent with it. 'Just . . . go to hell.'

'Go to hell yourself.' Michael was halfway down the stairs when he heard the bedroom door slam and felt the stale air move around him.

In the kitchen he opened the fridge and squatted in front of it. There was a slab of ham standing on a plate in its own congealed grease. He cleared a space on the counter top, pushing aside some unwashed dishes, a spanner, a copy of the *Cork Gazette*. He sawed off a couple of slices of soda bread and a slab of ham. The first bite of his sandwich was bulky and dry in his mouth. Up in the bedroom Kieran had gone back to his violin practice. Again and again the same half-dozen notes scuttled upwards as though attempting to take flight.

*

It had felt almost as if it might rain, but by next morning there had been no change. Weary with the heat, Michael stared at the racks of shirts and ties and braces in O'Connor's gentleman's outfitters and listened to Dennis O'Connor quizzing his father.

'And how's herself? That's grand, Jack, that's grand. And this is your fourth? And the older ones up at the university. What a credit to you and Moira. And you'll be following one day soon, I suppose.' O'Connor had turned to Michael. 'Wasn't it yourself I saw yesterday evening below at the river with a book in your hand? Sure, you're a great reader like all of them, I've no doubt. And tell me what was it you were reading?'

Michael blinked. A girl with an armful of socks stood watching him. She chewed gum with her lips drawn back from her teeth. She was Michael's age, more or less. There was something insolent in the steady way she looked at him.

'It was Schopenhauer,' Michael said. '*The World as Will and Idea.*'

'God help us but the lad's got a rare head on his shoulders, would you not say?' O'Connor faced the others theatrically, as though Michael was his performing monkey and he was about to pass the hat round.

Michael felt exposed. He had trapped himself by answering honestly. He should have made something up.

'He's got his mother's brains,' Jack Cartwright said.

Pillar of Englishness, Michael thought, *disdainer of shopkeepers, persecutor of the afflicted, dungheap of smuggery.*

'Indeed he has, indeed he has, and a fine-looking young man he is too. And we'll find a suit that will do him justice.'

While O'Connor looked along the rail, Michael spoke urgently to his father, lowering his voice so as not to be overheard by the girl. 'Honestly, Dad, what do I need a suit for?'

'No one's going to employ you dressed like a punk rocker.'

'I'm not a punk rocker.'

'Like an anarchist, then.'

'I'm not an anarchist, Dad. Everyone dresses like this.'

'Nobody I know. There'd be raised eyebrows if the new trainee at W. H. Smith's turned up to work dressed like an anarchist.'

Michael wanted to know what W. H. Smith's had to do with anything, but O'Connor had returned with a selection of suits. Since he didn't like any of them, Michael tried on the first one he was offered. It was tight where it should have been loose, and loose where it should have been tight. The lapels stuck out like wings, and the trousers, unbelievably, were flared. It was a suit a teacher might wear, one of the lay teachers, like Mr Hughes who explained rugby tactics on the board when they were supposed to be doing European history.

The girl who chewed gum looked up from the shelf she was stacking. Michael felt the heat rising to his face and a prickle of sweat on his skin. His father was nodding cautiously.

'It's a touch long in the sleeve,' O'Connor said, 'but we can fix that for you so you'd never know the difference.' He turned one of the sleeves under and caught it with a pin he found in his own lapel. 'I could have it down to you at the house later this morning, Jack. What do you say?'

When Michael came out of the changing room in his own clothes, the girl appeared by his side, with her arms full of trousers. 'Schopenhauer,' she said. 'He'd be a philosopher, I suppose.'

Michael shrugged. 'I only got it out of the town library to annoy Father Kenton. He's my RI teacher at school. I don't know anything about philosophy, really.'

'And what does Mr Schopenhauer have to say about the world and the will?'

'Well, I haven't finished it yet, but as far as I can make out he says the world is basically like a shadow of what's really behind it, which he calls the idea. A bit like Plato.' His voice had become hoarse. Tasting the dryness of his mouth, he swallowed and cleared his throat. 'And the nearest we can get to reality is art. And about will he says you can't control anything because life is basically suffering, so morality is irrelevant. Sorry, I've got that a bit muddled.'

'I think you must have. Morality irrelevant, indeed! I'd like to hear what Father O'Leary would say about that.'

Michael laughed. 'When Father Kenton saw me reading it before class, he said it's good to know what the opposition thinks and why don't I try *Das Kapital* next or the Koran, but I couldn't tell if he was being serious because you never can with Father Kenton . . .' He stopped, embarrassed to be talking so much.

The girl's eyes had widened, as though Michael had let her in on a conspiracy. 'Well, Michael Cartwright, you're a wonder all right.' She smiled, and pink strings of gum stretched between her teeth. 'Will we be seeing you at the dance later?'

'I don't know. What kind of dance?'

'Just a dance. In the hall over by the church.'

'I don't dance, really.'

'Who cares? It'll just be girls gabbing and lads getting drunk, anyhow. Who wants to dance in this heat? You can maybe tell me some more about Schopenhauer.'

'I'll have to ask.'

The girl glanced at O'Connor, who was following Michael's father to the door. 'I'll look out for you, so.' She gave him one last look at her teeth and the plug of chewing gum, before turning back to her work.

Michael made himself scarce for the rest of the morning. When he showed up at the house, the atmosphere in the living room was murderous. His mother stood in front of the fireplace, hands on hips, face taut with anger. Katherine squatted on the staircase.

Hunched in a chair staring at the floor, Kieran was muttering, 'All I said was no. You don't have to go on about it.' The violin lay on the table beside its open case.

Jack came in, sweating from his work on the roof.

'Oh, Jack!' Moira said, choking back tears. 'To be humiliated and made a laughing stock, and in front of Dennis O'Connor, and his nephew who's practically a priest.'

'For pity's sake, what now?'

Michael saw his new suit hanging from the curtain rail and understood without needing to be told. O'Connor had called, bringing Fergal Noonan with him, and Kieran had refused to play his violin.

Kieran was still scowling at the floor. 'Well, why couldn't you just leave me alone?'

'Oh yes.' Moira's voice shook with scorn. 'It would be a fine thing if we'd all just leave you alone to starve in the gutter, and when you'd cut yourself off from your family you'd quickly learn how little help you'd get from those clever friends of yours who teach you to talk down to your mother.'

'All right, then, play it yourself.' Stung to a fury, Kieran jumped to his feet and swept the music from the stand, thrusting it in his mother's face, the pages flapping at the end of his arm. 'Here, take it, you stupid woman. If you want to hear the blasted piece, you practise two hours a day for seven years and get backache and a sore wrist and a red lump on your neck and then you can play it when-ever you bloody well like.' He hurled the music towards the ceiling. It fluttered above Moira's head and took a swooping dive towards the fireplace.

Before it had crumpled on the hearthrug, Jack Cartwright's hand caught Kieran on the side of the head. 'You're not too old,' he said, grabbing him by the arm. 'I'll take a stick to you.'

'She started it.'

'Talking to your mother like that.' Jack's jaw was clenched with the effort of a second blow. It landed awk-wardly, as Kieran, white-faced and gasping, squirmed free and made for the door.

Michael felt the old fear clutching at him, but a kind of exaltation also, as though bobbing on the wake of his brother's defiance. He had a sense of the system cracking under pressure, its lunacy unmasked. He thought of Caligula appointing his horse to the senate – Father Kenton's favourite image of the pagan world – and the tension in him broke with a snort of laughter. Then, from nowhere, he felt inclined to cry. Standing in his grandparents' sooty living room, among the rage and the sobbing, he felt the weight settle on him. He was to blame, not Kieran, because he'd upset everyone with his results. And there was no excuse for it – they were right about that. It wasn't that the work was too hard. It was just that after all these years there was so much of it. It was like the basement at home, so crammed with junk you wouldn't know where to start.

Later Moira Cartwright fussed over Kieran at the tea table. Was the fish not done the way he liked it? Would he eat more potato, or the last of the peas? There was something abject in her tone that made Michael want to hurt her.

Only Jack remained buoyant, giving a brittle performance of unconcern as he read extracts from *The Times*. He practised his elocution on Israel's bombing of Beirut. 'You should all be taking more of an interest in world events,' he said, offering as an example the troops Reagan was sending to Lebanon. His tone altered when it came to the British news. 'They're still going on about the sinking of the *Belgrano*.' He shook his head in disbelief. 'We liberate the Falklands, and the lefties can't bear it. Can you imagine Churchill having to worry about exclusion zones? He didn't defeat Hitler with a bunch of lawyers looking over his shoulder.'

No one rose to the challenge. An uneasy peace settled on the room as they ate. Michael picked at his food. His suit hung at the window, a dark shape against the evening sun.

The first person he recognized at the dance was Fergal, looking even more out of place here in his cassock than at the cattle market.

Fergal seemed relieved to see him. 'You came, then. Peggy said you would.'

'Peggy who?'

'My cousin Peggy. Uncle Dennis's girl.'

So she was O'Connor's daughter. 'I almost didn't. They would have stopped me if they could. My dad would probably lock me in the cellar if he could get away with it.'

'I'm sorry to hear that.'

They stood for a moment, watching the band and the dancers, pretending that these things interested them. Michael wondered why he had said that about being locked in the cellar.

'I'm in trouble too,' Fergal said. 'Peggy's in a mood, and who can blame her – lumbered with me.'

'Why did you come, then?'

'Because Uncle Dennis insisted.'

'You could have said no.'

'Like your brother, this afternoon, when your mother asked him to play his violin?'

'Oh, that. Was it awful?'

'A little tense, I'd say.'

'After you'd gone, Mam had a meltdown and Dad went ape-shit.'

'Is that any way to talk of your parents?'

'You don't know them. They're lunatics.'

'That might be an exaggeration.'

'How would you know?'

Seeing Fergal's discomfort, Michael repented his sharp response. 'They're angry,' he explained, 'because I failed my O-levels.'

Fergal looked surprised. 'They didn't mention it.'

'They're hardly going to talk about it, are they?'

The band wore velvet suits and frilly shirts. They played synthesizers and sang in sobbing voices about a woman called Mona, who'd left the backstreets of Havana, and locked her feelings in a cupboard to prowl the catwalks like a leopard, like a tiger, like a puma, poor loveless Mo, oh, oh, ona.

'You shouldn't worry,' Fergal said at last. 'There's more than one way to skin a cat.'

Michael wanted to ask what the hell this was supposed to mean, but someone lurched against him, spilling beer down his T-shirt and onto his jeans. It was an older boy with a strong pockmarked face, who was turning unsteadily to see who had knocked into him, saying, 'Will you fuck off out of it, you fucking heathen.'

'You mind your mouth, Dan Sheahan.' Peggy O'Connor was coming towards them from the dance floor. She wore ankle boots and a pea-green dress. 'My cousin Michael doesn't want to be listening to language like that. My cousin Michael's a rare reader. He knows all about the world and the will. Isn't that right, Michael?' She eyed him mischievously through clumps of hair.

'Not really,' Michael said.

'And how about the flesh and the devil?' Dan Sheahan asked him. 'Are they on your reading list too?'

'I don't think Schopenhauer believed in the devil,' Michael said. 'I'm not sure, I haven't got that far yet.'

'Well, fuck Schopenhauer.' Dan Sheahan grabbed Michael's shoulder, breathing alcohol fumes in his face. 'I believe in the devil, right enough, strutting through Derry and Belfast, seeking whom he may devour, with his automatic rifle and his road blocks, and he's a fucking Englishman.'

'Ah come on, Dan, you might show a little more politeness to a guest in our country.'

'If it's a guest he thinks he is, and not the landlord come to visit the peasantry.'

'I'm sure Michael doesn't think that, do you, Michael?' Peggy said.

With his mouth open to speak, Michael found himself jostled towards her. She smelt of musk and calamine lotion. Her bra strap was slipping down across her arm.

'Well, Michael,' she said, 'what was it you were saying?'

'I'm only half English.'

'So then, maybe the Irish half will ask a girl to dance?'

'Yes, of course. Sorry. To be honest, it's not really my kind of music.'

'Well, I wouldn't say it's mine either, but you take what you can get in Kilross.'

'So very sorry,' Dan said imitating Michael's accent, 'not really, to be honest, my kind . . .'

'Now, Peggy,' Fergal said, 'perhaps it's time we went on home.'

'I'm talking, do you mind?' She shrugged Fergal's hand from her arm.

Fergal shrank back into himself, biting his lip.

'Seven hundred years,' Dan said, 'and British soldiers still in our country, and what do we get from Thatcher's gang but more of the same.'

Peggy gave Michael a challenging look. 'So are you coming, or what?'

Without waiting for an answer, she headed into the crowd, her boots clacking on the wooden floor.

Michael turned to follow her, but Dan Sheahan held him by the elbow and spoke into his ear. 'Someone should put a bomb under that bitch.'

Peggy was bouncing up and down out of time with the music, pushing one shoulder forward then the other so that her earrings clanked. Her eyes were closed. Michael turned back to Dan, puzzled at his vehemence. 'She's only dancing.'

'Not Peggy, you eejit. I'm talking about your Prime Minister.'

'She's not my Prime Minister. I'd never have voted for her.'

'Now, Dan,' Fergal said, 'this is not the time for politics.'

'But this is the time, Fergal, no time better, and I'll give you ten good reasons why: ten good men dying a martyr's death in the Maze, ten families left to mourn.' Dan pushed his face towards Michael's and began listing the names. 'Bobby Sands, Patsy O'Hara, Mickey Devine . . .'

Michael knew about the hunger strike – the slow drama had played out on the national news and the older members of the family had argued over the dinner table about the rights and wrongs of it – but it was a shock to come face to face with Dan's anger, to feel implicated, to know that he had paid it too little attention.

Feeling Dan's grip slacken, he pulled himself free and followed Peggy onto the dance floor. He turned and caught Fergal's reproachful gaze. Dan, who had taken a swig from his beer glass, wiped his mouth with the back of his hand and winked. Michael shifted from one foot to the other, trying to feel like somebody dancing.

Peggy put her arms round his neck and spoke into his ear. 'Are you having a good time?'

The floor was beginning to fill up, but Michael could still feel Dan Sheahan's eyes on him. 'What is this music? Why do they call themselves Chateau Nuremberg?'

'How should I know?'

'Are they German, then, or French or what?'

'They're from Cork and they're shite.'

'Who's Dan?'

'Would you like to go somewhere we can hear ourselves think?'

'Is he your boyfriend?'

She was leading him past the stage. Her dress glinted as she moved through the lights. In the corner of the hall, half a dozen steps led down to a narrow door. The corridor beyond was cluttered with stacks of chairs and instrument cases. It was cooler under the stage and the noise of the band was dulled.

'Who is he, then, Dan?'

'Dan is a professional wanker.' She pushed open a fire escape and they stepped outside.

'So he's not your boyfriend?'

'Yes, no, maybe. What do you care? Are you proposing? Do you think we should run away together?' She was smiling at him.

'I was just curious.'

'I've been out with him a few times. Maybe he thinks he's my boyfriend. Come on, I want to show you something.'

She led him along the side of the hall on a narrow path between high brick walls. There was a faint stir of wind. It felt cool where his shirt was damp. At the back of the hall, the path turned along the edge of a graveyard. The stones stood like grazing cattle, oddly spaced. The ground rose towards an iron fence and a handful of trees. Peggy turned and met him with her mouth open on his. She kissed him energetically, tangling her hands in the hair on the back of his head in a way that seemed grown-up to him, like the way women kissed in films. Her mouth tasted of alcohol and stale cigarettes. He could feel the zip of her dress running down her back. So I'm to be thrown out of school, he thought, and I'll wear a suit from nine to five in W. H. Smith's, but there's always this.

She drew her head back and looked at him steadily. 'Are you being punished?'

'Punished? What for?' It was unsettling that she should ask this, as though she could read his mind.

'You tell me. Who'd come from London to buy a suit in O'Connor's?'

'I don't live in London.'

'From England, then.'

'It's your father's shop.'

'And he's welcome to it.'

As he moved to kiss her again, she turned her head to the side. 'Look at those sad tossers,' she said.

Michael turned quickly, thinking they were being watched. But she was pointing towards the graveyard. There were angels and crosses and stones with curved tops and the sky turning red behind them.

'It's what I wanted to show you. Half my ancestors are buried here. They're rotting down there in the soil, O'Connors and Sheahans and Doyles and Keneallys. And they were rotting before they died, half of them.'

'Some of my ancestors too, then.' It was strange to think of it. All these people he knew nothing about.

Peggy still had one hand in his hair, the other was at her mouth, the teeth tearing at a nail. 'There are those who'd have me live and die in Kilross, though I wouldn't call it living.'

'And will you?'

'Jesus, no! I shall be gone before anyone knows it. I shall do what your mother did.'

'My mother?'

'Did you not know she ran away from home? Set off to work, cool as you like. She had a bag of clothes hidden away. She phoned that night from Fishguard. She was fifteen years old.'

'Is that true?'

'That's the way I always heard it.' She leant back against the wall. 'It's why my father envies her.'

It was a new thought to him that anyone might envy his mother. 'Because she got away?'

'Yes, I suppose. But not that so much – getting away is our main occupation. We've always been good at boarding ships and planes and not coming back. And then writing songs about it – how cut up I am to be here in America when I could be starving back home with me ma, boo hoo. Your mother wasn't the first and she won't be the last. The way she did it, though – that was something. She's got spirit all right, your mother.' She gave him a look, as though he'd disagreed with her. 'It's not easy. It's not everyone's as free as you.'

'How do you mean?'

She frowned and pulled him towards her. 'If I had your brains I should conquer the world.' She was teasing him, but he didn't mind. She levered one foot from its boot and moved it between his legs. He could feel the heat of it.

'I've never kissed a cousin before,' he said.

'Jesus, I'm not going to have your baby.'

He let his body lean against hers. Her ribcage rose and fell as she breathed. When he closed his eyes, there was nothing but sensations – her tongue in his mouth, her leg snaking behind his knee. The boom and thud of the music reached them through the brickwork. Her hand had found its way under his T-shirt and was warm on the small of his back.

After a while they heard voices, and she pulled him into an angle of the building where there was a smell of potato peelings and cabbage. His feet kicked a dustbin as they settled against the wall.

It was dark already, starless and moonless and still warm enough that the strengthening breeze felt good where it touched his skin. He wasn't sure what he should do with her clothing, except feel his way underneath it, exploring the limits of what was allowed. She pushed against him as if she couldn't get close enough. Then she was breathing against his neck, and her hands had left his hair and his back and his chest, and were unbuckling his belt, slipping the button from the buttonhole, tugging at his zip. And she was holding him, putting her hands where no one's hands had ever been except his own. It flashed into his mind that she was investigating an outrage, presenting Exhibit A – that her gesture meant *How dare you?* and *What's the meaning of this?* – before he understood it as an act of blessing. She had touched the deepest source of his shame. It was a feeling of relief that surged through him, gathering into a rushing sensation, and with a groan he felt all the tension leave him and his legs go weak.

'That was quick.' The rebuke came out in a rush of breath. 'Are you always that quick?'

'I don't know.' He leant against her, as though he had lost the strength to stand. At first the feel of her hand at his waist was reassuring, until he realized she was wiping it on his shirt.

She held him for a bit, loosely around the neck, while he straightened his clothes. Then she said, 'Jesus, what time is it?'

'I've no idea.'

'I have to be somewhere. I'll be late altogether.'

He knew it was just an excuse to get away from him.

'You'll be leaving soon, I suppose,' she said, 'going back to England?'

'Tomorrow, yes.'

'Well, I'll probably not see you again before you go.'

'Probably not.'

'That's a pity.' She hesitated. He sensed it in the

darkness – her wanting to leave, feeling bad about leaving. 'You'll be all right?' she said.

'I'll be fine.'

'Travel safely, then. I'll see you, maybe, in London.'

'I don't live in London.'

'Well, then, when you do live in London. When you're on your way to conquering the world.'

And she was gone. He was glad she was gone, because he thought he might cry. He lay down on the grass by the gravestones. He pictured himself decomposing, settling into the earth. He thought of Bobby Sands, voted into Parliament while he starved to death in his cell. People wouldn't forget that name in a hurry. Who would remember Michael Cartwright if he dwindled out of existence?

'Is that you, Michael?' Fergal's cassock merged with the shadows of the hall. Only his face caught the stray light from an open door. 'What are you doing here among the dead? Are you drunk?'

'No, are you?'

'Maybe a little. I thought I might find you here. I came to look for you earlier, to look for Peggy. I was wanting to go home, and not wanting to go empty-handed to her father, and I thought maybe I'd found you, but then I wasn't so sure. It was just noises I couldn't make head nor tail of. A donkey, was it, I wondered, nibbling the grass at the edge of a gravestone?'

Michael heard the sarcasm and sensed the embarrassment behind it. He sat up. 'You were spying on us?'

'I was not spying, Michael. This is a public place.' Fergal breathed noisily in the darkness. 'Peggy is my cousin, and a child still. I am, so to speak, in loco parentis.'

'But not to me, you aren't. I've got more than enough parents of my own.'

Fergal moved away and circled back again. Michael heard his shoes squeaking on the grass. 'I've no right to lecture you, I'm sorry.' He spoke more softly, his face hovering above in the darkness. 'Can I help you to your feet?'

'I'll manage.' Michael took hold of the nearest gravestone and pulled himself up.

'I'm sorry. It was pompous what I said. I meant to be of help. I've learned what can be learnt from books about the way people think. I'm sent to the cattle market to see how cattle are bought and sold. But what goes on between a man and a woman, Michael, though I have it in theory, I couldn't truly call it knowledge. Do you see? You can't study always with your head. Something has to enter the heart also. Even the Trinity is nothing but a trick with numbers, until you open your heart to its mystery.'

'What are you going on about?'

'What am I to tell Uncle Dennis?'

'Bloody hell, Fergal, you don't have to tell him anything.'

'He worries over her.'

'What about the seal of the confessional? Nothing happened, anyway.'

'The seal of the confessional doesn't apply. Nobody's confessed to me.'

'All right, then, I'll confess. Father, forgive me for I have sinned, it's six weeks since my last confession, maybe seven . . .'

'Seven weeks!'

'It's the summer holidays. I was supposed to go last Saturday when we first got here, but I couldn't face it.

Your Father O'Leary's a bit of a weirdo. Anyway, here are my sins. You can't refuse to hear my sins.'

'I'm not yet ordained.'

'Well, you can practise. I was mean to my sister, Emily, and I talked back to my mother . . .'

'How many times?'

'I don't know. Twenty.'

'Which – being mean or talking back?'

'Both. What difference does it make? And I failed most of my O-levels. Now everyone's in a bad mood, and Mam's suicidal because I'll never get to university, and Dad's going to send me out to work, and I had a fight with Kieran because Kieran's a creep. My father says I'm idle. But I'm not idle. I'm always doing things – just not the things people want me to do. Nothing happened with Peggy. We kissed, that's all. Anyway, whatever it was, how could I talk to you about it? Or Father O'Leary, or Father Kenton at school? One day, I'm going to hitch a lift to somewhere miles away, Bristol, or Birmingham, and go into some church where nobody knows me and confess everything and make a fresh start . . . That's it.'

'That's it?'

'That's it. Now you can give me absolution.'

'No, I can't. I couldn't even if I was ordained. You have to make a full confession.'

'Well, tough! I've confessed as much as I'm going to. And now I'm going home.' Michael set off down the path beside the hall, moving carelessly through the darkness.

Fergal hurried to catch up with him. 'You shouldn't make fun of a sacrament of the Church.'

'Why shouldn't I? What if it's all nonsense?'

'What if it isn't?'

'Then I'll go to hell, I suppose. My mother thinks I'm going to hell, anyway.'

'You won't go to hell, Michael. There are theologians who believe no one will go to hell. Through the mystery of God's love and mercy, all of humanity will be brought to salvation.'

'What's it for, then? Why have hell at all? Why build a torture chamber if there's no one to torture?'

'Who teaches you such things?' Fergal sounded shocked. 'There is no torture chamber. Hell is the absence of God. It's where we put ourselves when we shut the door on God's love.'

Michael grunted, scornful of the evasiveness of this account, the way it relieved God of responsibility for his judgements.

They left the shadow of the hall and turned into the road, and there was more light. They'd walked a hundred yards in silence when the music reached them. It was no more than a murmur at first, a suggestion of drums. Individual instruments became distinct as they approached – a fiddle and a pipe. The texture thickened, the intricate patterns rising above the noise of their footsteps on the pavement. They turned a corner and the sound swelled into a wild squirreling melody. The door from the bar opened onto the street.

'Hang on a minute,' Michael said. He had to duck his head to pass under the lintel. Peering through the smoky light, he saw the musicians sitting in the far corner. They stared down at the table, which made Michael think for a moment that their music was written there, but there was no music, only a clutter of glasses. The fiddle-player was a girl, thin-faced with straggly hair. Next to her, gnarled fingers scurried over the keys of an accordion. A younger man blew into a tin whistle from one side of his mouth. There was another girl making a din on a drum. From where Michael stood only her hand was visible, turning rapidly at the wrist to strike the skin with both sides of the stick. Sitting among them, pumping with his elbow the bellow of his pipes, was Dan Sheahan. A cigarette in an ashtray sent a thin coil of smoke rising across his face.

It seemed to Michael that these people had nothing to do with the notes that poured out of their instruments, that it took no more effort than if they had sat scattering coins across the floor. It was not new to him, this music, but he felt he had never really heard it before. It was like a tree that took root in the floorboards between one breath and the next, pushing its branches through the yellowed ceiling. It came to him that this was what he had been looking for in Kilross without knowing it, without knowing that he was looking for anything, this living thing that his mother cared nothing about and his English father had no part in. He was sorry now that he hadn't stayed to hear Dan Sheahan explain about Ireland instead of following Peggy onto the dance floor. There was so much he didn't know about his own history.

The drinkers who stood listening to the music split and regrouped, and Michael saw that it was Peggy who played the drum. Her eyes were closed. So it was true what she'd said, that she had to be somewhere else. Not wanting to be spotted, he stepped back out into the street. There was no sign of Fergal.

The music pursued him as he walked home. Dwindling from a din to a whisper, it dipped below the hum of the wind and emerged again at a street corner, reproaching him.

He let himself into the house. His grandmother sat playing cards with Emily in the glow of a lamp. His new suit still hung in the window. He stood for a moment and watched the card game. Emily was wearing her pyjamas. She waved at him, as though he were out of talking range, and gave him a secret smile. There were clanking noises from the kitchen and the soft sound, from somewhere upstairs, of his mother singing. Emily threw a card down and scratched her leg. Old Mrs Doyle panted, scattering cigarette ash on the table. She muttered, 'Ah, here now,' and peered at her cards.

Emily said, 'Michael's back,' and smiled at him again.

Mrs Doyle turned with a start. 'As handsome as your father,' she said, 'and out breaking young girls' hearts.'

The kitchen door opened, spilling light across the linoleum. Jack Cartwright stood wiping a spanner with an old tea towel. 'Ah yes,' he said cheerfully. 'The wanderer returns.' His mind was on his plumbing.

Michael lay for a moment hot and encumbered with blankets. There had been no transition from sleeping to waking, no dream that he could remember. He found himself instantly alert, his body buzzing with energy, a sensation on his skin that was a memory of Peggy O'Connor. The wind made the casement rattle. He turned his head and saw that Kieran was gone and he was alone. His pulse was racing. There was a rumble of thunder and something banged against an outside wall. The picture above the fireplace stared down at him – Jesus with his heart exposed and dripping blood. He kicked himself free and sat on the edge of the bed.

According to the alarm clock it was five-thirty. Twelve hours from now the ferry would be landing and they would be on the road home. Beyond that, his life was hard to imagine. There would be no more afternoons in the art room, that much was settled, and no more waiting for the convent minibus to see Salema Nikolaidis, head bowed, stepping shyly onto the drive. There would be the suit and whatever came with the suit.

He took a step towards the window and lifted a corner of the curtain. Across the river the trees staggered like drunks. He walked out onto the landing in his underpants and down the stairs. While he drank from the kitchen tap, he listened to the thunder and the creaking joints of the old house. There was a muffled thud. He was chilled by a gust of air, and the noise of the storm was inside. Stepping into the living room, he saw that the front door had blown open, hitting the back of an armchair. He took hold of the door to push it shut. A pale figure was standing in the street, pyjamas flapping. The sky flickered with lightning and for a moment Kieran was illuminated.

Leaving the door swinging, Michael went back to where his suit hung from the curtain rail. He reached the trousers down from the hanger and then the jacket and quickly pulled them on. Outside, he felt a surge of excitement that made him want to laugh. He pushed into the wind, careless of his bare feet on the tarmac and the jacket flapping at his chest. Reaching his brother, he held him gently by the arm and spoke his name, but the sound of his voice was lost in a crack of thunder. Then the rain came. It trickled down his neck and seeped through the fabric. Through streaks of sodden hair, Kieran, suddenly awake, stared at him with a shock of recognition.

FEBRUARY 2003 LONDON

In the foreground a tram window streams with condensation. Obscured by the wet glass, an old man stands outside on the pavement. His face is emaciated. His hair is white and cropped into stubble. Behind him on the wall someone has daubed a gibbet with a five-pointed star at the end of a rope. There are some words in a language Michael can't read and a fixed look in the man's eyes.

He clicks to the next image. A railway line receding between birch trees and snow. He took the picture in colour but there is no colour. The tree bark is grey and silver like the tracks.

Another tram, this one from the outside. Stocky women, muffled and anonymous, rush forward. This is Warsaw, out in the suburbs. There was a small dog, he remembers, just before he took the picture, sniffing at the edge of the road, pushing its nose into the grille above the drain. As the tram had come grinding towards them, he'd heard a cry of alarm from one of the women. Somewhere the dog was yelping, and the tram seemed to gather up these other noises into a single metallic scream. The dog was fine, it turned out, but the women in the picture don't know that yet.

Then a young woman on a park bench looking up at the

camera, smiling warily – Irena Lipska. It's a jolt to see her, not in his mind but on the screen. She's in the wrong file. He'll see to it later. His hand shakes on the mouse as he brings up the next picture. The glass bottles glow with refracted sunlight, their blue surfaces undulating like water. In the background are the glazing bars of a window and, beyond that, a blur of trees. An old bottle factory in Latvia. This one almost made it into the Latvian guidebook.

The Rootless Guide series, for which Michael has been working, favours the kind of offbeat images that appeal to people who don't like to think of themselves as tourists. These pictures on Michael's screen are the rejects, too offbeat even for Rootless travellers. Now that he's taken a break from the job, Michael can see what he's left with. Maybe some of these pictures with no other function will fall into the category of art.

When the intercom buzzes he looks around vaguely, not sure for a moment where the noise has come from. Ten days he's been in the flat but the sound is still almost unknown to him. He stands up and lifts the phone from its base on the wall. It buzzes again, so he presses the button.

'You have a visitor.'

'Are you sure you've got the right number?'

'It's a girl. Says she's your niece.'

'My niece?'

'That's what she says. Should I ask her name?'

It's the Russian boy speaking, the one they called Yuri.

'Yes, if you like. Or just send her up.'

'So what name should she say? What is the name of your niece?'

'Bloody hell, Yuri!'

'I'm sorry?'

'Why would anyone pretend to be my niece?'

Yuri isn't listening. Michael can hear him asking questions, and a female voice answering. His niece – but which of his various nieces, he wonders, of those old enough to turn up alone? And how did she know where to find him?

'Yasmin,' Yuri says, 'she says she's called Yasmin.'

'Yasmin? That can't be right. Are you sure?'

'Wait, though.' There's more conversation that Michael can't catch, then Yuri's voice murmuring into the mouthpiece. 'Now she says Trinity. Is this a name?'

'Trinity. Yes, of course. And she's got a friend with her?'

'No, just this girl, who says she's your niece.'

'Yasmin, you said.'

'Exactly. One girl, two names.'

'Well, whoever she is . . .'

'I thought I should check, OK, only because she looks sort of . . .'

'Sort of what?'

'Nothing. I'm sorry.'

'Just tell her what floor I'm on, all right?' Yuri has hung up.

So Trinity is here, calling herself Yasmin after her grandmother.

Michael opens his door and looks along the corridor towards the lift. From the other direction he hears a key turning in a lock, and a woman is walking towards him, smoothing her skirt, adjusting an earring. She's older than Michael – in her forties, probably – but shapely and elegant, dressed for an evening out. He inhales and feels the breath entering his lungs, is aware of the pulse of his own blood.

He discovers that he's still in his dressing gown, a shabby cotton thing pulled unironed from a suitcase. At some stage during the day he's added socks to keep his feet warm, but that's it for clothes. He raises a hand awkwardly to his face and feels the stubble. He nods to the woman as she passes. She glances away towards the lift with a tight smile. Michael stands for a moment to watch her go, detecting a new self-consciousness in her posture. The trail of scent is a reminder of something neglected.

He puts the door on the latch and retreats to the bedroom to dress. With one leg in his trousers, he hears the rap of knuckles on wood, and the door swinging open.

'Uncle Mike.'

'Hi, just a minute.'

'Can I come in?'

'Of course. I'll be right there.'

There's the flump of a bag hitting the floor, slow footsteps, shoes squeaking on vinyl.

He finds her in the living room, staring out the window. Her clothing is sombre – a dark knee-length dress, pants as floppy as pyjamas. The trousers make the dress look like a kurta – perhaps it is a kurta, though the whole outfit seems improvised, gathered from charity shops and other people's wardrobes, and the denim jacket thrown on top. She wears a headscarf tied at the back so that her dark hair is visible only at the neck.

She turns and puts her arms round him, her face against his chest, holding on with a tight grip. Her hands are cold. He feels the tension go out of her. When she looks at him again there are tears in her eyes. Her face is leaner than it was, though not as delicate as her mother's.

'You're growing a beard, Uncle Mike,' she says, pulling out a tissue. 'I can't imagine you with a beard.'

She turns abruptly to take in the room, a white box with a desk at one end by the window, a table and four chairs at the other end where the kitchen is. The walls are blank, except for the screw holes and picture hooks left by a previous occupant.

'So this is where you live.'

'Not exactly. I've borrowed it from someone at work.'

'Can I see the rest?'

'If you like.'

She steps across the hall. Michael is reminded of a cat circling a piece of ground before settling. Reappearing from the bedroom, she says, 'No clutter, anyway. That's something. You should see our place. One day we'll tunnel our way out and leave it to the spiders.'

Her indignation makes him smile. He sees the child in her. It's the headscarf that makes her look older than seventeen. She has inherited her mother's complexion. Was it this, the scarf holding the hair back from her face, the skin ochre-brown, that triggered Yuri's suspicion?

She joins him at the window and they say nothing for a moment, looking across the rooftops towards Battersea Power Station. The thinning of buildings in the middle distance suggests the curving path of the river. Scaffolding rises from the backstreets immediately below. There's a grinding noise from a demolition site.

'Trin, is everything OK?'

'Of course, everything's great.' She hits a brittle note with that last word and looks for a moment as though she doesn't trust herself to keep talking.

Michael is caught off balance by a memory of Salema, the time he found her in the street outside his digs in Brighton, distracted and incoherent, as though she'd woken among the litter and broken bottles and had no idea how she'd got there.

Trinity has her hands out now, palms towards the floor, like a conductor lowering the volume. She lets her breath out slowly. There's a glimmer of a smile. 'Not Trin, though,' she says, 'and not Trinity. Not any more. I've given up all that one-in-three, three-in-one business. I'm using my middle name.'

'I didn't know Yasmin was your middle name.'

'Well, who's to say it isn't? I mean, honestly, Uncle Mike, what was she thinking?'

'Your mother?'

'Wasn't it enough that she was in and out of the nuthouse? Couldn't she at least have given me a name that suggested a more integrated personality?'

Michael laughs. 'She always took her religion seriously.'

'So why not Mary? Why not Bernadette?'

'Bernadette had visions, you know. Mary too, if you count the Annunciation. Nuthouse material both of them.'

'I like Yasmin, anyway. It's who I am.' She delivers this with a shrug, turning to continue her inspection of the room, opening a cupboard above the sink, running a hand across the counter top.

'Do you miss her, your grandmother?'

'I never saw enough of her to miss her. It's Granny I miss.' She meant his mother, of course – dead almost a year. 'Why didn't you come to the funeral?'

'I was in Warsaw.'

'There are planes. Even in Warsaw, probably.'

In Warsaw – in pursuit of Irena Lipska, who stared at him wide-eyed, when he told her finally that he loved her, and arranged her lips in an O as though to blow bubbles. *O, how inconvenient! O, I'm so sorry! O, what a ridiculous delusion!* For Irena Lipska he missed his mother's funeral – the first act, anyway, of her funeral. Katherine explained it all in an email. Moira Cartwright had asked in her will for her body to be donated to a teaching hospital. There would be a cremation later. Meanwhile her mortal remains must be inexpertly filleted by a student, and the family must make do with a requiem Mass. And Michael would stand in a leaf-strewn park searching Irena Lipska's face for meaning as the O formed on her lips and her gaze flickered towards the frosted flowerbeds.

'Were people upset that I wasn't there?'

'I don't know. I was upset. It was horrible when she died. The house seemed so cold. She used to serve tea in the sitting room, and all the nuns would come, and the parish priest sometimes. I remember her fishing out a pile of newspaper cuttings from under the piano, and every cutting was about one of you lot winning a prize or getting a scholarship.'

'Probably not me, in fact.'

'Dad, anyway, there were lots about Dad, and Uncle Chris and Auntie Eileen.'

'And they were only in the paper because she'd written them herself and sent them in. She was a one-woman publicity machine.'

'But she was so proud of you all. And I laughed at the time, because there she was with her bum in the air, groping under the piano. I shouldn't have laughed. I should have paid more attention. I couldn't eat for days when she died. Dad went weird, and Granddad who was always weird got even weirder, but I thought at least I'd get to see you.'

Michael is startled by this declaration of attachment. He wonders what he's ever done to deserve it, apart from leaving the country. 'Tell me, Trin . . .'

'Yasmin. You can call me Yas if you like.'

'Yas. How did you know where to find me?'

'Auntie Kath told me you'd been doing this Rootless Guide thing. I googled it and phoned the office and explained who I am.'

'That was enterprising of you.'

She looks at him defiantly, as though he has criticized her. 'OK, so I'm a cyber-stalker. Everybody does it.'

'I don't mind. I'm glad to see you. Really.'

'What, then?'

'Does Kieran know you're here?'

'I'm nearly eighteen. I go places all the time. I go out with my mates.'

'In London?'

'Sometimes. Why not?'

'Maybe you should phone him.'

'If you think that's such a great idea, why don't *you* phone him?' She flops onto a dining chair. With her elbows on the table she rests her head in her hands.

Michael hesitates. *Because, to be honest, I find him intimidating* – he could tell her that. Instead he says, 'Because I haven't got a phone.'

She looks up at him open-mouthed. 'Even Dad has a phone. How do you manage?'

45

'To do what?'

'You're in a strange mood, you know that?'

'Yes, I probably am. Sorry. I haven't been talking to people much. I'm out of practice.'

She shrugs. 'I know this area, anyway. Mum was in hospital for a while in Camberwell. Now she's in Peckham, in a kind of halfway house.'

He has a glimpse of what it must have been like for Yasmin, with her mother migrating between home and else-where, between reality and psychosis – so many cracks to fall through – and what it must have been like for Kieran raising her.

'You haven't run away, have you?'

'Don't be so dramatic. It's only for the weekend.'

'Isn't this Thursday?'

'And tomorrow's Friday.' She stands up, sighing as though his questions are tedious. 'So is this where you work.' Her pacing has brought her to the desk. She touches the mouse and the monitor is full of colour.

'At the moment, yes.'

'What's this one for?'

It's the Latvian bottles. He doesn't feel ready to talk about art, if that's what it is, if that's what it might become. 'I haven't decided yet.'

'It's beautiful.' She gazes at it with fresh attention. 'Is it going in one of your guidebooks?'

'No. I'm taking a rest from guidebooks.' It sounds fright-eningly blank when he puts it into words. 'We're about to launch an online magazine – weekend breaks for the price of a toothbrush. I'll be working on that for a bit.'

She laughs. 'Well, don't tell Dad, that's all.'

'He wouldn't approve, I suppose.'

'You know Dad. It's the kind of thing that makes him go mental. He never flies. He won't drive a car. He shaves in rainwater – he does, honestly. We'd scavenge for food in bins if it was up to him, and wrap ourselves in old newspapers.'

Michael hesitates. Caught between contradicting and colluding, he finds himself saying nothing, and with his eyes on Trinity's his silence seems to take on a meaning he hasn't intended. He's aware that whatever he says next will seem artificial. 'I haven't offered you anything. A cup of tea? I've got coffee, if you don't mind instant.' He crosses the room to the kitchen and opens the fridge. 'There's some cheese in here, and a couple of tomatoes. I've got pasta, if you like pasta.'

'Is that it?'

'I was going to go out later. What do you fancy? There's a place down the road that does all-day breakfast.'

She gives him a withering look. It turns out she has a plan already. She remembers this little Greek restaurant not far from the National Gallery where Eileen took her on her fifteenth birthday.

Michael shaves and takes a shower. He finds himself unsettled by this visit. It's as though an exotic bird has landed on his windowsill – he's inclined to hold his breath. He likes her, this child of his brother's who used to call herself Trinity. He's always liked her. And if he's tempted now to give her twenty quid and tell her to get herself a pizza, it's only because he isn't quite ready for the West End. Unthinkable of course, to throw her out, not to protect her when she's put herself in his care. He sees her as a glass about to fall. This fear is a reflection of his own fragility, he knows that much. He has caught it glinting back at him from harassed mothers struggling at bus stops, and timid children clutching their schoolbags, and all the cyclists weaving along the Walworth Road. Everything's breakable, and he feels too raw to watch.

After Warsaw, after Irena Lipska, he moved northward and eastward, negotiating Rootless projects that took him from the Baltics to St Petersburg, and from St Petersburg to Krasnoyarsk and Irkutsk, seeking the solace of isolation and physical discomfort. For nearly a year the work kept him going until his editor persuaded him to take a break. For ten days now he has floated in his mid-rise bubble, working obsessively on a project that seems to remain just beyond his grasp, interacting only with the West Indian women in Tesco's, and the Afghan men in the corner shop, and the boys at the front desk who come from various parts of Eastern Europe. Carrying his dislocation like a hollow space in his chest, he has felt that this is as much of a homecoming as he can cope with. He has thought of phoning Katherine or Eileen – intends to phone them someday soon, once things are more settled – but has not imagined that Kieran's child would come to drag him out of his isolation.

Yuri, with the phone to his ear, nods as they cross the lobby. Scuffing through litter in the street, Michael asks if he gave her a hard time, the Russian boy at the desk.

'Not really,' she says. 'He probably thought I was a Chechen, which makes a change.'

'From what?'

'From being a Paki.'

They walk beside the railway arches, turning their heads from the gusts of cold wind. Grass and weeds sprout between the brick piers and the tarmac. Under one arch is a motorbike repair shop. Under another, a place that sells mattresses. One of the archways is boarded up. Posters advertising obscure bands and prayer meetings and South London clubs have spread haphazardly across the wood. There's a new one for a cafe, with international phone calls and cheap rates on money wired to Nigeria. Michael lingers to take a few pictures. From habit, he's brought a camera with him.

Trinity is complaining about school, the way everyone goes on at her about university. 'And Dad's no help. Do something useful, he says, like law. I mean law! Dad, I say to him, do I look like a lawyer?'

That makes Michael laugh – the vehemence, but also the movement that goes with it, head shifting sideways, fingers pointing to the ground.

'I suppose he wants you to be successful, have a steady income.'

'No, he wants me to devote my life to defending the kind of people who live up trees and break into agrochemical factories. He thinks it would more useful than his piddling newssheet and his blog that nobody reads. And he's not wrong about that. Basically he's terrified I'll just mess everything up like he did.'

'Did he mess everything up?'

'It wasn't his dream, was it, to live at home with his parents and be a science teacher. I do know that much.'

'Is that what he is, a science teacher?'

'Environmental workshop thingy facilitator person, then.'

They cut through a housing estate to the roundabout

by the Elephant and Castle. The homeless in the underpass doze or mutter their requests for change.

'And then there are the things he never mentions.'

'What things?'

'How do I know? He never mentions them. That's the point.' Trinity's indignation echoes from the concrete walls.

They come up past the subterranean market stalls, the urine smell giving way to street food and incense and musty clothing, and take the stairs to the tube station.

When they emerge by Trafalgar Square, the light is fading. They head up through squealing crowds of sightseers and workers streaming from shops and offices, their breath visible in the cold air.

'It's somewhere on that side, I think,' Trinity says, and steps off the pavement towards St Martin in the Fields.

Seeing the danger before she does, Michael pulls her back. A fleet of police motorbikes is roaring downhill towards the sprawling junction at the corner of the square. They fan out sideways to the traffic. Anonymous behind their visors, the riders straddle their machines, holding up gauntleted hands, their helmets and boots gleaming. A fat exhaust pipe flashes.

'What's going on, Uncle Mike?'

'I've no idea.'

More appear from the same direction, followed by a van with obscured windows, which hurtles through the cleared space, collecting the first fleet of bikers behind it.

And everything is as it was. A few heads are still turned, the traffic nudges forward cautiously.

'There were prisoners in that van, weren't there,' Trinity says.

'I suppose so.'

'Brown people, probably.'

'You think so?'

'Well, what do *you* think? That's what's happening in this country. And I bet they didn't need to come this way, all through the middle of London. It's just intimidation.'

'That doesn't seem likely.'

'It is, I bet you. Because of the march on Saturday. They're hoping people won't come. They'll pull all kinds of stunts like this.'

Michael knows about the march. And he knows that the war will happen anyway. On the move, with just enough Russian to get by, he tried not to think much beyond the present. But the Internet chatter was unavoidable – Afghanistan was not enough, Iraq would be next. And the leaders and opinion-formers who imagine democracy growing wild like a weed on a bombsite seem only to gain strength from opposition.

So when Trinity invites him to join her on the march he declines. She pleads with him, skipping sideways on the pavement to confront him with the urgency of the cause.

'I'll think about it, OK?' In his reluctance he recognizes other motives – an instinct to protect himself from human contact, and an older resistance to joining anything.

'Of course, Dad doesn't approve. Unless everyone comes on bicycles. He says it's trivial anyway – just a fight over who owns the deckchairs. I said, Dad, just because there's sand in Iraq that doesn't mean it's one big beach.'

'He was probably thinking of the *Titanic*.'

'And you know this how?'

In the Greek restaurant, a woman who shuffles like a penitent leads them to a table at the back behind a wrought-iron grille. She smoothes the tablecloth, puts down two menus and lights the candle, before returning to her stool near the door. While the waiter pours water, Michael orders a glass of the house red and asks Trinity if she'd like one. She shakes her head.

'You're old enough.'

'I know. It's not that. I just don't like it, that's all.'

'We could have a toast.'

'To what?'

'Anything. Your future.'

'I don't drink! OK?'

'In water, then.' He lifts his glass towards the candle flame. 'To your wonderful career, whatever you decide to do.'

Trinity pushes her water glass away from her. 'I wish people wouldn't pressure me all the time.'

'I didn't to mean to upset you.'

'I'm not upset.'

'OK, you're not upset.'

He waits for a response. Then he leaves her staring at the menu and follows the signs to the toilet, a single room in the basement opposite the kitchen. The harsh light exposes the crudeness of the plumbing, the carelessly spaced tiles, the extrusions of grout and mastic. He imagines his father wincing at the workmanship. There's a thread of graffiti in various hands running down the wall towards the basin.

Too many fucking foringers in London.
Learn to spell u twat.
Fuck off Paki lover.
Bigots have small brains.
True. And small cocks.

Michael makes that three out of five in favour of foringers. Sixty per cent. It could be worse. When he's run his hands under the tap and dried them on his trousers, he takes a couple of pictures, getting the shadowed lumps and indentations in the plaster, and a piece of mirror in which are reflected the soil pipe and a crescent of toilet seat.

Back upstairs, his glass of wine has arrived and some bread and olives. Trinity seems to have recovered.

'When it says meat souvlaki, here, Uncle Mike, what kind of meat is that, do you think?'

'I'm not sure. It's probably lamb.'

'But it says lamb in these other things where it's lamb. Do you think meat might be pork?'

'I suppose so. Why don't you ask? What's wrong with pork? Have you given it up for Lent?'

'It was just a question.' Trinity looks at him quickly and down again at her menu. There's a sudden intensity in her eyes, and one hand goes up to her neck in a defensive gesture.

And he understands. The headscarf, the new name – it all falls into place. He's alarmed at his own obtuseness. She hasn't given up pork for Lent, she's given up Lent. When the waiter comes, Michael orders a kebab and Trinity asks for something vegetarian, carelessly as though it suddenly doesn't matter what she eats, as though she's been dragged here against her will.

'Tell me, Trin . . . Yasmin. Is something the matter? Is there something we should talk about?'

She glares at him, and the subject seems to be closed.

Michael has his glass to his mouth when Trinity asks him, 'What happened before I was born?'

The immensity of the question makes him snort wine up his nose. Still spluttering he says, 'How far back should I go?' He realizes too late that he seems to be laughing at her.

'You see.' She stands up, knocking her chair back against the wrought-iron screen. 'This is exactly what I'm talking about.'

'Trinity.'

'Yasmin!'

'Yasmin, please sit down.'

'Tell me first.'

'I don't know what you want to know.'

She hovers for a moment as though she might speak and then turns and walks out of the restaurant. Michael follows, aware of the heads turning from the other tables, bored couples ready to speculate. A father coping with a moody teenager? A creep chasing a girl half his age? He reaches the door a few seconds behind her.

The old penitent calls to him from her stool. 'You're going already?'

'I'll be right back.'

A gang of women clatter along the pavement, trailing balloons. They wear heels and feather boas and dresses too thin for the weather. Michael pushes his way among them, leaving them behind to catch up with Trinity by the crossing. 'Please come back and eat something,' he says. 'You'll feel better if you eat.'

'I don't want to feel better. I want to know.' She turns back to face him, challenging him to answer. Her face is wet with tears. 'What happened to make everything so weird?'

Michael shrugs. 'Lots of things happened. Life happened.'

'You're twins, you and Dad, but you never even talk. What's up with that?'

'Fraternal twins. We were born at the same time, so everyone assumed we wouldn't mind sharing everything. I met an American woman in Berlin who told me that I was still searching for a womb of my own. She reckoned it was why I wouldn't move in with her.'

'Why do you have to make a joke of everything?'

'*She* didn't think it was a joke.'

Tinny music comes from the pocket of Trinity's denim jacket. She pulls out her phone, lifts the cover with her thumb, scowls, and shuts it again.

'Is it Kieran? Is it your dad?'

'No, it isn't. Why do you keep asking?'

'Because I assume he'll be worried about you.'

'Why would he be worried?'

'Because he's your father.'

'And what if he isn't my father?'

He searches her face for meaning. 'What are you talking about?'

'I'm talking about an eleven-month pregnancy, which is only possible for a horse, and in case you hadn't noticed my mum isn't a horse, and neither am I.'

The women with balloons are all around him, and Trinity has left again, heading in the direction of Covent Garden, stepping on and off the pavement to dodge cyclists and pedestrians and taxis, a bird startled from his window-sill, only her movement identifying her in the dusk. He follows more cautiously, feeling overwhelmed now he's here in the thick of it, north of the river, down at street level. He finds her weeping in an alley between restaurants. Smells mingle from competing kitchens. He reaches out a hand to touch her arm.

'I heard them arguing about it,' Yasmin says. 'Mum and Dad, after Granny's funeral that you couldn't be bothered to come home for. They had a horrendous row about everything. What he'd done to her, what she'd done to him. I was in my room with my headphones on but I could still hear them. Mum was saying she'd never neglected me because she was always watching from a distance, like she's my guardian angel or something. And that's when Dad said it.'

'What? What did he say?'

'It was miraculous, I suppose, he said, like your eleven-month pregnancy. And I didn't hear the rest because I climbed out the window and went up on the roof.'

'Up the scaffolding?'

'How else? My whole life it's been there. Anyone could climb into my bedroom. They might as well put a sign up, rapists welcome. They wouldn't care, anyway, because basically my mum abandoned me and my dad isn't my dad. So where does that leave *me*?' She gives way to her tears, snatching breaths, and pushing them out again in little sobs.

Michael raises his hands to her shoulders and draws her gently towards him. 'That thing about an eleven-month pregnancy – your mother used to make up stuff like that all the time.'

'But it was Dad said it.' Trinity's voice is muffled against his coat. 'Like he was accusing her of something.'

'Of talking crap, probably.' He moves his hand across her back, wanting to smooth the ripples out of her breathing. 'She was always making up miracles, spinning her own kind of hysterical mysticism out of nothing.'

She settles against him, making small noises in her throat. He hears laughter behind in the street and hurrying footsteps and the ringing of bicycle bells.

† The Church of St Ursula and the Virgin Martyrs

Friday 14 February 2003

Dear Michael,

If this reaches you, you will perhaps be wondering
why I am writing after a silence of so many years.
You have been in my mind. On my conscience, I
should say. For what reason, I cannot precisely say.
There are things for which I owe an explanation,
and when I think of explaining – when I find myself
putting the words together in my head – it is, more
often than not, to you, Michael, that I speak. I have,
then, rehearsed what should be said, and so the words
should be ready. That would be logical, would it not?
But the words are not constant from one rehearsal
to the next. Only the pressure to speak is constant.
That pressure builds. And I find now that time also
is pressing. But I am rambling.

Father Gerard, who was my first parish priest,
once observed that I had a mind suited to theological
disputation. He meant, in his kind way, that I was
useless at comforting the grieving widow, the
husband struggling with an addiction to the bottle
or the horses, no earthly good in the pulpit or the
confessional. You asked me to hear your confession

once, do you remember – as a joke, I think. But why should you remember? I was drawn to you the first time we met. You were more interested in my cousin Peggy. And she in you. And why not? I was too old and too awkward to be your friend. Do you remember that day at all, I wonder. The heat? And me sweltering in my soutane? You left me in the cattle market, and again at the edge of the dance floor in the parish hall, and a third time in a bar where Peggy was playing, into which you had led me. And it was almost a year before I would see you again.

I had offended you, I know, by my clumsy intrusion on your privacy. My presence had been an embarrassment to Peggy all evening. Later we were all somewhat embarrassed, I think, even Peggy, though you might not have thought so to look at her – all her life, she would have the world believe she was a pagan, not subject to shame. And you had indeed surprised me, the pair of you, in the shadow of the church among the gravestones, making noises in the dark. I felt awkward then, and I feel awkward now. I have been a curate, Michael, and a parish priest for almost a dozen years, and have been called upon to prepare couples for marriage and to counsel couples who experience difficulties in marriage, and I have learned a language to help me through such occasions. But I still stumble when I am pulled from my text. I say this without pride, I hope you understand that. If there was ever a time in my younger days when I felt myself to be above such matters, I have no such feelings now. It is a weakness entirely.

I had a sheltered childhood, of course, but the
disabling innocence that I carried with me through
adolescence into early manhood could not be blamed
on the narrowness of my upbringing. My grandmother
was a pious woman. She was old-fashioned, and would
not have a television or a record player in the house.
I wish I had more to say about my grandfather. He was
under my grandmother's thumb, that much I know.
He travelled in ecclesiastical accoutrements – wafers
and altar wine, charcoal and incense for burning in
thuribles up and down County Wicklow. These were
the staples. More costly items could be ordered from
the catalogue – vestments and embroidered linens,
cruets and chalices and other vessels, Stations of the
Cross engraved and framed behind glass. If he drank
while he was on the road, I knew nothing of it. He
certainly never drank at home. He had taken the
pledge as a young man, according to my grandmother,
though I never heard him speak of it. There was a deal
of things in that house that were not to be spoken of.
I too was under my grandmother's thumb.

But I mingled with my schoolfellows when it
could not be avoided. I saw them at play in the school
yard, and heard their jokes in the classroom when
Mr Ryan would hurry for the lavatory before the bell
had rung or Father Byrne would arrive late having
crossed to Farrell's for a tin of pipe tobacco. Girls
passed in the street, and travelled with us on the bus.
I registered the coarseness of my contemporaries with
a sense of humiliation I could not then explain. Was
it for them, that they could say such things? Or for

myself, that I could not? And whatever took place among them of a sexual nature I observed as though through the grille of the confessional, hearing the words that were spoken, but seeing in darkness and in fragmentary pieces. This was a blindness that I carried with me into the world. The conduits by which others learn the customs of cursing and fornicating were blocked to me. My grandparents are not to blame for this, for who depends on the adults who rear them to induct them into these mysteries?

My grandmother was a pious woman and she taught me the habits of piety, which have helped me all my life. She was a mother to me in all things. My own mother died when I was barely three years old. She was not a strong woman. She died of complications during her second pregnancy. When the life was nearly out of her, the child she had carried for eight months in her womb was delivered by caesarean section. The child, the girl who would have been my sister, did not survive, and so half our family was ripped away. I remember my mother, though people all my life have told me that this is impossible, that the mind of a three-year old is too soft to retain the imprint of a memory, or that any such memory would be buried too deep under the clutter of later impressions. There are the photographs I grew up with, and the stories of my infancy. Out of these, I am told, I constructed my memories. But I carry sensations in me that could not have been planted. I remember my mother to sing a song while she would hang the washing out, and the sudden

dampness of a sheet across my face, and her calves in
their nylon stockings that I clung to for comfort.

Which is why I envied you your family – such
entanglements, such music-making and arguing.
From the start I was half in love with you, I think.
You, Michael, and all of you collectively. I envied you
that first summer in Kilross. You saw your parents'
anger. I saw their fierce commitment to you all, your
mother's most particularly. How could you know how
cunningly, how deviously she worked for your future
good? I heard not long ago that she had died from
a stroke, and was sorry not to have heard earlier so
that I might have attended her funeral. It was a grand
gathering of the family, I have no doubt. I wrote to
your father but heard nothing.

We exchanged letters, your mother and I –
I wonder did she ever tell you that – while I was
still studying in Dublin, and later when I was a
curate in London and felt myself a failure. My
grandmother saw so many causes of offence, there
were so many things I could not tell her about, that
I wrote always to please her. In my letters to your
mother I wrote to please myself – to take the edge
off my loneliness. The letters I got back from her
were a great comfort to me in those years. I have
them all somewhere. She worried about all her
children, but you especially at that time excited her
concern. You were working for your father, painting
his houses, attending courses at the technical college
that she feared would lead nowhere. She told me
more than once that you seemed lost.

But I see that my attempt to explain myself has stumbled, and my story has scarcely moved beyond our first meeting.

I shrink, of course, from speaking openly about myself. This is not an *apologia pro vita sua* I have embarked upon, but a laying-out of what has been hidden. I had in mind, as I wrote 'laying-out', a simple image of things presented to view, but I see now that it suggests also a body prepared for the grave. And it reminds me that this letter is prompted by another thing I have not yet told you of. The time approaches when I must make things right with God. And before I can hope to receive absolution, I should attempt to repair whatever damage I have done.

I wonder if I can still count on your friendship. I think I can. But the writing of this letter must be an act of faith. I am not sure what I have to ask of you, except to read it to the end. I hope by then it will be clear to both of us. And much more will have become clear, perhaps, by the time this account has been completed and posted to your parents' address – your father's, I should say – which is the only address I have for you, and delivered, God willing, into your hands.

I have squandered an hour, and now I have duties to attend to. I have requested a leave of absence and there is a great deal I must organize in the parish. I will make a fresh start on this tomorrow, or when I can.

DECEMBER 1982 CHELTENHAM

Mr Koppel reached over Michael's shoulder to point at something in his drawing. His index finger was stained with nicotine around the nail, and smudged with charcoal. 'This is beginning to work,' he said, 'this knee.' His voice was a rumble. 'Just a few lines, see, and there's the shape of the bone under the skin. But here, look, the chin doesn't seem attached to the neck. This line's a bit crude, too, don't you think? And check the proportion of the foot. There should be more foreshortening from this angle. Do you see what I mean?'

'Yes. Sorry.'

'And don't, for Christ's sake, be so anxious about it. There's plenty of time. You're doing all right. All right?'

'All right.'

He moved on, and Michael found that he'd been holding his breath.

As the class was packing up, Mr Koppel urged them to practise. 'We've got a vacation coming up, ladies and gents. Don't get rusty. It's like riding a bike. Keep moving or you'll fall off. Draw your relatives over Christmas. Catch them on the move – one-minute sketches. They won't mind. They'll be too busy stuffing their faces. Auntie Mavis having a bit of a snooze after Christmas dinner. Get your pad and pencil out. P'raps she'll take her clothes off, if you ask her nicely.'

'Mr Koppel!' one of the girls said, while the boys grunted in amusement.

Mr Koppel's mouth opened in a laugh that rearranged all the crevices on his face. It was a coarse, rasping laugh that showed his teeth, which had little dark cracks in them like old pots. Michael found it interesting that this sack of a man inspired the respect of the class. It was his skill, of course, that they responded to – his ability to lay down pencil lines as neat as fish bones, or to evoke the human form with a few bold sweeps of charcoal.

In the entrance hall someone had put up some tinsel, but there wasn't much else to suggest that Christmas was approaching – nothing like school, where there would be Advent carols, and the traditional forms of licensed disor-der. Normally Michael liked this about the Tech, that it was so grown-up and businesslike – that there was noth-ing to waste your time, just an hour on each subject every day, and if you didn't show up that was your lookout. It felt good, normally, to be in this place where they left you alone, where the name Cartwright meant nothing and you could turn over the page and live a new story for yourself. But today, walking out into the dark street, with the air crisp and smelling faintly of wood smoke, he registered a pang of regret for the familiar end-of-term rituals.

He walked towards town, between Georgian houses, under brown-leaved beech trees, feeling the cold at his neck, wishing there was someone he could have a laugh with about Mr Koppel and his idea of drawing Auntie

Mavis in the nude. He might tell Kieran later, but Kieran
would probably be practising with Salema.

It had been a shock the first time Kieran had mentioned
that they were going to play in a concert together. 'Salema
Nikolaidis,' Kieran had said. 'You know, that convent girl
who plays piano with the orchestra sometimes.' And then
she'd begun turning up after school, and Michael had had
to get used to knowing she was in the house but not with
him.

A number seven was pulling away from the bus stop.
He'd have to wait. He stepped inside the newsagent's for
the warmth. There was the face of Nigel Lawson, one of his
father's heroes, staring up from a newspaper with a headline about rising unemployment. His eyes strayed to the
magazines on the top shelf.

'Michael?'

He looked around. It was Father Kenton from school.

'Daydreaming?'

'No, Father.'

'I was asking how you got on with Schopenhauer.'

'Oh! All right, I suppose, Father.' It was months since
he'd thought of Schopenhauer.

'Good for you. I always admired your elevated tastes.'

Michael wondered if that was a dig. Had Father Kenton
caught him glancing up at the porn? He was annoyed to feel
himself blushing.

The priest was still eyeing him. 'You may not believe
this, Michael, but I was sorry to see you go.'

'I didn't have much choice, did I?'

'Well, I don't know about that.'

A blur of green caught Michael's eye, and he turned to

the window to see a bus pulling away. 'Damn!' It was another seven. So it was early. Or the other one had been late.

'Your bus?'

'Yes, Father.'

'I'll give you a lift, if you don't mind waiting a minute. I just have to score some recreational drugs.'

It was the kind of thing Father Kenton used to say in class to let you know that he was all right, that he knew what went on, even though he was a teacher, even though he was a priest. He wore his Carmelite habit with a certain style, scapular twisted to one side, the loose end of the belt dangling. Michael waited while he bought a packet of cigarettes and some mints, then they walked out together to the car.

'So your brother tells me you're doing some courses at the technical college.'

'Yes, Father.'

'How is that?'

'It's fine. It's good, actually.'

'It's good?'

'Yes, Father.'

'And you're OK with your subjects? What is it you're doing? I think Kieran told me . . .'

'Just art and economics. I have to work the rest of the time.'

'Art and economics. That's an interesting combination. Why economics?'

'Because it's a one-year course, like art.' And also, he might have added, because it was a subject he hadn't failed yet.

'If you had one more subject you could apply for town planning, or something.' They pulled forward into the flow of traffic. 'What are you reading these days?'

'All sorts. A lot about Irish history.' There was a silence and Michael felt he should say more. 'I had no idea it had been going on so long.'

'Irish history? For as long as there have been Irish people, I should think, and someone to write things down.'

'No, I mean the terrible things the English have done to the Irish.'

Father Kenton raised an eyebrow. 'Are you sure you're reading the right books?'

Michael shrugged. 'They were in the town library.' He wasn't in the mood for sparring. 'Is this your car, Father?'

'It belongs to the order. To each according to his needs. We invented communism long before Marx. I needed it for an ecumenical meeting over at the Methodist chapel.'

'Sounds like fun.'

'It's better when *we* host it. The Methodists don't serve booze, which is a drawback. They were all there, the Anglicans, the Baptists, the Quakers. I'm all for breaking down barriers, I told them. Our doors are open, whenever you want to come home. Always raises a laugh. They think I'm joking.'

Michael attempted a chuckle. Father Kenton's style, which he had always enjoyed in class, was somehow overwhelming when there were just the two of them.

'It wasn't necessary, you know,' Father Kenton said, taking his eyes briefly off the road. 'I'm sure we could have worked something out.'

'How do you mean, Father?'

'We would have had you back. You could have done some retakes, some catch-up classes. We would have designed a programme for you.'

They were crawling up the High Street, past the bright windows, under the Christmas lights.

'You're very quiet, Michael. Is there something on your mind, something troubling you?'

'No, Father.' This was a lie, of course. There were lots of things troubling him, an unsorted pile of things. Father Kenton's kindness had caught him off guard. He felt cut adrift from the school he had always hated. It was more than Salema. It was the sadness of a door closing, the wreckage of unread books and unfinished essays that he'd left on the other side.

'Tell me something, Michael. I don't mean to pry, but I'm curious. You've always been something of an enigma to me. A bright young man, such as yourself, doing so poorly. Is there trouble at home, would you say?'

'What sort of trouble?'

'Well, I don't know. It's hard for you, I should think – with all those brothers and sisters – no place of your own. How many did you say there were of you – seven, was it? And you right in the middle of them all.'

'Me and Kieran.'

'Quite. So you don't have a bedroom to yourself, I assume.'

'I share with Kieran, Father. And Christopher some-times, when he's back from uni. It depends how many lodgers we've got.'

'How do you cope with the lack of privacy? Do you find time for yourself alone?'

'I run sometimes. And I go out with my sketchbook.'

'At home, though, is there any privacy for you? In your bedroom, I mean, or in the bathroom. I assume there's a lock on the bathroom door.'

It was an odd question, Michael thought, and Father Kenton had an odd way of asking it, his voice dropping until it was just audible above the hum of the engine. Of course there was a lock, an old six-inch bolt his father had salvaged from a demolition site. What kind of house didn't have a lock on the bathroom door? He was conscious of Father Kenton's eyes, glancing sideways to look at his face then back to the windscreen. They'd left the department stores behind, moving now between the haphazard lights of flats and office buildings. The priest was clearing his throat, preparing another question.

'Because I was wondering . . . whether you'd say you had been brought up to feel comfortable with your body?' His smile was even thinner than usual.

The silence became oppressive while Michael wondered how to answer this, what feeling comfortable with one's body might consist of.

'And I was wondering if there are ways in which we let you down at school. Our disciplinary procedures, for example, might be considered . . . insensitive. I don't know if you yourself . . .' Father Kenton paused as though struggling to express a complicated thought – 'if you yourself were ever caned?'

Michael began his answer with an ambiguous noise. He sensed that he couldn't rely on his voice to remain steady. The simple question had acquired an unfamiliar weight. 'Yes,' he said at last.

'And where were you caned? You don't mind me asking, do you, Michael?'

'I suppose not, Father. In Father Brendan's study, usually.'

Amusement flickered across the priest's face. 'I meant, on the hands, or where?'

'Oh yes, the hands. Except when Father Ignatius did it. But that was only a few times.'

'And it was . . . different?'

'He had me bend over a chair.'

The priest breathed in sharply, moving as though in response to a spasm of discomfort. The silence in the car hammered at Michael's ears. His limbs seemed clumsily elongated. He had the illusion that his head had detached itself and was suspended at an airless altitude. Below him the car continued to throb and sway, pulling the road towards it like a rope. On the pavement, a boy pushed his bike past terraced houses, a woman in a sari unlocked a door and stepped inside.

'You shouldn't bury these things, Michael.'

It startled him to hear the voice so close beside him.

'I could help you, you know. We could talk.'

'I'm sorry.' Michael unclipped his seatbelt and started fumbling with the door handle. 'I forgot something. I need to go back to town. I should get out here, really, I can walk from here.'

'What are you doing?'

'I can catch the bus.'

The door swung open, and Michael found himself tilting out over the blur of tarmac.

'I'm pulling over. For God's sake!' The priest's hand was grabbing at his arm.

The hubcaps scraped the kerb and they stopped. Michael put his foot out on the pavement and sat for a moment. A woman looked at him as she came out of the Star of India holding her takeaway in a plastic bag. Then she walked off, past the hardware shop that was shut for the night with metal bars across the window.

'That was very dangerous.' Father Kenton's voice was shaking.

Michael pulled himself up out of his seat. 'I'll walk from here, then.'

'Is that all you have to say for yourself?'

'Sorry. I didn't mean . . .'

Now the priest was on his feet, watching Michael across the roof of the car. 'Michael! Please!'

Michael waited with his eyes on the pavement.

'That was insensitive of me. I should have realized – this is painful for you.'

Michael felt the air cold in his throat, great lungfuls of it as though he'd been running. 'Thanks for the lift,' he said, and set off along a side street, hugging his bag. Behind him, he heard the car doors slam, first one then the other, and the car move away with a scrape of aluminium on concrete.

When he'd walked enough to calm himself, along streets of red-brick terraced houses and bay-windowed semis, he circled back towards home. Clouds covered and uncovered the moon, and the shadows on the old house deepened. On the columns of the portico the paint flakes shifted and settled like moths. The front door would be locked. He scrambled up the bank that rose around the side of the house, pulling his way through the scaffolding.

Reaching the veranda, he walked under its glazed canopy past piles of timber, surplus scaffold poles, a stack of folding chairs with the canvas rotting off them. The glass above his head was cracked and stained. There were rectangles and jagged-edged rhomboids of sky. Wisteria branches braided the wrought-iron supports. Stopping in the light from the sitting-room window, he saw Salema. His mother was saying something to her. Katherine and Emily hovered as though the house was shrunk to this room and there was no other oxygen to be found.

Salema was standing on tiptoe by the mantelpiece with a framed picture in her hand. It would be one of his mother's cuttings from the local paper – someone in the family with a music trophy or a letter about a scholarship. What would Salema think of such showing off?

He stifled a sneeze. Katherine turned away from the others to peer through the window. Michael stepped out of sight, and went round to the back door.

The kitchen was full of old baby clothes, table and kitchen surfaces and chairs draped with hats and dresses and tiny knitted mittens. Four pairs of lace-edged booties were lined up on the breadboard.

Katherine came in from the hall. 'It's you. I thought it was you.' She watched him shyly, as he looked about the room.

'What's all this?'

'Mam's having a sort-out.'

'But why baby clothes?'

'It's in case Eileen's pregnant.'

'Does she think she might be?'

'Mam isn't sure, but Eileen phoned to say she's getting married.'

Emily came in, singing, 'Ei-leen's get-ting mar-ried, Ei-leen's get-ting mar-ried,' hopping from foot to foot. She took Katherine's hand. Half-heartedly Katherine joined in, self-conscious in front of her older brother.

'Ei-leen might be preg-nant,' Emily sang. 'I'm going to be an aunt-ie.'

Moira Cartwright bustled into the room with the teapot. Her face was furrowed with anxiety. 'Michael, you're back. Shut it, you two. Michael, I'm run off my feet. I've been talking to that friend of Kieran's, the Indian girl.' She rested the pot on top of the Aga, and moved the kettle onto the hot plate. 'Do you have any idea what's going on between those two?'

Michael shrugged. 'Don't ask me.'

'I just don't want him to make a silly of himself. Here's Eileen now telling me she's marrying some boy we know nothing about, and her not even done with her studies. Kieran has years ahead of him before he'll be a doctor. And she's a heartbreaker that girl, anyone can see that. Sure, I paid no attention when it was once a week, but she was here Monday and Tuesday, and here she is again. I may as well make up a bed for her and be done with it. Do we even know if she's a Catholic, or what religion she is?'

'They're rehearsing, that's all. The concert's coming up.'

'There'll be more to it than that, you mark my words, even if Kieran knows no more about it than you do. You haven't the sense you were born with, either one of you.'

'Where is Kieran, anyway?'

'At the church with Father Dolan and the parish choir. He's to play the harmonium for midnight Mass. Father Dolan's hoping you'll sing with them.' She glanced up at the clock. 'He should have been back half an hour ago.' Lifting the kettle with an oven glove, she refilled the teapot. 'Come in with me a minute, Michael, and talk to her.'

'About what? She isn't here to see *me*. And you can tell Father Dolan I'm not going to midnight Mass, or any other Mass ever again.'

'Take this in right now and no more of your nonsense.' She handed him a tray with the teapot on it and an extra cup and saucer. 'I don't know what's got into you. I'll be in in a minute, tell her, with some cake. Katherine, stay here and peel the potatoes.'

Katherine crossed her arms with a sigh and gave Michael a stricken look. He went with the teapot to the sitting room, Emily trailing after him.

Salema was studying a pottery ornament that was hanging on the wall. Above her head was a framed print of the meeting of Dante and Beatrice. The whole house had been furnished from auction-room bargains and lucky finds on demolition sites. The sitting room specialized in shabby grandeur – brass lamps and old rugs and leather armchairs with horsehair showing at the seams. The stuffed fox that prowled the mantelpiece fixed Michael with its glassy stare. Salema hadn't noticed him yet.

'How's it going, then?' Michael felt his heart beating and heard the unsteadiness in his voice.

Salema turned round and looked at him vaguely. 'This is a holy water font, you know.' It was true. There was a bowl for water and a squat little cherub hanging over it. 'It's not just for show. You should hang it by the door and put holy water in it. That's what it's for.' Their eyes met for a moment, before hers darted away towards the window.

'OK.' He put the tray on the coffee table, next to the empty cups and the milk jug, and straightened up. He was aware of his hands now that they had nothing to do. He was ashamed of his shapeless paint-smeared trousers and his scuffed shoes.

Salema was neat as always in her school uniform. Her straight black hair, gathered at the back in a ribbon, fell across her shoulders like a mantilla.

The stand was ready by the piano with Kieran's music on it. 'So how's the piece going?'

'All right, thanks. Actually it needs more work. Kieran has a wonderful technique, of course.' She focused on Michael as she said this, then her eyes darted sideways again as though the contact was too intense. 'But sometimes you can tell that he's not there yet. My piano teacher says it's not enough to play the music, you have to let the music play you. Your brother is something of a tabula rasa, don't you think?'

Michael tried to remember what a tabula rasa was and whether it was a good thing or a bad thing. Emily was standing in the doorway, swinging the door back and forward, humming to herself, which made it hard to concentrate.

'In what sense is he a tabula rasa, exactly?'

'He hasn't suffered yet.'

'I think he's suffered.'

'But not enough. He idolizes you, of course, in some ways.'

'No, he doesn't.'

'He looks up to you even though you're only ten minutes older.'

'Seven minutes.'

'He told me you could have been at least as good a musician as he is . . .'

The idea was left hanging in the air. He could have been, if he'd worked at it. Always it came down to this. He wished he could tell her about his drawing class, how hard he worked at art now that it was all he had left. Instead he said, 'I'm sorry about the piano. I know it's rubbish. I'm sure you're used to better pianos.'

'Michael.' His mother had come into the room, carrying a plate. 'There's no need to apologize for the piano.'

'How would you know?' He was instantly enraged by the interruption. 'Have you ever played it?'

'I've got ears, haven't I?' She sat in an armchair, setting the plate on the table. There were two slices of Battenberg cake. 'Now we'll be eating shortly, Michael, so don't spoil your appetite.'

Michael turned to Salema. 'It cost Dad ten quid in an auction. It came out of a pub. They must have thrown it out. That's how bad it is.'

'We don't know that, Michael.' Moira leant forward to deal with the tea. 'We don't know that it came from a pub.'

'It's got beer rings on it, look, and the dampers are worn so all the strings jangle whatever note you play.'

'Sure, it's not that bad. It's good enough to practise on.'

'It doesn't matter, anyway,' Salema said. 'There's a Steinway in the town hall.'

Michael could think of nothing more to say about the piano, or about anything else. He cursed himself for being such a child in front of Salema.

'Michael,' Emily said, 'can I have your marzipan?'

'If you like.'

Squatting by the table, she took one of the Battenberg slices and began peeling it.

Moira absentmindedly tapped the side of her teacup with her wedding ring, as though signalling her agitation in Morse code. 'Now, Michael,' she said, 'Salome was telling me earlier about her father, God rest his soul.'

'It's Salema, Mam.'

'Yes – Salema. Salema's father was born in Greece and her mother in India – did I get that right?'

'Yes, Mrs Cartwright.'

'Isn't that interesting, Michael?'

Michael glared at his mother. 'Yes, it's very interesting. It means she's probably Orthodox or Hindu or something.'

Salema's eyes widened with shock. 'My father was a Catholic and so am I. My mother's a Muslim, if you really want to know, but I'm a Catholic, like you. More than you, probably.'

'That wouldn't be hard, because I'm not a Catholic at all.'

'Michael!' His mother laughed, pretending to find this amusing. 'Don't listen to him, Salome dear.'

'I used to be a Catholic,' Michael said, 'but I gave it up, when I realized it's all crap.'

His mother put her cup back on its saucer with a click. 'If you can't be civil, Michael, you may leave the room.'

'Well, it's true. The priests pretend to be so holy and they're not. Father Kenton, for example.'

Emily paused in lowering a strip of marzipan into her mouth. 'I thought you liked Father Kenton. You said he was your favourite.'

'Emily, dear, don't talk with food in your mouth.'

'It's not food, Mam, it's only marzipan.'

'I never said Father Kenton was my favourite. He's a creep and a hypocrite. He smokes when he thinks nobody's looking, and he drinks. He tries to get the Methodist minister to drink.'

'Well, for goodness' sake, where's the harm?'

'He wanted to know all kinds of things about the house. If we have locks and things.'

Emily raised a hand, as though she was in class. 'Perhaps he's a burglar.'

'He's not a burglar, Emily,' Michael said, 'he's a priest.'

'Well, why can't he be both? Burglars have to be something else or people would know they were burglars. Perhaps he breaks into houses . . .'

'No, he doesn't!'

'Perhaps he breaks into houses where Protestants live, and consecrates their bread, and then they eat it and they're Catholics without knowing it.'

'Shut up, Emily.'

'Shut up yourself, mean pig!'

'Now that's enough, both of you,' Mam said. 'What will Salome think?'

'Salema, Mam,' Michael said, 'her name's Salema!'

The floor began to vibrate, and there was a rumbling noise from below.

'God help me,' Moira said, getting up out of her arm-chair. 'It's the washing machine. It needs a good seeing to. I must speak to Jack about it. Come on, Emily, you can help me take the load out.'

Emily hung back as her mother left. 'Salema,' she said, 'can I have your marzipan?'

'I'm not very hungry, actually.'

Emily peeled the slice quickly, dropping the sponge squares back onto the plate, and skipped from the room.

There was silence for a moment before Michael spoke. 'I'm sorry about what I said. About you being a Hindu. I didn't mean to insult you. I know you're not a Hindu.'

'That's all right.'

'My mother's so annoying.'

'I like coming here. You should see *my* parents. At least yours believe in something.' She looked as though she had nothing more to say. Then she started again with new urgency. 'My mother isn't really a Muslim. She converted when she met my father, but everything's skin deep with her. She only married him to get a British passport, because he had one already, and she became a Catholic so that he'd marry her. That's what she's like. She uses people. And my stepfather is worse. He has this satanic influence over her. He murdered my father, actually.'

'He murdered him? Was he arrested?'

'Of course not.'

'How do you know, then?'

'It's obvious. It was obvious the first time I met him. You can't hide murder. It's one of the four sins crying to

BESOTTED

heaven for vengeance. Defrauding the workman of his wages, that's another one. And that's what he does for a living, basically, because he's a tax inspector. It's too perfect. My father hated tax inspectors, he called them agents of the secular state. He used to say we should be allowed to pay a tithe to the Church instead. It's so ironic that she should end up with a tax inspector. It's more than ironic.'

Michael had never heard her talk so much. He was flattered that she confided in him but wished they could talk about something other than sin.

She was staring at her knee. After a moment she asked him, 'Have you really left the Church?'

'I don't know. Father Kenton gave me a lift today and he said things . . .'

'What things?' She leant forward and stared into his eyes. Her complexion was perfect, a deep brown with a subtle undertone that was almost mauve. You only saw it in certain lights, and if you were close enough, like a glow under the skin. It made Michael aware of his own blotchy pinkness. He searched for a response, something that would keep her eyes fixed on his. But she had already slumped back into her chair and refocused on her flawless knee. 'I know what you mean about priests. They can be so disappointing, can't they. The nuns are worse. I don't think they believe in anything, most of them. I'm going to join Opus Dei when I'm old enough.' She looked up suddenly. 'That's something I haven't told anyone.'

'I won't tell anyone either. What is it, though, Opus Dei? I've never heard of it.'

'Nobody has. My father told me about it before he died. You look like an ordinary person and you can be a doctor or a barrister or anything, but underneath where it matters, where only God can see, you suffer.'

'Inside, you mean? Emotionally?'

'I mean under your clothes. When you join you have to wear this thing round your thigh. I can't remember what it's called. It's a Latin word. It's like a necklace or a bracelet, except you wear it here, high up like this.' She raised her right foot onto the seat, and demonstrated with both hands around her leg, bunching her skirt so that it fell away from her knee. 'And it has little spikes on the inside so you know it's there all the time you're wearing it and you're reminded of Christ's agony.'

'I had no idea.' Michael's voice had become reedy to his own ears and his mouth was dry. 'Do people really do this?'

'You mustn't tell. It's actually a secret. I only know because of my father.'

It confused him to find himself conscious of her body in this entirely new way, to be thinking about her naked with this bracelet thing around her thigh, to see her gasping with the discomfort of it, biting her lip so as not to cry out. There was a silence during which he held his breath, and then he heard Kieran's footsteps in the hall, and Katherine chatting to him. When they came into the room, he found it hard to believe that his carnal imaginings weren't laid out for everyone to see. They were as visible to him as the teacups and the denuded Battenberg cake.

'Those blasted altos,' Kieran said. 'They can't get a thing right. We had to go over it and over it. Hello, Sal. Sorry I'm late.' He threw his music case onto the settee.

'That's all right. I was talking to Michael.'

'My legs ache from pedalling that sodding harmonium.

I hope you're going to come, Mike. It'll be so much better with you. You'll halve the average age and multiply the average talent by about ten. They've only got two tenors and they're both rubbish. Mr Simcock hisses and Mr McLaren bleats like a goat, and between them they sound like a leaky bagpipe. Please come. It's so boring when you're not there.'

'I'll see if I'm needed at work.'

'At midnight? On Christmas Eve?'

'There might be an emergency.'

'Oh yeah, an emergency paint job. Puce alert! Send five gallons of white emulsion and a stomach pump.'

Michael laughed, pleased that he'd been missed.

Emily drifted into the room, humming her Eileen tune.

Kieran took his coat off and threw it over the back of an armchair. 'Which reminds me. Have you seen what Dad's done to the bathroom?'

'No,' Michael said. 'Is it awful?'

'The left-over-paint monster strikes again.'

'What colour?'

'Egg-yolk yellow.'

'I like it,' Katherine said. 'It's a happy colour. It's better than it was before with all damp patches.'

Salema stood up and touched Kieran's arm. 'Maybe we should do some practice.'

'Yes, of course. Sorry, Sal. Clear off, you lot. We've got work to do.'

Michael was the first to the door. 'Not you, Mike. Why don't you stay and criticize.'

'I'll stay and criticize,' Emily said. 'Let me, Kier, please. I promise I'll criticize a lot.'

'Get her out of here, Kath.'

Holding a block of rosin in his left hand, Kieran moved the bow across it from tip to heel and back again. 'Otto just gave me my last lesson until after Christmas, and you know what he said, just as I was leaving . . . I don't think I told you this, Salema . . .' Kieran went into his Otto impersonation, head held high and in profile, preparing his mouth for the Hungarian accent. 'Good luck with the concert, my boy, and just remember how little mistakes matter.'

Sinking into an armchair, Michael laughed at his brother's performance. Salema smiled vaguely. She was preoccupied with her part, playing a passage in the air above the keys.

'He's right, though,' Kieran said. 'Every detail has to be perfect.' He began bowing the strings in pairs, listening to the intervals. Then he touched them lightly with his middle finger to hear the harmonics. 'OK, so let's see if we can get through it without mistakes.' He raised the dog-eared corner of his copy, ready for a quick turn of the page, and settled the violin on his shoulder.

'Unless,' Michael said, 'he meant the opposite.'

Kieran stopped with the bow poised and looked at him. Salema too had turned from the keyboard.

'About mistakes, I mean – how little they matter.'

Kieran lowered his violin. 'Are you going to help, Mike, or are you just going to play with words?'

'Well, he might have done.' Michael sat forward in his chair to argue the point. 'It's ambiguous, if you think about it. Remember how little mistakes matter? He might have meant either.'

'He's my violin teacher. I know what he meant.'

'But his last words before your concert . . .'

'Exactly. He's relentless about details.'

Michael was acutely aware that Salema was watching him. 'I was just thinking, that's all,' he said, 'about the way people make us feel bad all the time for getting things wrong.' He wasn't sure what he was trying to say. 'Going to confession, for example. Week after week we're supposed to list all the things we've done wrong. Nobody ever asks us to list all the things we've done right. Nobody pays attention if you do something right unless you get an A in an exam or win a prize or something.' He was surprised by the strength of his feeling and his urgent need to express it. 'I watch Mr Koppel in art going mad all over the paper with charcoal and this amazing picture appears out of nowhere, but he must have done thousands of crap drawings to get that good, and I can hardly make a mark in case I get it wrong.'

'What are you talking about?'

'I don't know. Maybe we shouldn't even list the things we've done right. Maybe we should just stand up in church and say all our sins and everyone should applaud because it means we've at least been doing something, we've at least been living.'

Salema turned back to her music. 'That's what the rest of the world is for,' she murmured, 'to reward us for our sins.'

'No one's ever rewarded me for my sins.'

'Look, Mike, if you're just going to sit there talking drivel . . .'

'I wasn't . . . I only meant . . .' Unable to trust his voice, Michael waved a hand to indicate that the conversation was over and sat back in his chair. He felt the moisture pricking his eyes. He should have known not to talk, not while Salema was there, not in this personal way.

When Salema began to play, and Kieran after her, he closed his eyes and let the music wash over him.

FEBRUARY 2003 LONDON

A man with an ornamental birdcage is standing by the
entrance to the Royal Academy. Something in his posture
holds Michael's attention, a contained energy that reminds
him of his father. He stops walking and holds the shifting image in his viewfinder. The bird man stands erect
with his feet together, his sharp features framed by a flat
cap and muffler, his jacket buttoned, holding the cage by
its wrought-iron handle. He's wearing fingerless gloves.
People pass between the camera and the subject, some with
placards, some chanting. They obscure and reveal the man
and the cage while Michael takes pictures, ignoring the
cold. When everything falls into place – a bird opening
bright wings in thwarted flight, the man peering suddenly
towards the lens, an unfocused profile encroaching from the
right – Michael touches the shutter button one last time.

He lowers the camera and the bird man is talking,
calling out to him. The words are lost in the din of protest,
but the sarcastic tone cuts through. Thin-lipped and beady
eyed, he has the look of a bird himself. His words come
out in clouds of condensation.

Michael is walking again, but the bird man is on the
move too, edging through the crowd towards him, holding
the birdcage high as he eases his way between marchers.

'Having a jolly time, are you? Bit of a singalong?'

Michael looks around him, hoping it's someone else the bird man has in view. He finds himself among an elderly group. Two of the men hold up a CND banner.

'That's nice. Nice for Saddam's torture victims, that is.'

'Are you talking to me?'

'You're here, aren't you?'

The birds hop and flutter in the cage, scrabble at perches, open their beaks in little bursts of song.

'There's a prison called Mahjar. There's another called Abu Ghraib. Course, you lot wouldn't know about them, would you. You wouldn't know about the torture and the rape. Just here for a jolly time, bit of a singalong. Ever been to Iraq, have you? Ever met any torture victims?'

'Not as far as I know.' Michael is anxious not to lose sight of Trinity. She was beside him when he stopped to take the picture. Now he spots her twenty yards ahead, the earth colours of her scarf, the ink-black hair at her neck. She's been cheerful today, energized by the cause, but he senses the fragility of her mood.

'Making you uncomfortable, am I? Upsetting your sense of moral superiority? You'd like me to shut up, and I can't say I blame you. Just here for a jolly time, after all, bit of a singalong.'

'I wish you'd stop saying that.'

'Course you do, son. Not my problem – that's your message. Long as I got clean hands. Not in my name. Keep me out of it. It's nice and cosy here with my head up my bottom.'

'Now, listen . . .'

'Don't get me wrong. I'm not saying I've got all the

answers. That's your department.' With his free hand he gestures at the crowd, nodding as he looks round as though the very sight of them proves his point. Michael looks round too, not to appease the bird man but because he's lost sight of Trinity again. He takes in the placards, the bouncing effigies of Bush and Blair, the women in black with the cardboard coffins, the couples with their toddlers in pushchairs, the girl on stilts, the man walking backwards with a megaphone, the chanters and the conversationalists, the group in red-streaked T-shirts who have taken each other's hands to improvise a meandering dance of death.

'I'm more interested in asking questions,' the bird man says. 'You're scared of questions, I can understand that. The right question might weaken your exclusive hold on moral discernment. Better to stick your fingers in your ears and keep singing.'

'Haven't you got anyone else to talk to?' Michael picks up his pace. He can't have overtaken her, so she must have gone ahead.

The bird man hurries to stay alongside. 'These are my birds by the way.' He raises the cage to the level of his chest. 'You don't mind them, I hope. You're not allergic. Some people are allergic. Finches, canaries, cockatiels, I've been collecting them. You like birds?'

'They're OK, I suppose.'

'Like them or hate them, son, they're all God's creatures. You'll be wondering what I'm going to do with this lot.'

'Not particularly, no.'

'Well, people ask, and I always tell them, the day Saddam's prisons are liberated, I'll open the cage door. It'll be my own little gesture of solidarity. I wonder if I could tempt you to join me. I have a piece of paper here with my address on it.' He reaches inside his jacket. 'There's a lovely little roof garden the landlord allows me to use.'

The red-streaked dancers are snaking back towards them. They have acquired a trailing band of drummers and whistle-blowers, and a man in a top hat playing a reeded instrument that might be the chanter from a bagpipe. They forge a path between Michael and the birds. Swept sideways, Michael glances across to see if he is being pursued, but the bird man has latched on to a woman with long white hair, one of the Aldermaston veterans, who dips her head to listen. There's a flutter of wings as the man lifts his cage towards her.

Someone with a megaphone starts a raucous chant. *What do we want? No war! What do we want? No war! What do we want? No war!*

Michael catches a glimpse of Trinity up ahead by Green Park tube station waving her arm in time with the words. He feels the chill of the air blowing across from the park. The caged birds have put him in mind of his mother, lying in some hospital, chemically preserved for anatomical dissection.

What do we want? No war! What do we want? No war!

His phone is ringing. When he pulls it out of his pocket it stops. It's new, bought with Trinity's encouragement. He has owned many phones – his last one was stolen in Irkutsk while he dozed at a railway station – but he is happy to let Trinity think that her thirty-six-year-old uncle needs help with modern technology. She has thoughtfully programmed it to sound like a tinkling bell, thinking perhaps that he grew up in an age when you had to crank a handle.

He has also taken her advice on how to dress for a demonstration. 'If it's all the same to you,' he told her, looking from his flat down onto the neighbouring roof garden where the pots glistened with frost, 'I think I'll just concentrate on not freezing my arse off.'

'But those trousers, Uncle Mike. Whoever told you to buy trousers with double pleats?'

'They're fashionable in Estonia.'

'Nothing is fashionable in Estonia.'

'You've never been to Estonia.'

'And I don't want to if they all dress like you.'

'You argue without any logic, you know that? In complete circles. It's beautiful to watch your mind on the move.'

'You're just like Dad. He's obsessed with logic.'

'And how are his trousers?'

'Identical to yours.'

'Estonian imports, probably.'

'No, he found them in a skip.'

'How extraordinary!'

'What is?'

'Genetics, moving in mysterious ways.' He took in the cityscape to the west, towards the heroic wreckage of Battersea Power Station, and thought of the vast influx of people converging invisibly on central London to assert a single proposition. He felt an energy to join them that was suddenly more than a willingness to please his niece. Something stirred inside him that he recognized as love – for Trinity, because she had come to find him, and for Kieran, who was perhaps waiting to be found.

Trinity was clattering crockery behind him in the kitchen.

'Think about it, though,' he said. 'I'm in a street market in Narva about to expire with the cold, and two thousand miles away Kieran's rooting through a skip in the gentrified backstreets of Cheltenham, and we both stumble across the same pair of trousers. It's enough to make you believe in wormholes. Think of those trousers popping up simultaneously in two different locations in the space–time continuum, and Kieran and me with a leg each, tugging for all we're worth.'

'I'm making more coffee. Do you want some?'

'We'll be peeing all the way down the Strand.'

'Don't be gross.'

'Unless the whole world is just one big womb – nothing but me and your dad, still hoping to be born, dreaming one vast interlocking dream.'

Shuffling now along Piccadilly in denim jeans approved by Trinity, with an icy draught at his legs, he misses his Estonian trousers. The river of protestors stretches ahead and out of sight. When the phone rings again he's ready for it. He has difficulty hearing at first. Then he recognizes Kieran's voice.

'Trinity, is that you?'

'No, it's Michael.'

'Michael? Christ! Where are you?'

'In London.'

'Is Trin with you?'

'Yes, more or less.'

'Thank God for that.'

'She didn't tell you?'

'No, she bloody didn't. I've been frantic. Where in London? What's all that noise?'

'Piccadilly. By Green Park.'

'You're on that march. Of course. I assumed she was in Peckham. Then Salema phoned to read me some article in the *Catholic Herald* about Cardinal Ratzinger, as if I care, and I ask her how Trinity's doing and she hasn't seen her for days. I nearly had a heart attack. Then Trin left a message with this number. Naturally she isn't answering her own phone.'

'Look, I'm sorry about that. I kept telling her to call you.'

'So you're back in England.'

'Just about.'

'How's the march?'

'Big.'

'Who's there?'

'Oh, you know, the usual crowd, the pacifists, the anarchists, the Islamists, the revolutionary socialists. Plus half a million other people who seem to have got off at the wrong stop. They were probably looking for Madame Tussaud's.'

'People of all faiths and none, then.'

'Yes, and I even saw the nun.'

'Those papists sneak in everywhere.'

'You should have come, Kieran, it would have been good to have you here.'

'A bit late to suggest it now.'

'Trinity said you didn't approve.'

'If you wanted my opinion you should have asked.' Kieran's tone is suddenly sharp.

There's a silence and Michael wonders if they've been cut off. 'Are you still there?'

'To be honest, Mike, it's a bit much having her confiding

in you after all these years. There were times when I might have been grateful for your help. This, though – sharing secrets with her . . . Is she calling herself Yasmin, by the way?'

'Yes, she has been.'

'You're not encouraging it, I hope.'

'I don't imagine she cares what I think one way or the other.'

'You'd be surprised.'

'Look, Kier, I didn't mean to undermine you . . .'

'It's not easy raising a child alone, you know. And she still is a child, though she talks like she knows what she's doing.'

'Yes, I know she is.'

'You should have called me.'

'I assumed *she* would. I told her to more than once. She thought I was pestering her about it.'

'*Before*, I mean. You should have called me when you got back. It would have been nice to know.'

'Yes. Sorry. I've been a bit preoccupied. It's only been a week or so.'

'Well, anyway . . .'

The conversation lapses into silence.

'I've got these Estonian trousers.'

'What?'

'Trinity says you've got a pair just like them.'

'Like what?'

'Like mine. Some old pair you found on a skip.'

'Old Etonian trousers? I don't think so.'

Michael thinks it's a joke, but can no longer be sure. It's hard to hear subtleties with the noise of drums and hooters. Then they lose contact.

It bothers him to be caught in this role – conspiring with Trinity against her father. They've got along pretty well, these last couple of days. She's spent two nights on the couch in the living room, and they've had to manoeuvre around each other. But it's been OK, except for those moments when there's been nothing to say and the silence has developed an edge like an untuned violin. A couple of times he's been tempted to say, 'OK, Trinity Yasmin who-ever you are, let's talk about your mother's miraculous pregnancy that wasn't, and while we're at it what's with the non-pork diet?'

He suspects her of praying. He's almost certain that he caught her at it that first evening, after their aborted Greek dinner – just a glimpse through the half-open door. She moved suddenly, raising her head from the floor by the dining table as he came out of the bathroom, letting the scarf drop to her shoulders. It makes him sad for her. It must be hard to crouch among domestic furniture at con-stant risk of exposure. His mother would sink to her knees anywhere for a quick fix of the rosary, propping herself on the back of the chair or the edge of a table, but she was born to it. Anglicans would never kneel on their own kitchen floors, Michael is pretty sure of that. Most of them can't hack it even in church, preferring the half-crouch from the edge of the pew. He has watched men davening at the Western Wall. No kneeling there, but a jerking motion as though to bounce oneself into the irrational. All of it, he thinks, is an affront to human reason, a distraction from the real challenge to make life tolerable.

As he turns towards Hyde Park Corner he glimpses his niece by the gate. To his left, beyond the railings, is an area of grass cluttered with monuments to old wars – a naked David with a sword as high as his shoulder, a preening fusilier fresh from the defeat of Bonaparte. Ahead is the gate to Hyde Park with the lion and the unicorn in wrought iron, gaudily painted. And there's Trinity with a handsome Asian boy and a couple of girls. The stark plane trees of Hyde Park rise up behind her. She has her phone in her hands and is texting someone, or more likely, Michael realizes, entering the boy's phone number. He feels a surge of anger at her thoughtlessness.

The boy is dressed in a dark suit with a collarless jacket. His hair is swept back behind his ears. The girls are in ankle-length dresses and long white headscarves that cross under the chin and fall neatly over the shoulders, leaving exposed only the smooth ovals of their faces.

Michael strides towards them. 'Trinity.'

She turns round, glaring at him, and mutters her new name, glancing sideways at the boy.

'I've just had your dad on the phone.'

'Yes, I gave him your number.'

'You told me you'd call him.'

'I left a message.'

'You've had since Thursday. That's three days. He's not in a very good mood.'

She pouts and rolls her eyes. 'Not three days. Not even two, actually, if you think about it.'

The Asian boy steps forward and pushes a flyer into Michael's hand.

Michael glances at it. 'What *is* this?'

'We're calling for the restoration of the caliphate, yeah?'

The girls in white headscarves hang back, one on either

side of the boy like acolytes. He seems insolently aware of his power over them.

'Would that be a good thing, then, the caliphate?'

'Course it would.'

'What would be good about it?'

'A state for Muslims, yeah? All Muslims. We'd be ruled by sharia law.'

'But I'm not a Muslim, so I'd be stuffed wouldn't I, basically.'

'Like I'm stuffed here, you mean, living in a Christian country.'

The girls simper, admiring the boy's wit. Trinity watches Michael warily, afraid that he might do something to embarrass her.

Michael looks the boy up and down. 'You seem to be doing all right.'

The bolder of the two girls speaks up. 'Everyone would be welcome in the caliphate. Christians, even Jews.'

Michael turns to her, his face animated as though she has said something impressive. 'Even Jews!'

'Why not?'

'So generous.'

'There'd be no conflict,' she says, 'that's the brilliant thing about it. All living under the same law, see?'

'So could your citizens vote out your caliph and install a secular government?'

The boy shakes his head with a patronizing smile. 'That's just not going to happen.'

'You wouldn't let it happen, you mean.'

'He means,' the bold girl says, 'why would anyone want to do that?'

'Islam is designed by Allah,' the shy girl explains, 'to make people happy – that's the whole point. So if they truly experienced it, they wouldn't want anything else.'

'But it's still OK if I'm not a Muslim. I can come into this new country under this caliphate without having to convert.'

'If you want to.' She glances sideways to check that the boy approves.

'No worries,' the boy says, 'course you can.'

'And I can bring my gay lover?'

'You what?'

The bold girl sniggers.

'My gay lover – can I bring him?'

'Course not.' The boy's lips twist into a sneer. 'That would be against the teachings of the Qu'ran.'

'Well, you've lost my vote, then.' Michael crumples the paper. 'Come on, Trinity.' Dropping it to the ground, he turns to go through the gate.

The boy moves quickly to intercept him, standing in his way. 'You should show more respect.'

Trinity hasn't moved.

'Sorry, didn't mean to offend you, but the conversation's over.'

'It's not me you've offended. There are verses from the Qu'ran printed there. You want people stepping on them?'

'That's ridiculous. You've got piles of those things. Most of them are going to be thrown away . . .'

'Here.' Trinity has stooped to pick up the flyer and is smoothing it out. 'Take it. He didn't mean any disrespect. He doesn't understand, that's all.'

'Well, you explain to him, sister.' The boy turns away and the girls follow.

Michael rounds on his niece. 'I understand perfectly well. They want to impose their religion on everybody. I don't think we should let them.'

'Isn't that a bit racist?'

'If you think that's racist you don't know what racism is.'

'I bet I know a lot more about racism, actually, than you do.'

Marchers jostle past them into the park, fanning out among the limes and horse chestnuts, crowding the avenues. A pair of pigeons flap up into the air, finding a perch on the rim of Achilles' shield.

'Look, Uncle Mike, you're a Christian, basically, even if you don't believe in it. And this is a Christian country, so you don't notice. If you were a Muslim you'd notice. We're ruled by Christian laws.'

'No, we're not, thank God. We're ruled by laws that stop people killing and robbing each other, laws that establish rights of property and enforce contracts and allow us to vote and believe whatever the hell we like. There's no law against worshipping idols. There's no law against coveting your neighbour's wife.'

'Well, perhaps there ought to be. Perhaps we'd all be happier if people stayed married and looked after their children.'

'Yes, and you could have your mother flogged for abandoning you.' Michael regrets the words as soon as they are out of his mouth.

Trinity looks as though he has struck her. Tears come

to her eyes. 'That's a horrible thing to say.' She turns to go, pushing her way through the crowd towards Park Lane.

'Don't go, Trinity.'

Marchers within earshot turn curious eyes on them.

'Leave me alone.'

'Trinity! Yasmin, don't go – not like this.' He realizes too late that making a point at her expense is a humiliating achievement. He has acted like his father, letting his words do his thinking for him. 'Trinity, please! When will you be back?'

'That's none of your business, really, is it.' She has stopped to look at him. Her face, alive with defiance and pain, is obstructed and revealed again as people pass between them. 'You're not my dad.'

'I never said I was.'

'Exactly. Nobody ever says anything.' She glares at him, challenging him to respond.

What do we want?

No war!

What do we want?

No war!

Michael looks round with fury at the source of the noise. When he looks back, Trinity has gone.

Her phone is switched off, or she's choosing not to answer. He's on the pavement, heading back towards Piccadilly Circus, moving against the tide. They keep coming, the opponents of Blair's war. Trinity's departure distresses him in complicated ways. His annoyance snags against his fear for her and a delayed recognition that she has said something important.

He hears his name. He raises his head to scan the approaching faces. He knows the voice but can't place it, a female voice, an Irish accent. Then he sees the eyes fixed on his, the mouth half open.

'Good God!' She is not as he remembers, not at first. It takes him a moment to recognize her. 'Peggy O'Connor.'

'Michael Cartwright. You look just the same.'

'So do you.'

'Liar. I'll look a fuck of a lot better, though, when this demonstration's over and I can get in a hot bath.' She looks into his face. 'Are you all right, Michael?'

'I've lost my niece, that's all.'

'Your niece. Not Kieran's child.'

'That's the one.'

'How old is she now?'

'Seventeen.'

'Well, Jesus, she hardly needs you to take care of her. Remember what we were getting up to at that age.'

'I do, and it scares the hell out of me.'

It rises up between them, the memory of themselves at seventeen, a knowledge pressing on the senses. Michael sees his own awareness reflected in Peggy's shifting posture. She turns for a moment to watch some drummers pass. When she looks back she's smiling. 'Ah well, we didn't do too bad in the end.'

'How do you know?'

'You look pretty good to me.' It's the familiar smirk, unmodified by age. 'Fergal's here somewhere. But we'd never find him in this mob.'

'Fergal's here?'

'You wouldn't get a word out of him, anyhow – he's taken a vow of silence for the day. He likes to make things difficult for himself. He had it written on a card when we met. I said to him, "Jesus, Fergal, who's going to care whether you're talking or not with all this din?" And he took the card and wrote on the back of it, *Who'd care anyway?* Then he smiled to show me it was a joke. He's an odd one, that Fergal. His head's always been in some other place. His silence is for God, of course.'

'Ah yes, God.'

It's a shock to see her, bouncing up out of the past, and not so different now that he's had a chance to look, except that her hair lies more evenly on her head without the hindrance of rubber bands.

She scrabbles in her shoulder bag. 'I know I had a pen in here somewhere. Sure, this'll do.' She takes out an eyeliner. 'You wouldn't have a scrap of paper, would you?'

'How about this?' Michael picks up a discarded flyer from the road. It's the one calling for a new caliphate.

She writes her number on the back of it in large purple figures, resting the paper on her shoulder bag. 'Get in touch if you feel like talking about old times.'

'And if I can't face old times?'

'Get in touch anyway.' She squeezes the paper into his hand and moves on without looking back, mingling quickly with the other marchers.

† The Church of St Ursula and the Virgin Martyrs

Sunday 16 February 2003

When Peggy told me she had seen you yesterday,
Michael – I hardly know how to describe the effect
it had on me. I am still in a state of turmoil. I felt
that in embarking on this letter I had summoned you.
And Kieran's child was with you on the march, Peggy
said. Was Kieran with you at all, I wonder? Peggy
didn't say. Strange to think of us all gathered for
those few hours and now dispersed again. Even now
I struggle to find a place of calm to put my thoughts
in order.

   Had I seen you I would have broken my silence,
though I had made a solemn promise not to utter a
word. Just as well then. Better that I say in this letter
what must be said. As it was I kept my promise from
sunrise on Saturday until the first words of the Mass
this morning – In the name of the Father, and of the
Son, and of the Holy Spirit. How strange the words
felt in my mouth after a silence of only a single day,
which would be nothing to a Trappist. I was light-
headed, I think, when Peggy spoke to me afterwards.
She comes occasionally – out of friendship rather than
faith, I suppose, and God bless her for that. I had not

eaten since Friday, having accompanied my silence
with a fast, and would have sworn I had seen you
kneeling beside Peggy in the pew at the very moment
of consecration while I stood with the host and the
chalice in my hand. It was a vision of the ordinary
kind that will come to us often if we are open to
them. You have no time for such things, Michael,
I know. I assume your views are still as they were.
You always had a firmer foothold on what is
commonly known as reality. But I have been subject
all my life to a kind of slippage, a dizzying sense that
what has been solid is insubstantial and that the light
that plays on the surface of mundane objects is a
glimpse of the eternal.

When I was a child I would cycle to school along
a road that took me past a farmyard. Built against
one end of the cowshed was a stone grotto where
a life-size St Bernadette knelt to the Virgin. One
winter evening I cycled home at dusk and saw from
the corner of my eye the Holy Mother move her
hand in blessing. The frost in the yard shone for that
moment with unaccountable light, and I knew then
that I would be a priest. More wonderful visions
have come to me, and more terrible ones also.

But they must wait. I have always let words run
ahead of me, leading me down distracting byways.
And so I hold my tongue for one day and think I have
done something.

Amongst the endless words spoken for and against
this war, in fear and judgement and anger, it is so hard
to find God. I have tried to hold myself back from

all of it. I have taken to saying vespers during the
nine o'clock news, selfishly to shut my ears to the
noise. A handful of parishioners join me.

My childhood was shaped by political conflict,
Michael. My father died when I was seven, in an
area of Belfast called the Ardoyne. Shot like a dog
in the street by a Protestant bullet – that's how
my grandmother spoke of it, when words were
unavoidable, her lips scarcely open as though the
truth must be dragged through them. It was the
summer of 1969 and my father, a schoolmaster, had
been teaching in Belfast since my mother's death.
We didn't live in the Ardoyne, my father and I, but
he was there for a civil rights meeting. I remember
a kitchen, and me on a stool in a corner with biscuits
and a glass of milk, an older girl who might have
been ten, and a crowd at the table, and my father
telling someone to calm down. He was a calm man
usually, my father, but not so calm himself that night.
And I remember a bigger gathering in a schoolroom,
long after bedtime, and the fear in people's voices.
You have read, perhaps, of those times, Michael.
You must know of them anyhow. The demands for
equal rights in voting and employment and in the
allocation of housing, and the violent reaction of
the Protestants – of some Protestants, I should say,
for there were Protestants who marched alongside
my father and the others. And there was fear on
both sides, no doubt, Protestant as well as Catholic.
But demonstrations in Derry had been put down
brutally by the constabulary. It was madness, of

course – policing the streets with armoured vehicles and machine guns. My God, what were they thinking?

The cause for which my father gave his life was a rare thing in my country's history. It was a moment of blessing. Angels had descended for that brief season to bring light into men's hearts. You will laugh at me, Michael, I know, but when I speak of angels it is angels I mean. The moment was crushed, the breath squeezed from it. I will not place the blame on one side only. The campaign for civil rights, which I knew at the time as sleepless excitement and the smell of printer's ink and sitting on the shoulders of strangers to watch my father speak, was, as I now understand it, an acknowledgement of a historical reality – an implied acceptance of the partition of Ireland. We will take part, the people said, if you will let us. We will vote. We will be equal citizens in this province that is not our country but only part of our country, over which the foreigner, our ancient enemy, still presides. For some, still committed to a unified republic to be fought for by whatever means however murderous, this alone was a betrayal. And the Loyalists, loyal to their own status if to nothing else, were ready for them. And so the angels retreated, driven out by guns and bombs, leaving my father to die. I have never seen a dog shot in the street, Michael, though I doubt whether a stray bullet from a machine gun is the way you would choose to have the job done.

So my grandmother lived in bitterness. It grieves me to say this – loving one's enemies was for her a theoretical requirement that must be waived for the

mother of a murdered son. She hated Protestants
above all. Her hatred of the British was not political.
The English soldiers stationed on Irish soil had stood
by while her son died, that was all.

It was not many years later that she lost her
other child, my Aunt Maud – not killed but buried
in disgrace. Maud had married Dennis out of necessity,
it seems, rather than love, and poor Peggy was only
eleven when Maud left them both for a Cork man,
a poet or an actor – a scandal much chewed over in
Kilross and, for all I know, in Cork, but never
mentioned at home.

My grandmother harboured another source of
bitterness. I could not be in that house all those years
and not catch a whiff of it. It was because of my
mother that my father moved to the North – because
of her, therefore, that he was killed, though she had
been long dead already by then. My mother was
Spanish and had moved to Belfast to work in the hotel
trade. People spoke of her as Corrie, but I heard once
that this was part of a longer name, Corazon del Sol,
which I jumbled in my childish way with the flapping
sheets covering and uncovering the sun, and her above
me in the dazzling light.

And so I grew up in a house of unspoken
certainties, prejudices expressed in sniffs and narrowed
eyes and pursed lips, where words were spent as
sparingly as silver coins. This was not a contemplative
silence, you understand. This was not the silence
that invites the presence of God. This was a dinning
muteness that clamoured throughout the house.

My visits to Kilross, though a welcome relief, were too infrequent and I remained a stranger in my uncle's house and an embarrassment to my cousin Peggy. Little wonder that I was enchanted by your family. There were certainties there too, of course, no shortage of them, and I knew that you chafed against the opinions of your mother and father and resented their authority, but there was too much noise and bustle for secrets and I sensed that anything that must be said would burst out one way or another. And indeed there was anger enough, God knows, that first time I was taken to visit all of you in your grandparents' house on Strand Street, and I thought I would see blood spilt, and all about nothing – about whether Kieran should play his violin (I can't remember now were you there at all? I don't see you in the room as I picture it) – but I loved your mother in her anger, as I would later love her in her grief and in her pride and, most often, in her fretfulness. We spoke more that evening at the church after confession, when she approached me to apologize, not for her own behaviour but for the scene Kieran had caused and the poor light in which the whole family had been cast. I imagine you smiling at that, Michael, believing your mother to be at fault entirely, but it was a small enough thing she had asked of Kieran. I am inclined to think you would have done it for her.

It was a great thing for me to know, when I was back in the seminary in Dublin, that I had cousins in England, for I was in no doubt that I would be sent to that fearful land of Protestants once I was ordained.

Don't laugh at me, Michael. I had dreamt that spring of dragons and of a knight who would help me fight them, and woke in the knowledge that I had been visited by St George, the patron saint of the English. If I had thought more deeply about that dream I might have understood that the dragon I would have to fight I would be taking with me on my journey, and that it was a dragon I was singularly ill-prepared to defend myself against.

I planned to leave early for my new parish in London so that I would have time to stop in Cheltenham for a few days on the way, a town known back home for the racing, so I took some teasing from Uncle Dennis that it was to put money on the horses I was going and not to visit the Cartwrights at all. I had looked forward to spending time with your whole family, though it was you, Michael, most of all that I longed to see. Meeting your mother again I anticipated with mixed feelings. It was she, of course, who had urged me to come, but I was a little shy, having opened up to her in my letters on the strength of so brief an acquaintance.

I had little idea what complications would come with me across the water.

JUNE 1983 CHELTENHAM

A moth-eaten bell pull hung beside the mantelpiece in the dining room. As children Michael and Kieran had swung on it, imagining ghostly servants listening in the attic bedrooms. At some stage in its decline the house had been divided into flats, and the glazed partitions cutting off the stairwell at each floor still had their letter boxes and their doorbells whose wires now led nowhere. Meaner subdivisions had followed. There was a bedroom split in two with plywood and corrugated plastic, another with a gas cooker and hot-water geyser, disconnected but never removed.

The scaffolding that curtained the building was brown with rust. It had stood there for as long as the twins could remember, and longer – ever since Jack Cartwright had rescued the place from demolition. Ivy from the side wall of the house had strayed out along the putlogs and down the diagonal braces to mingle with the grass and weeds.

Stone steps led up from the road to the portico, whose columns supported a conservatory. One corner had settled, leaving a trail of spidery cracks across the panes. It was from here through the distortion of the glass that Michael watched the truck pull up. He saw his father climb out, then Fergal from the passenger side. The sound of their conversation floated in through the open window. They

were talking about Eileen's wedding. Michael had heard
his father's line on this. He was sorry to see Fergal drawn
into this argument before he'd even got through the front
door.

'A travesty is what it is, Fergal.'

'Moira tells me he's a Catholic boy, Jack, and a good
student. That's something, isn't it?'

'But this is a doctrinal issue. As a priest you can grasp
that, surely, even if my family can't.'

Michael was turning from the window, on his way to rescue Fergal, when a second passenger stepped out onto the
road, red ankle boots first, then spiked hair and a woollen
coat. It had an odd effect on him to see Peggy O'Connor after
almost a year, a swooping feeling in his stomach.

Jack was pulling the suitcases from the back of the truck.
'Before Christmas, when Eileen announced this brilliant
match, we assumed she must have got herself pregnant.
Now, Fergal, without a scrap of shame, she tells us that she
has no intention of having babies. Your so-called marriage
will have no meaning then, I told her. The contract will be
null from the moment you make your vows.'

Peggy looked pale and subdued, and held her coat
closed, though it was a mild evening.

'And if I were to attend the ceremony, knowing what I
know, if I were to lend my tacit support to this ... this ...'

'I do see what you mean, Jack.'

'... this fraud, well I'd be an accessory, wouldn't I.'

'On the other hand, Jack, Eileen is part of your family.
No one would condemn you for attending your daughter's
wedding if you have done your best, which I'm confident
that you have, to counsel her appropriately.'

'Counsel her? Do you imagine any of my children come to me for counselling?'

Passing Emily, who was hovering by a pillar, Michael joined the visitors where they stood on the road under the canopy of trees. Fergal brightened at the sight of him and shook his hand vigorously, saying how great it was to see him looking so well.

'I hope your mother won't mind the change of plan, Michael,' Peggy said. 'If there's no bed for me, I'm sure I can find somewhere to stay. It's only for a few days. I'll be on my way to London shortly.'

Michael felt himself blush. 'There'll be a bed for you somewhere. The house is full of beds.'

Moira appeared in the doorway, pulling her apron over her head. Relieved of his duty, Jack got back in the truck saying he hadn't yet been to vote. Michael led the visitors up the steps, past the Conservative Party poster that leaned out from a rhododendron bush, lugging Peggy's suitcase. In the hall there was large fireplace with a print of Monet's lilies propped against the grate. The stone staircase spiralled upwards.

Moira took Peggy's hands and moved around her with a kind of gaiety that Michael knew not to trust. When she turned to the light he could see that her eyes were still red from crying. 'How nice that you came, Peggy dear. And how is your father?'

'He's well, thanks, Mrs Cartwright.'

'You look pale, dear. If I'd known you were coming, sure, I'd have made up a bed.' Raising her head, she sang Katherine's name up the staircase.

'What now?' Katherine appeared above them, leaning out over the balustrade.

'You'll be sleeping with Emily tonight. Peggy O'Connor's here, come with Fergal.'

'Hello, Katherine,' Peggy said, tilting her head back. 'Sorry to take your bed.'

Katherine shrugged. 'That's OK.'

'They'll want towels, Katherine,' Moira said, 'and show Peggy where the bathroom is.'

Katherine glared down at the top of her mother's head.

'Now, Fergal, you'll be sharing with Michael and Kieran. I've invited some people for a drink. I thought you'd like to meet our parish priest, Father Riley.'

'That's very thoughtful of you, Moira.'

Michael showed Fergal the spare bed and left him to unpack. Downstairs, the sound of the violin drew him to the dining room. Kieran was practising an orchestral part. Salema was sitting at the table doing her homework. Beside her Kieran's metronome was ticking.

He lowered his violin. 'Mam turfed us out of the sitting room.'

Salema looked up from her writing. 'Apparently there are people coming.'

'I know. Sorry. I mean . . . it's because of Fergal.' What gave Salema this power, Michael wondered, to reduce him to such a state of incoherence? Even Peggy, who had appeared suddenly from nowhere, didn't have quite this effect. But Peggy was just an ordinary Irish girl who thought about ordinary things, whereas Salema was half Indian and half Greek and half mortal and half spirit and half of what she said was entirely mysterious to him and the very sight of her scrambled his brain so that he was incapable of replying sensibly to the other half. The metronome didn't help, measuring the silence with its little explosions of sound.

'How about a drink later?' Kieran asked him. 'What about it, Sal, can you stay for a bit?'

'How long's a bit?'

'Long enough for a drink with Mike.'

Salema gave Michael a startled look as though she'd only just discovered he was in the room and let her gaze slide towards the ceiling. 'Maybe,' she said. 'I'll have to see.'

'There you are then, Mike.' With a flash of irritation, Kieran raised his violin to his shoulder, shifting his jaw to accommodate it. 'That probably means yes.' His fingers were already moving experimentally across the strings.

In the kitchen Katherine was buttering bread rolls. She had managed to make her hair look vaguely like Peggy's, with clumps sticking out in odd directions. Through the window, Michael caught sight of Emily leading Fergal on a tour of the garden. Whatever it was she had found to say about the tomatoes, Fergal was listening carefully, leaning in towards her. Peggy came into view, kicking her way through nettles and dandelions in her red boots. She turned her head to gaze up at the house. Michael felt a rush of desire and anxiety at the sight of her. Kieran's music, an angular piece of Shostakovich, cut through from the dining room, adding a disjointed soundtrack.

'Watch out,' Katherine said, 'Mam's in a funny mood.'

'Why, what's she been doing?'

'Crying. About Eileen, mainly. And then laughing and getting all excited. She started a novena to the Virgin Mary. She lit a candle on top of the telly. She wanted me to join in. I said I had homework.' Katherine was about to say more, but stopped herself.

There were footsteps in the hall and Moira came in, zipping her skirt up at the side. She held a matching jacket under her arm. The music came more clearly through the open door. 'This blouse buttons up at the back, Michael. Would you mind?' She lifted her hair for him to fasten the buttons. 'That little madam's still in there with Kieran, I suppose.'

'Her name's Salema, Mam, and I don't know what you've got against her.'

'So aloof, she is, so haughty, keeping her thoughts to herself.' She pulled away before the last button was done. 'When those baps are buttered, Katherine, you can open a tin of salmon.' She walked across the kitchen, putting the jacket on and adjusting the shoulder pads. Then she turned to face Michael, tilting her head self-consciously. 'Well, what do you think?' The suit was a synthetic blue. The blouse was cream with mauve flowers and a mauve bow at the neck. She had no shoes on, only pale tights, with white reinforcement at the toes. 'I found a hat to go with it, on the table, look, and a handbag. It'll do, won't it?'

'I suppose so,' Michael said. 'For what?'

'Oh, Michael, don't be so aggravating.'

They heard the flush of the downstairs toilet and the sound of water running in the basin. 'That'll be your father. Now, Michael, I ran into Father Kenton at the co-op and invited him. He was your favourite at school, wasn't he? You were always talking about him.'

'Father Kenton?'

'And I thought, since Father Riley's invited, and Fergal's here . . .'

'But, Mam!'

Jack came in from the hall smiling at his newspaper. 'You should read this piece, Moira, on the Labour manifesto. Even their side are calling it the longest suicide note in history.'

'You invited Father Kenton?'

Moira had arranged the hat on her head – blue felt with a matching bow and a neat brim. 'Well, Jack,' she said, turning towards him. Her eyes flared in anticipation of trouble. 'What do you think? It was on sale in Marks and Spencer's. Hardly any price at all.'

Jack looked up from his paper. 'A bit much for a drink with Father Riley, isn't it?'

Katherine giggled. 'You look like Maggie Thatcher.'

'You mind your mouth,' Moira said, 'or you'll get what's coming.'

'Well, you do, doesn't she, Mikey?'

Moira faced Katherine, hands on hips. 'Did you open that tin of salmon yet? And what in heaven's name have you done to your hair?'

'Salmon!' Jack said. 'We're not having salmon, are we?'

'And why not salmon, I'd like to know?'

'People won't want to go around smelling of fish.'

'What are you talking about? Perfectly decent people eat fish all the time.'

'We should have cucumber sandwiches, anyway, if you're going to wear that hat.'

Moira sighed with exasperation. 'It's my outfit for Saturday, Jack, not for tonight. It's for Eileen's wedding. There's a handbag as well here somewhere.' She rummaged among the bags and papers on the kitchen table. 'It was forty per cent off.'

'Eileen's wedding? I've told you what I think about Eileen's wedding. And Fergal agrees with me.'

'Oh, does he?' Moira's face hardened with defiance. 'Does he indeed?'

'Yes, he does. You'll make yourself look ridiculous, turning up dressed like that.'

'Honestly, though,' Michael said, agitated almost to the point of tears. 'What on earth did you invite Father Kenton for?'

'Well, Mam? Am I supposed to be opening this salmon or do you want something else on the rolls?'

'So! I'll look ridiculous, will I?'

'A lot of punks and lefties. And those two playing at getting married, making a mockery of a sacrament of the Church.'

'Father Kenton, of all people, Mam! Don't you ever listen to anything I say?'

The back door was pushed open. Emily stood looking in from the garden with Peggy and Fergal behind her. Everyone inside was suddenly quiet.

'And this is the kitchen,' Emily said, 'where Mother cooks meals for the family and we eat, and sometimes we watch the news on the TV, and *Dallas*, and next I'll show you the coal shed.' In the dining room the Shostakovich stopped for long enough for Kieran to shout, 'Bugger and bollocks!' The back door closed and Emily and the Irish guests were gone.

Katherine made a choking noise that grew into a snort that might have been laughter.

'Well, that's it, then.' Moira threw the hat onto the table and was pulling off the jacket. 'You like nothing better than to gang up against me, making a joke of everything I do.' She began to weep as she unzipped the skirt and stepped out of it, leaving it on the floor.

'Moira, for pity's sake!'

'You care nothing for my feelings, and you care nothing for me.' Standing in her blouse and tights, she rounded on Michael. 'And as for you . . . I've done everything I can think of to make your life happy. Do you think you'd be going to the art college next year if it was up to your father? And for you to turn on me now . . .'

'I didn't turn on you. I just said . . .'

'All of you laughing at me behind my back, getting Fergal to side with you against me.'

Katherine banged the tin down in exasperation. There were tears in her eyes. 'Do I open the salmon or not?'

'Do what you like. I'm done with the lot of you.'

Jack winced as she left, slamming the door in his face. 'For heaven's sake, Moira,' he said, and then, more quietly, speaking to himself or to Michael, 'I think this crack is opening up again.'

Michael was relieved to see that his mother had found something else to wear by the time Father Riley and Father

Kenton arrived, and had recovered herself enough to put on a show of sociability, a brittle surface under which her emotions churned. She greeted the guests with the mixture of deference and flirtatiousness that she reserved for priests, showing them into the sitting room, where Fergal waited. Emily clung to the sleeve of Fergal's jacket as though afraid he might float away. Dreading an encounter with Father Kenton, Michael would have lurked in the attic or the basement, but he didn't want to behave like a child with everyone there – everyone being Peggy, probably, and Salema, and maybe Fergal.

Father Riley officiated from the leather armchair by the fireplace, knocking back Moira's sherry. Father Kenton chipped in with humorous comments. In his nervousness Fergal laughed too loud and agreed too emphatically, which made Peggy turn aside to quiz Kieran on his fiddle-playing – did he know any Irish tunes and could he play by ear? – while Salema drifted off around the edges of the room, fingering the ornaments, and the shabby curtains. Katherine stood sullenly with her plate of buttered rolls, sliced now into squares and supplemented with cubes of Cheddar and tinned pineapple skewered on cocktail sticks. She had forgotten the reinvention of her hair until, moving at an angry signal from her mother to offer the plate to Father Riley, she caught sight of herself in the mirror on the mantelpiece and, suddenly embarrassed, began pulling surreptitiously at the plastic slides and rubber bands. Peggy, who hadn't felt able to eat on the journey, reached indiscriminately for whatever food caught her eye. A passing reference to liberation theology from Father Kenton set Jack off on a rant. And when, from across the room, Father Kenton's gaze settled as though by accident on Michael, the priest's mouth twitched and his eyelids flickered as conflicting feelings struggled for control of his facial muscles, which might settle at any moment into an expression of fear or pleading or mockery.

'Yesterday was my father's birthday,' Salema said later, in the Coach and Horses. 'Eighth of June. He would have been fifty-two.'

'He's dead, then?' Peggy asked her.

'Yes, he's dead. But my mother doesn't care. The tax-man invited his brother to dinner last night and he brought his disgusting girlfriend and I had to eat with them. And all the time I wanted to be able to think about my father.'

'How long ago was it he died?'

'Eight years.'

'And do you miss him a great deal?'

'I do, yes. I miss him terribly.'

'Well, I hope he wouldn't have been drinking shandy on his birthday.'

'I don't know. I can't remember what he drank.'

They sat without speaking for a while. Then Peggy said, 'My mother walked out when I was eleven. Went waltzing off with her lover.'

'How awful.'

'I'm over it now. I wouldn't have her back. My dad would, but I wouldn't, not if she crawled all the way from Cork on her knees.' Peggy's face, pink-cheeked now from the warmth and the drink, was attractive to Michael in movement and expression. Salema didn't need to do anything, or say anything, or even think anything to be worth looking at. Michael had concluded that this was what was meant by beauty and he had begun to chafe against the effortless tyranny of it.

Salema's lips had begun to quiver and a tear rolled down the side of her nose.

'I'm going to get you a brandy,' Peggy said, 'and sure, we'll drink a toast to your dad.' She got unsteadily to her feet.

'No, really. I don't.'

'Well, it's about time you did. I'll be right back.'

'Eighth of June,' Kieran said.

Salema took out her handkerchief and dabbed her eyes. 'That's right.'

'Albinoni was born on the eighth of June.'

'Albinoni?' Michael twisted his vowels into an approximation of a New York accent, reaching across the table to flick Kieran on the arm with the back of his hand. 'Tomaso Albinoni?'

Kieran followed his lead. 'Who wants to know?'

'Antonio Vivaldi. Call me Tony.'

'How ya doin, Tony?'

'What you got in that violin case, Tomaso?'

'I got an adagio that'll blow your head off.'

'And also,' Salema said, 'Saint Alphege.' She picked up her shandy and took a sip.

Kieran looked sideways at her. 'Saint who?'

'Alphege, tenth-century bishop and martyr. He became the Archbishop of Canterbury. My father revered Saint Alphege, partly because they shared a birthday, but also because he was a musician.'

'Alphege?' Michael had drunk enough to find the name irresistibly comic. 'Alphege? Ere, Alphege, what you bin doin?'

Salema raised her voice to be heard. 'You shouldn't laugh, you two. Alphege was a great and holy man. He built a huge organ that could be heard a mile away. It needed twenty-four monks to operate it.'

The organ had reduced the boys to helpless, stomach-clutching laughter. Kieran was clinging to the table.

'Ere, Alphege,' Michael managed to say, 'er indoors says you bin pesterin er wiv your huge organ.'

'It's not funny! Really it's not! The Vikings killed him with an axe. There were miracles after his death.'

'Do you really believe that?' Kieran asked her, recovering somewhat. 'You believe that there were miracles?'

'Yes.'

'Such as?'

'Well, his body was uncorrupted, for one thing. They opened his tomb years later when Thomas à Becket was archbishop and it hadn't even begun to rot.'

'This body,' Michael said, 'it was in the ground, was it?'

'I don't know. It was probably in the cathedral – in the crypt, or something. He was venerated.'

'Exactly, so they buried him in a nice dry stone coffin.'

'Of course,' Kieran said, 'and then they eviscerated him.'

Salema looked bewildered. 'They did what?'

'They gutted him.'

'How do you know? Why would they do that?'

'Where else did they get all the relics? Little slices of his internal organs. That's all the enzymes gone. They weren't going to chop his fingers off, were they?'

'What relics?'

'There had to be relics. That's what people wanted from a medieval martyr. Body parts.'

'Yes!' Michael said. 'Exactly! Dry coffin. No enzymes. No wonder it took him so long to rot.'

Salema turned from one to the other. 'What are you talking about? Why are you being so horrid?'

It gave Michael a surge of uneasy joy to collude with his brother against Salema.

Peggy was back from the bar with a large glass of brandy.

'Go on,' Peggy said, 'force yourself. In memory of your dad. It'll do you good.'

Salema picked up the brandy and poured it into her mouth. Gulping it down, she spluttered the last of it onto her chin.

'Well, Jesus,' Peggy said, 'you're a girl who knows how to have a good time.'

Salema burst into tears.

'Come on, Sal,' Kieran said, 'we were only messing about.'

'You're not usually like this,' she said.

Peggy nudged Michael with her elbow. 'What have you boys been doing to her?'

'Nothing.'

'Honestly,' Kieran said, 'we were only joking.' He seemed torn between remorse and irritation.

Salema had pulled her feet up onto the bench, hugging her legs. With her head down against her knees, she rocked forward and back and forward again. Across the rim of the table Michael could see the backs of her thighs, dark and flawless except for a horizontal mark like a welt from a beating, and a white triangle of underwear.

Her head moved and she was peering at him through strands of black hair with an ambiguous expression. He forced himself to look at the drunk over by the bar, at the fat women giggling by the window. The welt, he realized in a rush of private embarrassment, was only the indentation from the edge of the seat.

Kieran had raised a tentative hand to touch her shoulder. 'Don't cry, Sal, please.'

There was a grumbling noise from her throat, and she curled round towards Kieran, her knees against his chest, her arms round his neck, and began kissing his face. His head straightened suddenly against the wall from the shock of it. Then his hands began a tentative progress across her shoulders. When their mouths found each other – Salema almost sitting now in Kieran's lap, having turned her slender back on the table – Michael half rose from his chair, sat down again, picked up his glass and drank from it, staring at the tarnished horse brasses hanging above Kieran's head and the fox-hunting scene in its silver frame and the imitation parchment lampshade. Two contradictory thoughts had come to him at once – that Salema and his brother had never kissed before, and that Salema knew a lot more about kissing than he would have supposed.

Peggy was speaking into his ear. 'Come on, Michael. I think these two need some time alone.' She finished her drink and stood up. Taking his hand and pulling him to his feet, she led him towards the door.

They stumbled out into the narrow street, turning towards the promenade where the lights were brighter. Now that there was room they moved apart. The music was fading behind them. They reached the corner, and there was the fountain – the water tumbling over Neptune's horses in the changing colours of the traffic lights – and the unhurried movement of people, some of them hand in hand or with their arms round each other's waists, as though it had all been settled – the guesswork and negotiations, the shifting alliances, all over and done with.

'You have a thing for that girl, don't you.' Peggy's voice reached him from the edge of the fountain.

'What kind of a thing?'

Laughing, she leaned back against the stone balustrade. 'You tell me.'

'I don't know what you mean.' He couldn't help smiling. It excited him to be questioned by Peggy in this intimate way. 'Anyway, I don't have a thing for her.'

'She's not the one for you, Michael Cartwright.'

'What makes you so sure?'

Peggy's jaw dropped in mock amazement. 'Were you not sitting beside me when she started climbing all over your brother? Your mam sees what's going on, even if you don't. I heard her telling Fergal. She thinks Little Miss Perfect is going to gobble that boy up and spit him out.'

'Doesn't sound like something Mam would say.'

'Maybe not – that was the gist of it, anyhow. And I'd say the gobbling has begun, wouldn't you?' Dissolving into giggles, she set off across the street to where the shops were.

Michael caught up with her by the window of a department store. She was staring in at the display. 'Can you believe the stuff they want to sell us?' The models behind the glass were dressed for corporate power, triangles teetering on slender feet, exaggerated shoulders and skirts tight at the knees.

'You'd look good in anything.'

She twisted round to face him, slumping back against the glass, and gave him her insolent look. 'Are you practising?'

'How do you mean?'

'Things to say to Little Miss Perfect.' Her lips parted in mockery or challenge. As he leant in towards her, she turned aside and his mouth collided with a plastic hair grip just above her ear. Her mood had changed. 'Oh, no, no, no, I shouldn't be doing this.' She spoke more to herself than to him.

'It was OK last summer.'

'Last summer! We were kids last summer.'

'What does that mean?'

She made a noise that might have been the beginning of an answer. Then she said, 'Isn't that them?'

They were fifty yards off in the middle of the promenade. Kieran had his hands in his pockets. Salema clung to his arm, her head resting on his shoulder. They reached the pavement in the glare of a jeweller's window, and disappeared.

'They came a different way.'

'Dirty beasts.' Peggy faced Michael, her eyes full of mischief again. 'Let's catch up with them.' She took his arm and pulled him forward into a run. Reaching the jeweller's, they took a curving path into a dimly lit side street, Michael animated by the exertion, Peggy skipping and whooping beside him. A woman stepping out of a restaurant backed into her husband to avoid a collision and for a moment Michael retained the image of their snooty disapproval – a moment of clarity in the blur of street lights and shop fronts and dark spaces behind wrought-iron railings.

Up ahead where the lights were sparser and the buildings more dingy, a skip blocked half the pavement and stuck out into the road. Somebody stood in the shadows by the wall. There was a movement and it was two people, Salema with her hands held up to Kieran's face. Michael accelerated towards the skip and threw himself up at it. With his forearms on its rusted rim, he kicked the side, scrabbling for a foothold. The thudding resonated in his belly and echoed back from across the street. He could hear Peggy's whistles and catcalls, and felt his own struggle weakened by laughter. Then someone had taken hold of his foot and hoisted him so that he toppled forward on his hands and knees into the rubbish. There was a muffled crack of glass and glazing bars. His feet found the rim and he stood up, arms flailing. Dizzy with the sudden movement and the alcohol buzzing in his head, he saw Kieran below preparing to break his fall, Salema hanging back in the darkness, Peggy clapping, while the flickering street lamps and the slate roofs and chimneys shifted around him.

Finding his balance, he looked down again at the skip. Beyond the broken window was a pair of feet, naked with the soles towards him. The legs descended at a shallow angle into a pile of fashion magazines and cardboard boxes. He took a couple of tentative steps over the glass and squatted to take a closer look. He reached out, with his heart racing, and found himself touching hard plastic. He took the mannequin firmly by the ankles and tugged. It slid towards him, skinny arms dragging, bald head lolling to one side. Taking its weight, he staggered backward and righted himself. He heard a wolf whistle from Peggy, and the horn of a passing car.

He dropped the mannequin into Kieran's arms, a better trophy than the catseyes they had once gouged out of the tarmac together in the middle of a country road.

Peggy lolloped over to give Kieran a hug. The plastic feet poked up between them. Salema stood ten yards away, shoulders hunched, arms tightly folded, feet together, as neat and detached as a mannequin herself.

'Well?' Kieran said in a sudden rage. 'What?'

She turned away and started walking.

Michael squatted down and sat on the rim of the skip, letting his legs swing. 'Will she be all right, Kier?'

'Do you know what she was saying when you turned up just now?'

'What? I want your sexy violinist's hands all over me? I can't wait to get inside your trousers?'

'She wants us to rededicate our lives to the Divine Mother.'

'Fuckinell.'

'Sometimes I think she's mad. I mean, clinically insane.'

An image came into Michael's mind of men in white coats leading Salema into the back of a van, and Salema, sedated, her feet naked on the pavement, turning to him in mute appeal. Then a struggle to rescue her, a chase through dark city streets, and Salema at last in some place of safety curled up on his lap. But it was Kieran's lap she was sitting on, curled up in the corner of the Coach and Horses, and he shook the picture out of his head.

They straggled home, the three of them, the boys taking it in turns to carry the mannequin, and talking about what to do with it. They'd prop it up by the cooker with an apron on. They'd fill the bath with water and leave it sitting there for their father to find in the morning.

'Or Fergal,' Peggy suggested. 'He's always up at six. It's a habit with him.'

The collision of Fergal's habit with the naked mannequin had them choking and snorting, and prompted a burst of nun jokes, so that Peggy christened the thing Sister Benedict after a young teacher at her school in Kilross who had been the object of girlish fantasies because she was suspected of sleeping with the gardener.

When they reached the house, it was Michael who suggested that they lug Sister Benedict up the ladder onto the scaffolding. They gathered by a bedroom window at the corner overlooking the street, breathless with the fun of it, shushing each other not to wake the parents. The trees and houses fell away ahead of them, roofs of tile and slate, with their chimney pots all different, stepping down into a valley and rising again to cluster round the tower of the Anglican church. There were little rectangles of light scattered up the slopes of the hill beyond, and the edge of the escarpment was dark against the sky. They stood for a while, breathing from the exertion.

Then Peggy said she was starving, and Kieran offered to get some bread and cheese.

'And some fruit if there is some. Oranges maybe. Pickles too if you have any.'

'Anything else?'

Kieran was being sarcastic, but Peggy just grinned and said, 'No, that'll do me for now.'

He slid the sash window up and disappeared into the darkness, clambering over Emily, who grumbled sleepily. Peggy smiled at this, and Michael moved closer to her where she stood leaning on the outer bar of the scaffolding. There were some stars out and a hazy impression of the moon.

'Can I kiss you now?' he said.

She pulled a face. 'You know I'm on my way to London.'

He shrugged.

'So what would you be kissing me for?'

'Just because I want to.'

'Or because you can't have your Indian princess, so you'll make do with me?'

The sound of cheering on a neighbour's television floated up from an open window. Peggy looked at him. 'You could come with me if you like.'

'How do you mean?'

'To London. You could get a job. Why work for your dad? You could earn as much on any building site. You can paint and do carpentry.'

'I'm going to art college. I'm going to do a foundation course.' He saw the road below as a dark river he could leap into and follow wherever it would take him. But it was just a fantasy, this London idea, just a game she was playing. 'So what will you do, when you're in London?'

'I don't know. It depends. There's a thing I have to take care of, then I'll decide.'

Before he could ask what it was, this thing, she put her hand on the back of his head and kissed him. Her breath was warm and her mouth tasted of rum. He remembered the feeling of everything being lifted inside him.

She pulled back with a sigh. 'Come with me to London, Michael.'

He laughed, excited to be asked, excited to be kissed, not thinking she meant it.

'I'm not joking. You have to be serious too. It's not something to joke about.' She turned away and he knew he'd disappointed her.

They heard Kieran's whisper behind them. 'Here, grab hold of this.' He passed a plate of food out through the open window. Michael took it, losing an apple, which landed with a soft thud. Finding a crack between scaffold boards, it rolled away along the side of the house, until Peggy took a few quick steps and stopped it with her boot.

'And this lot,' Kieran said, bundling some clothing out towards Michael. It was the outfit their mother had bought in Marks and Spencer's. 'We can dress her in these.'

As Kieran climbed out, Emily appeared behind him in the open window. 'Dress who? What's going on, Kier?'

'Sister Benedict. Now go back to sleep.'

Katherine peered out, yawning and bleary eyed. 'Who's Sister Benedict?'

Peggy took a few bites out of her apple and, with sudden energy, set about dressing the mannequin. She had dressed mannequins before, Michael realized. He watched her twist the arms back to get the jacket on, and slide the skirt up over the narrow hips. Propped against the wall, Sister Benedict tilted drunkenly on her toes, and then slid down onto the boards, leaving her hat behind her on the windowsill.

Coiled nearby was a length of rope their father used to haul up loads of roofing slates and mortar. Michael slung an end over a higher pole and began to tie it in a loop around Sister Benedict's neck. 'Here, Kieran,' he said, 'find something to attach the other end to.'

'My God,' Peggy said, 'I can't believe you boys are hanging your mother.'

'Sister Benedict,' Kieran corrected her.

'And we're just keeping her upright,' Michael said.

'Not Sister Benedict any more, not with that suit on.'

'Can I hang her too?' Emily said. 'Please, Mikey. Please, Kier.'

'Go back to sleep, Em,' Katherine said, climbing out to join them. 'You're too young.'

'I'm not too young. Really I'm not.'

Kieran made a hushing noise. 'Keep your voice down, Em. You'll wake Mam and Dad.'

'They haven't even gone to bed yet. They're in the living room, with Fergal, watching the election.'

Katherine had stood on something and stooped to pick it up. It was the handbag that had dropped from Kieran's bundle. 'Here, Mikey,' she said, 'what about this?'

Michael arranged one of the arms so that he could hang the bag over the wrist. Straightening the hat, he too was reminded of his mother in her new wedding outfit, and his rage against her, which felt urgent and inexplicable.

Down under the beech trees, a car swept past on the

road, music blaring. It stopped with a squeal of brakes, and backed up at high speed until it stood outside the house. The volume rose as the passenger door opened.

Michael moved to the edge to get a better view. Someone was getting out, a boy with shaggy hair, wearing an old combat jacket. He opened the back door and pulled out a bag. He leant in to say something and slammed the door shut as the car pulled away. He stood in the street for a moment. Then the sound of their feet on the boards drew his eyes upwards.

'Is that you, Peggy darling?' he said.

'No it's not,' Peggy said, 'so fuck off out of here.'

He dropped his pack by the wall and began climbing, not bothering with the ladders, just swinging and hauling his way up.

When he reached their level he took in the scene, his craggy unshaven face breaking into a grin. 'I see I'm in time for the hanging.'

Kieran stood awkwardly by the wall, the mannequin beside him. The younger ones sat on the windowsill. Michael and Peggy were together at the outer edge, leaning against the pole. 'I suppose you're drunk, Dan Sheahan,' Peggy said.

'I may be, Peggy darling, but I hope you're not.'

'What if I am? What's it to you?'

'You should be taking better care of our baby.'

'And you should mind your own business.'

'Whose business would that be if not mine?'

'Who is he, Mikey?' Emily said in a loud whisper.

Spinning round to talk to the others, Dan stumbled, looking for a moment as though he might lose his footing and slip from the edge.

Peggy reached a hand out and took his arm. 'Dan, for heaven's sake . . .'

Recovering his balance, he slipped his arm around her waist and pulled her towards him. 'I'm glad to see you, Peggy. I thought I'd lost you altogether.'

She twisted her mouth away. 'Be careful, Dan, you'll have us both killed.'

'And in front of Mikey too. You see how this girl takes care of me, Mikey? And you . . .' – he turned to Kieran – 'you must be the brother.'

'Yes.'

'You play the fiddle, I hear.'

'That's right.'

'And I see you're the rebel of the family.'

'Am I?' Kieran sniggered, glancing across at Michael. He played absently with his end of the rope, which had become an embarrassment to him. The mannequin slid a few inches down the wall, jerking the handbag and snagging the hat so that the front of the brim tipped over the eyes.

'Hang her in effigy today, Kieran, and tomorrow, you can go to Downing Street and hang her in person.'

'If she gets back in,' Michael said.

'Oh, she'll get back in, no doubt about that. The English love a good beating. The more Nanny beats them, the more they cling to her skirts. The first results are in, anyhow. We heard it on the road. It's set to be a landslide.'

Michael looked at Peggy who had given up trying to move Dan's arm from her waist. So she was pregnant, and everything she'd said while Kieran was in the house meant something different. Katherine and Emily were watching the Irish visitors from their windowsill, curious to see how this new drama would develop. Kieran, wanting to be done with his end of the rope, was tying it to a downpipe. There was cheering and laughter from one of the neighbouring houses. A bank of cloud shifted across the sky.

FEBRUARY 2003 LONDON

Michael sits in Izzy's, just off the Walworth Road. He feels comfortable in this hybrid place, where a Turkish proprietor cooks English breakfasts for Poles and West Indians. Business is slow today. It's early yet for Sunday shoppers. But the market traders drop by, standing in the doorway in knotted scarves and woolly hats to negotiate orders, letting in gusts of wintry air.

Trinity didn't show up last night. He hasn't seen her since she stalked off along Park Lane. Her phone is still switched off. Waking this morning, early, he found the sofa still unoccupied, the bedding folded on the chair, her bag just where she had left it before the march. He thought of phoning Kieran but was reluctant to identify Trinity's absence as a crisis. Instead he phoned Peggy, finding her number folded in the pocket of his jeans. And sleepy as she was, she responded as though calling her was the obvious thing to do, as though seventeen years were an insignificant pause in their friendship, and he felt a surge of gratitude and relief. She is on her way now on the bus from Pimlico.

His only lead is an address for Salema that he found in a notebook of Trinity's – the place in Peckham.

To calm himself he watches the outdoor scene through

his camera. The Indian shopkeeper across the street is setting out plastic bins and folding chairs, hanging dried flowers from the awning. A trader wheels his stall into view and Michael adjusts the lens to focus on the baskets of okra and chillies and red-brown yams. The name Izzy's is stencilled backwards on the plate-glass window. Sheets of laminated paper have been taped inside, translucent in the sunlight and darkened with the shapes of letters announcing today's specials. Elsewhere the glass is streaked with recent rain and enlivened with droplets from the eaves.

When Peggy appears, head down into the cold air, he puts the camera on the table and stands. She comes grinning through the doorway and gives him a hug. Stepping back, she compliments him with practised irony on the stylishness of his outfit – a fur-lined canvas jacket that he picked up in Poland and a knitted hat with earflaps.

He laughs. 'What about you, though?' She's wearing a tailored overcoat and a cashmere scarf.

'Ah well, I'm a business woman now, don't you know – I have to dress the part. I have a meeting later in town.' She carries herself, he notices, with more poise but hasn't lost the quickness of movement that he remembers. 'I'm glad you called, Michael, but you know you shouldn't worry about that girl. Sure, if she's anything like you, she'll be all right.'

'Why do you say that – if she's anything like me?'

'Just that it runs in the family. Your mother was practically on the streets at fifteen and look at the life she made for herself.'

He notices the tense and wonders if Peggy knows she's dead. 'I don't know if you heard . . .'

'I did, Michael. Fergal told me. It reached him on the Catholic grapevine. I'm so sorry.'

He shrugs, feeling fraudulent somehow and not deserving sympathy. He isn't sure what he's supposed to have lost, not having got round to seeing his mother except as a force to be resisted.

Peggy is still looking at him, her eyes full of concern.

'The thing is,' he says, 'she was always sort of common property. I'm not really entitled to more than a seventh of the normal allocation of grief. If you see what I mean.'

'I don't, actually. I think that's nonsensical. Love can't be divided in that way. There were a lot of you, but she was your mother, even so.'

The girl comes with coffee and toast, and cutlery wrapped in paper napkins.

'I was sorry to miss the funeral. I would have come.'

'I missed it too. Not a funeral, though. Just a requiem Mass. She left her body to a hospital and they're not done with it yet.'

'Did she have some rare disease?'

'No, it's a teaching hospital. They need cadavers for the students. She was always disappointed that Kieran dropped out of medical school, I suppose, so this way she gets to hang out in one herself.'

Peggy laughs. 'You're a terrible man, Michael Cartwright.'

They find the house at the shabbier end of the street. It isn't attached to the terrace, but stands alone on a corner, its ground floor hidden by a high wall. There's a wooden door in a round-arched doorway overhung with ivy, and a hollow in the brickwork with a rusting iron bell pull.

Michael rings the bell. 'She won't be here.'

'And what will you do then?'

'Phone Kieran.'

There are scuffing noises on the other side of the wall and the clucking of hens. Peggy gives Michael's arm a squeeze. 'There's probably nothing to worry about. She'll show up.'

'Meanwhile we have Salema to deal with.'

The door opens a few inches. An elderly woman peers at them through the gap. Hens gather at her legs and she turns to shoo them away. She wears a coarse grey tunic that reaches to her calves and a grey headscarf. She turns back, her eyes moving between Peggy and Michael.

'We were hoping to see Salema,' Michael says, 'Salema Cartwright.'

'Ah!' the nun says with a tranquil smile. 'Salema!' She turns again to shoo the hens, opens the door wide enough to let the visitors through, then shuts it quickly behind them. 'They like to have the run of the garden,' she says, 'but I daren't let them out for long or the fox will have them.'

The birds scatter and Michael and Peggy follow the nun along the brick path to the front door. In the narrow hall they hear the piano and feel under their feet the thumping reverberations of the dampers.

The nun smiles. 'Always making music,' she says.

Through a half-open door at the end of the hall, Michael has a glimpse of the kitchen – a woman scrubbing something at the sink, another sitting at the table, staring listlessly at a mug in front of her – before he follows the others into the front room.

Eyes shut, with the bay window behind her, Salema is playing Chopin. The tone is thin, and dominated by the creaking of the sustaining pedal. The room is sparsely furnished – an armchair with worn covers, a coffee table, some wooden chairs designed for church, with hinged kneelers attached to the back legs and pockets for prayer books and hymnals. There's a crucifix above the piano and a Raphael Madonna and Child over the mantelpiece, the naked infant clinging with a determined look, Mary gazing vaguely into the middle distance as though she'd rather be somewhere else.

Conscious of being watched, Salema stops abruptly and turns to face them.

'Hello, Salema,' Michael says. 'You remember Peggy?'

Salema has already risen from the piano stool and is walking towards them. Her pace slows. She stops, rises on her toes, and stands marooned. In her shapeless smock, she looks slighter than Michael remembers her. Her hair has been cropped.

He holds out the paper bag. 'We brought you some fruit.'

'Did you think I was sick?'

'No.'

'What kind of fruit?'

'Nectarines. We saw them when we got off the bus and they looked so . . .'

'So . . . ?'

'So orange.'

'It's a bit early, actually.'

'They're probably imported.'

'A bit early in the day. I haven't been to Mass yet. *You* could eat one if you like.'

'They don't have to be eaten right now.' Irritated by Salema's obtuseness, Michael wonders how he used to put up with it. 'They were just something to bring. Put them in a bowl, or something.'

The nun steps forward from the doorway. 'I'll take them. There'll be a bowl in the kitchen.'

'I'd offer you some tea,' Salema says, as though she'd rather not.

Peggy smiles. 'That's OK. We just had breakfast. If you could show me the loo, though.'

'This way,' the nun says.

Michael and Salema are left alone.

'It's nice to hear you play.'

'I'm afraid it's horribly out of tune.'

'Can't you have it seen to?'

'It's too old. I think maybe the frame is cracked. He can get it in tune with itself, the piano tuner says, if I don't mind it being a semitone below concert pitch. But when he does that I hear everything transposed into the wrong key. So last time I had him crank it up so that it was more or less right, but after a few days the strings started slipping again.'

'That's a pity.'

'He did warn me it wouldn't hold, and I said I'd have to offer it up to God.' She smiles. 'He assures me that in Heaven all the pianos are in tune.'

'The piano tuner does?'

'No, God. The piano tuner tells me that the mechanism can't take the tension.'

Michael smiles at this. 'I know what he means.'

'I'm sure. You were always good at mechanical things.'

'The thing is, Salema . . .'

'I just have to think of it as a penance. Sensual pleasure is a snare, in any case. It's only what is inward that matters – the divine indwelling.'

'The reason I'm here is I was wondering if you'd seen Trinity.'

'I see her all the time.'

'But I mean in the flesh – bodily.'

'Of course, bodily. What did you think I meant?' For a moment Salema's voice is fierce with indignation. 'She was here a couple of days ago, as a matter of fact. Thursday morning. She said you were back in the country and she had an address for you. I'm not mad, you know. You don't want to believe everything Kieran tells you.'

'I'm sure you're not mad. Kieran hardly tells me anything.'

'I'm sorry.' She seems shy again, and looks awkwardly at the floor. 'People make assumptions.'

'So she's not here now? She didn't spend the night here?'

'No, she never stays the night. She comes and goes. She has such a sturdy soul. She's a miracle, you know.' Salema's eyes burn suddenly into his, and he has a memory of the effect it used to have on him, the fleeting intensity of her gaze. 'The one really good thing we ever did.'

'We?'

'Kieran and I.'

'Yes, I see.'

'We're still married, you know. I still honour him. Even

if life under the same roof proved impossible. The Church doesn't require that, actually. That you share a bedroom or that you go to Tesco's together. All that stifling intimacy that we associate with marriage. That's just a modern invention, something people learn from watching television.'

'Yes, I suppose it is.'

'I've been reading Blessed Elizabeth of the Trinity.' She steps back to the piano and takes a book from a pile.

The sudden shift of subject makes Michael laugh. 'Sorry,' he says, 'not on my radar, that one.'

'She's sometimes called the Saint of the Divine Indwelling.' Salema is turning pages, looking for something. 'She was a remarkable person. A gifted pianist, with an incredible energy for life, but dead at twenty-six and already a great mystic. Here it is. Listen to this. It's one of her last letters. *My beloved Antoinette, I leave to you my faith in the presence of God, of the God who is all Love dwelling in our souls. I confide to you: it is this intimacy with Him within that has been the beautiful sun illuminating my life, making it already an anticipated Heaven: it is what sustains me today in my suffering.* Isn't that lovely?'

They hear the toilet flushing. A door opens and closes. There are footsteps. A murmur of conversation drifts along the hall from the kitchen.

'You'll let me know, Salema, when you have to leave for Mass.'

'I'll wait for Father David, probably. He'll come later to bring Sister Dominic Communion. She's practically bedridden.'

'And is that enough? For you, I mean. You used to be strict about that kind of thing.'

Salema glances towards the window, lets her eyes rest briefly on Michael's face, then stares at the floor. 'I don't always feel strong enough to go out. I'm not good at coping with people.' She looks up defiantly. 'Father David says I don't have to. He says we can put too much emphasis on the outward forms, when what matters is the life of the spirit.'

'Good for Father David. He sounds like a Protestant.'

Salema smiles. 'You always liked to tease me. I take it you're as much a heathen as ever.'

'At least.'

'And you're with Peggy now. She seems to have done well for herself.'

'I'm not with anybody.'

'Sorry. Of course not. Why should you be?'

'So this place is a convent, then.'

'There are only three nuns left. Most of the other women don't stay long, but they let me stay. I know you must be looking at me, at what my life is reduced to, and wondering what all the fuss was about. But it's not so bad. Really it isn't.'

'What fuss?'

'You used to think I was the prize and that you were always coming second. But how long would you have stuck with me, honestly? You'd have lost interest in six months. Kieran was always steadier than you.'

'I didn't know that was what you were after – steadiness.'

From outside comes the sound of the old nun talking to the hens and the hens talking back.

'So you're looking for Trinity?'

'I had an idea she might be here.'

'She'll show up. She follows her own rhythm. She's like me in that, only so much easier in the world. Do you remember me visiting you in Brighton?'

The question startles him. 'Of course I do.'

'How well do you remember it?'

'Well enough. It was a long time ago.'

'More than eighteen years. Trinity turns eighteen in September. Do you remember everything that took place between us?'

'I suppose so. It depends what you mean?'

'There are things, Michael, that I've never, in all the years since then, confided to another living soul.'

The stillness in the room is suddenly oppressive. Michael is conscious that his breathing has become shallow. Somewhere towards the back of the house a door opens and shuts. There are voices in the hall.

'If I were stronger, then perhaps I could live without secrets. But as it is . . .'

'It's all right,' Michael says. 'I won't say anything. I've never said anything.'

'I know. Thank you.'

Peggy comes in from the hall, with the nun who looks after the hens. 'Sister Clare has been showing me around, Michael. They have potatoes and runner beans in the back garden, and a beehive. They make their own honey.'

'We should probably go,' Michael says. 'I need to make a phone call.' He's shaken up, anxious to speak to Kieran, to confess that he's mislaid Trinity. This whole trip to Peckham feels now like an elaborate procrastination.

Peggy is giving Salema a hug. 'It's great to see you looking so well, Salema. You take care now.'

As they leave, the sound of the piano comes through the open door, beautiful in spite of the creaking pedal and the dissonance pulsing in the high notes.

Out in the street, Michael is inclined to move, to exercise his limbs, to put some distance between himself and the person he used to be.

Peggy hurries beside him. 'No word on Trinity, then?'

He has his phone out, listening once more to Trinity's message. He takes a deep breath and keys in the number he grew up with. After a few rings Kieran answers.

'It's Michael. You haven't seen Trinity, have you?'

'Why? You haven't lost her already?'

'I haven't seen her since the march. She didn't come back to the flat last night.'

'That was careless of you. Not so easy, is it, being a parent? Not something you can just take on casually . . .'

'I didn't take on anything, and I didn't phone to get a lot of crap from you. All right?'

Peggy turns towards him, searching his face.

'Well, you can relax, anyway,' Kieran says. 'She phoned.'

'She did? When?'

'Late last night.'

'So why didn't you tell me, you bastard?'

Reading Michael's tone, Peggy's expression softens from concern to relief.

'I assumed you'd know already.'

'So she's all right, then?'

'Apparently. She's in Woolwich.'

'Woolwich?'

'Yes. Sounds like she missed the last bus.'

'So she's with friends.'

'I suppose so. Why else would anyone go to Woolwich?'

'You didn't ask her?'

'I didn't speak to her. It was Dad who took the call, so it must have been after I'd gone to bed. She can be so inconsiderate.'

'Well, at least she phoned.'

'It was a pantomime getting the message out of Dad. He suddenly perked up at breakfast. You know he has this way of saying *Ah!* when he remembers something, as though inspiration has struck? Well, I'm giving him his porridge, which is all I can get him to eat in the morning these days, and he says – Ah! that blessed girl phoned.'

'He was annoyed with her, then?'

'No, that's just an old joke – you know, the blessed Trinity – but he uses it now when he forgets her name.'

'It's that bad?'

'It gets worse. Trinity's message, according to him, was that she'd been retarded in Woolwich.'

'Retarded? What the hell does that mean?'

'It took us a while to get it. Luckily Kath's here for the weekend. She's got boyfriend problems. Anyway, she's really good with Dad. She asked him if he meant Trinity had been delayed. Well, Dad's not sure about that. So Kath says, *What about held up?* and he says, *Yes, that would be it, held up* – as though they had to agree on a form of words before he could let the matter drop.'

'And it was definitely Woolwich? I mean, he can't even remember Trinity's name.'

'I asked him if he was sure, and he said, *She's with the*

Woolwich, and grinned as though he'd made a terribly witty joke.'

Michael was silent at the thought of his father's decline.

'Look, Mike, if you speak to her before I do, remind her that she's got school on Monday.'

'All right.'

'And A-levels in a few months. It's great that you're helping her sort out Blair's foreign policy, but if you could persuade her to apply to university while she's at it, that would be even better.'

'I'll see if I can weave it into the conversation.'

'And tell her, next time, to think about phoning before midnight.'

'We were the same, though, weren't we?'

'Were we really?'

'Far worse, if you think about it.'

'Maybe. But that was different. Our parents were off their heads.'

They're turning into Rye Lane as Michael closes his phone.

'It's funny to hear you,' Peggy says, 'the way you and Kieran talk. Exactly the way I remember it.'

'Not quite,' Michael says. 'Not the way it was when you were around. I wish you could have heard his end of the conversation. There's a kind of sourness under the surface.' He pictures Trinity's bag, abandoned in his flat, and feels a shadow of his earlier unease. *Retarded in Woolwich* – how reassuring is that? And if Trinity, angry as she was, went all that way to visit friends and took nothing with her, there's an unworldliness about it that is disturbingly reminiscent of her mother.

He shakes the thought away. It's a crisp February morning. The sun is rising above the rooftops. He's with Peggy. The women at the vegetable stall talk French, magnificent in their bright headwraps. Middle Eastern pop is blaring from the halal butcher's. 'I love this,' he says. 'Isn't this the most amazing place?'

'Well, it's a certainly a far cry from Muriel Spark.'

'Muriel who?'

'Do you mean to tell me, Michael Cartwright, that I've read something you haven't?'

'Did she write *The Prime of Miss Jean Brodie?*'

'Yes, but I was thinking of *The Ballad of Peckham Rye*, in which the foreign interloper has come all the way from Edinburgh.'

'Well, exactly. And look at it now. We could be anywhere in the world and we could only be in London. How did we get so lucky? After all those centuries of conquest, we should be shunned.'

'Sure, I never conquested no one, mister, so don't be blaming me.' They've reached the bus stop. 'Anyhow, you can afford to be romantic about it – you're just a tourist.' Seeing him frown, she takes his hand and kisses him on the cheek. 'Maybe tourist isn't the right word. But even when we were teenagers I had the impression you were just passing through. Not just in Kilross – at home with your family. It was part of your mysterious allure.'

'Say that word again.'

'Mysterious?'

'No, the other one.'

'Allure.'

'I like the way you say that word.'

'Are you laughing at my accent?'

The bus comes. The doors open with a sigh, and Peggy pulls Michael by the hand towards the middle. 'You have to stand here,' she says, 'in the belly of the beast,' and they rest against the rubber zigzag of the wall, which squeezes like an accordion as the bus pulls out.

'So tell me, Michael, what was it like to see her again?'

'Who?'

'Who! Mother Teresa – who do you think?'

'It was . . . peculiar.'

'Peculiar in what way?'

'Disturbing.' The bus takes a corner and the floor plates slide under their feet. 'It made me think about who she was then, compared with who I thought she was, which made me think about who I must have been.'

'I don't suppose you could manage to be a little less abstract?'

'All right, she's a bit mad, and it's curious to me that I used to find that so attractive. Except that she struggles with it, and there's something admirable about that.'

'You want to know what I think?'

'I'm not sure. Do I?'

'She was out of reach, so it was safe to fall for her. No chance of a result.'

'Ah yes, your tourist theory.'

'Exactly.' Peggy picks up a discarded newspaper from a seat and begins leafing through it. 'It was all about your mother, anyhow.' Her eyes flit between the headlines in the comment section.

'What was?'

'Everything you did.'

BESOTTED

'Well, thank you, Fräulein Doktor, for that penetrating insight.'

'And everything you didn't do, which is perhaps more to the point, you being a notorious waster of your God-given talents.'

'Was I?'

'Infamous, so you were, the length and breadth of your mother's kitchen. Not that I blame you, there being only two choices – jump the hoops or dig your heels in. Kieran jumped. You, on the other hand . . .'

'Bollocks.'

'What a fucking nerve! Look.' She holds the page out towards him.

The bus shakes and the paper is unsteady in her hand, but he can read the headline. 'What's it about?'

'I'm pretty sure it's about us.'

She settles against him so that they can read it together.

THIS WAS THEIR PHONIEST HOUR

Through the Gates of Hyde Park they poured, these armies of the chattering classes. Woolly hatted and fluffy brained, they marched to defend the right to feel good about themselves.

Old socialists who spent their youth defending Stalin joined Me Generation liberals and kids whose knowledge of history could be written with a magic marker on the back of an iPod.

What do we want? was the startlingly unoriginal question. No war! came the crashingly mundane answer. And so pleased with themselves they looked as they gave it, like contestants in a beauty pageant making their simpering request for world peace.

But for some this was no harmless weekend lark. There were those in the crowd with a firmer grasp on the geopolitical struggle.

Make no mistake, the Islamists behind this dewy-eyed demo, and their Trotskyite fellow travellers, know exactly why they want Saddam in power. And they know who will benefit from 9/11-style atrocities executed in the name of a psychotic god.

'Well, yes,' Michael says. 'That's us all right. He's got us to a T, I'd say, whoever he is.'

'Whoever he is, Michael? Look at the name – Daniel Sheahan.'

'Yes, but that's not . . .'

'Indeed it is. Do you not recognize the face? Admittedly there's more of it to see, now he's smartened himself up and had a haircut.'

'My God, it *is* him.'

'Isn't that what I'm telling you? I've seen his stuff before, but I didn't know he was taking this line.'

'Do you remember when he climbed the scaffolding to tell us that Thatcher had won the election?'

'No, but I remember the mad bastard pursuing me all the way from Ireland to try and persuade me to keep the baby.'

'Wasn't that the same night?'

'Was it? I can't remember.'

'The night we strung up that shop-window dummy.'

'Oh yes. Your mother in her wedding outfit.'

'My mother? I thought it was something political.'

The bus stops. A couple of small children climb aboard followed by a woman with a pushchair.

'Do you miss him, Peggy?'

'His clothes on the floor stinking of yesterday's fags, and me waiting half the night for him to come home? I don't think so.'

'So do you ever regret . . . ?'

'Not for a minute. How could I have cared for a child, the hours I had to work? And with no help from Dan. And her turning him into a hero, anyhow, and asking me why the hell did I have her . . .'

'Not that.'

'Because I could never have done what my mother did – walk out on her when I couldn't take it any more.'

'I didn't mean that.' He pauses, while he works out what it is he means. 'Do you ever regret that I didn't come to London with you?'

'When?'

'When you asked me?'

'Did I?' She frowns in an effort to remember, then the bafflement clears and she's mischievous again, eyes wide, mouth slightly open and a smile hovering. 'You'd have been mad to say yes.'

'Why?'

'Because I was brash and cocky and I knew nothing.'

'I should get off at the next stop.'

'Call me.'

'When?'

'Whenever. Soon. Tomorrow if you like.'

Gripping the bar above his head, he reaches across her to press the button and puts his mouth lightly against hers. The bus swings in against the kerb and they rock towards each other and away. Michael steps out onto the pavement.

As the doors close, drawing the reflections of shop signs across her face, Peggy puts a finger to her lip and smiles at him, still somehow elf-like in spite of being all grown up.

It turns out that Jack was right about Trinity, though he'd garbled her message. She *is* in Woolwich – at the police station. By the time she gets her phone back and calls Michael it's 5.30 on Monday morning and she's been there for more than twenty-four hours. She's not entirely coherent, and it takes him a minute to realize that she hasn't been mugged, but arrested. She doesn't seem to know whether she's been charged with anything.

Anxious for her safety and troubled by the feeling that there's more he could have done, Michael pulls on yesterday's clothes and hurries to the tube with his *A–Z* in his pocket. He suspects that she has been the victim of an injustice and arrives in Woolwich with words like *discrimination* and *racial profiling* buzzing in his head. His annoyance loses its focus when he sees that Detective Sergeant Ambrose, the officer dealing with the case, is black.

'You don't want to get shirty with me, all right,' Ambrose says. 'I'm concerned about your niece, and I think you should be too.'

Ambrose takes him to an interview room in the basement. A high window gives a view of the street, where it has begun to rain. Hungry and dazed for lack of sleep, Michael is impatient to see Trinity, wherever they're keeping her, and get her out. Ambrose perches on the edge of the desk drinking coffee from a polystyrene cup. He is paunchy and greying and not to be rushed.

'Thing is, see, when I came on duty this morning I had the advantage of viewing her case with a fresh eye. Two things struck me. One – this was more serious, potentially, than the arresting officer thought – way beyond criminal damage. You've got inciting racial hatred, for a start.'

Michael is struggling to catch up. The damage, Ambrose has already told him, consisted of graffiti on the brick wall of a carpet warehouse. The message – DEFTO IS REAL – meant nothing to the arresting officer. Trinity denied all knowledge of Defto as a person or a movement, and claimed to have been watching out for the police while an associate handled the spray can and another sat in the car with the engine running.

As it happens, the building is due for demolition to make way for luxury apartments, so the owner, a Mr Jahangiri, has decided not to make an issue of it. But Ambrose is troubled by this added dimension. 'You could be looking at a racially or religiously aggravated offence as defined in part five of the Anti-terrorism, Crime and Security Act of 2001.'

'But I don't get it,' Michael says. 'Racially aggravated? Because the owner's . . . what . . . Pakistani? It doesn't make sense. Trinity's . . .'

'Partly Asian herself? No, the thing I should have mentioned is that the warehouse was once – and still is to all appearances – a synagogue. Been decommissioned for a good forty years, the Jewish community having moved on. Nevertheless. *Defto is real* on the walls of a synagogue . . . semi-literate perhaps, but far from meaningless, if you take a step back and apply a little thought.'

'A synagogue?'

'Context is everything, of course, and allowing for care-less spacing and abysmal spelling we're only a short step from *Death to Israel* – a threat made for the purpose of advancing a political, religious or ideological cause, to quote the 2000 legislation – and I emphasize the word *purpose*, actual Jews to receive the message not being necessary, one could very well argue, as long as Jews were present in the minds of those delivering it. You see where I'm going with this.'

'Oh, God.' Understanding of the trouble Trinity might have got herself into comes at Michael in a wave of nausea.

'Which would allow us to detain her for a further twenty-four hours without charge, extendable to seven days with judicial approval. Which I would certainly consider if I could see any mileage in it.'

Michael sees a glimmer of hope in that conditional clause. 'Two things, you said – two things occurred to you.'

'Ah, yes. Well, it's unlikely to have been your niece wielding the spray can, isn't it.' Ambrose turns to pick up the file from the desk. He crumples the empty coffee cup in his other hand and flicks it into the bin. 'Nice handwrit-ing she's got. All neatly spaced. Bright kid. Better spelling than me, I shouldn't wonder. *Def to Isreal?* I don't think so.'

'No, of course not.' Michael is light-headed with relief.

'So you've got to ask yourself – what was she doing wandering the streets at four in the morning with a couple of anti-Semites from the remedial class. I'd be thinking long and hard about that one, if I were you.'

Trinity is in a draughty waiting room. She sits with her hands squeezed between her knees, staring vacantly at the tiles. When Ambrose tells her he's letting her go, she raises her eyes in a look of abject gratitude.

'And you'll remember what I told you?'

'Yes, I will. Thank you.'

The inner doors swing open and shut and there's the sound of Ambrose's heavy tread retreating along the corridor.

Trinity looks cold and bewildered. Michael puts his arms round her and her shaking turns into a series of deep, wrenching sobs.

It's not until they're on the train that Michael is able to get much out of her. She'd hooked up with Malik, the boy with the flyers. They'd gone in his car, she wasn't sure where. There had been a gang of them in someone's front room, home-cooked food, a lot of talk. She'd caught their indignation at the treatment of Muslim countries, their anger at being harassed outside mosques, strip-searched at airports – mundane humiliations that linked them with their brothers on the West Bank and in Kabul, and in Belmarsh Prison on the other side of London where you could disappear and never be heard of again.

And then, somehow, she was back in Malik's car, and Malik's cousin Mahmood was directing them to his dad's hardware store to get a stepladder and a can of spray paint. It wasn't clear to Michael what had happened to the rest of the gang, nor why, in the end, these two jokers had left Trinity to face the Woolwich police alone. Woolwich was, in any case, an accidental detour. By the sound of it, they'd never even found Thamesmead, let alone Belmarsh.

'Mahmood was supposed to be reading the map,' Trinity explains, 'but he couldn't tell north from south, he misread all the street names, he got the turns in the wrong order. I offered to take over, but they wouldn't let me, because I don't live in London, they said, and I don't drive, but really because I'm a girl. So Malik's getting more and more angry, and Mahmood's saying, *S'your fault, bro, should of got the sat nav fixed*, and I'm getting tired and carsick and generally fed up. Then Malik sees this synagogue.' They've stopped for breakfast at London Bridge, and Trinity continues her story between mouthfuls of scrambled egg. 'Malik should have let me do the writing as well. At least I'd have written something sensible in English that people could read. Free Palestine, or something, not that *defto* crap – I mean what the hell was that?'

'You don't know?'

'I do now, but only because that policeman told me.'

'You'd had all that time to think about it and you hadn't worked it out?'

'I just assumed it was Mahmood's tag, all right?' Her voice has risen defensively. 'You don't have to make me feel bad. You wouldn't be so clever, either, if you had people shouting at you and you were locked up in a cell with a metal toilet and a bed the size of a shelf with mad drunk people screaming all the time . . .'

Later, when she's had a shower and has sunk onto the couch, Michael asks her about the policeman, Ambrose, and what he'd said to her.

'When?' Yawning, she rests her head on a cushion and pulls a blanket over her feet.

'He said something to you that he wanted you to remember.'

'Oh, that. He said just because I've got delinquent parents it doesn't mean I can't make something of myself.'

'Nice one. I'll have to remember to tell your . . . dad.' He regrets the hesitation, a clumsy acknowledgement of the question that hangs between them. But Trinity is already asleep.

† The Church of St Ursula and the Virgin Martyrs

Monday 17 February 2003

I was interrupted yesterday – called away to visit a parishioner. He had been ailing for months, and just this evening died. I was in time, thank God, to hear his confession and anoint him. He was a difficult man, old Mr Hollingshead, a retired schoolmaster. He tried to be obedient to the Church, but was nostalgic for its old ways. He would often challenge me after Mass on some point of theological or liturgical difference, and I would try to avoid him, until I began to see that these arguments were for him a form of friendship. I was glad to be able to minister to him at the end. He once rebuked me for being too ready to anoint the sick – for 'dishing out the oil', as he put it, 'like ketchup in a fast-food joint' – so I was glad he had not lost faith altogether in the final sacrament or in my ability to administer it. Extreme Unction he called it, as all my older parishioners do. His daughter was visiting, whom I had never met, nor heard him speak of. She was a sour woman who seemed reluctant to have me in the house, but she left me alone with him as he requested.

I had begun the prayer – Through this holy anointing, may the Lord in his love and mercy help you with the grace of the Holy Spirit – and was about to put the oil on his forehead, when he turned his head away and took hold of my wrist. 'No, Father,' he said, 'not there.' 'Where, then?' I asked him. 'You must begin with the eyes,' he said, 'and then the ears, then the nostrils, lips, hands and feet, absolving me of all bodily sins.' 'No,' I told him, trying to soothe his anxiety, 'that's no longer the way it's done. The forehead and the hands are enough.' His hold on my wrist was strong, though he laboured in his breathing. 'Oh, but you must,' he said, 'and you must anoint my loins.' I was taken aback. But he persisted. 'You must lay your hand in blessing on my procreative organ.' 'That would be quite improper,' I told him. 'Sure, it hasn't been done that way for centuries.' 'But what of my sins of carnal delectation?' he said, using the old form of words, and I saw that twinkle in his eye and knew that he was teasing me – a thorn in my side to the last.

It was gone midnight before I returned to my desk and saw what I had written in this letter – about the trouble I brought with me on my first journey to England – and found I was too tired and too low in spirits to write any more about the past.

I meant Peggy, of course, who was a trouble mainly to herself. It was not until some weeks later that I discovered the true purpose of her journey to England. I was extremely angry with her, that she had lied to me. I felt it as a deep betrayal. She had travelled under my protection, drawing me into an unwitting conspiracy to deceive her father. At first I was too angry to speak to her. Then I was angry with

myself for putting this trivial injury to me above
the mortal danger to her unborn child. I have always
blamed myself for not fighting fiercely enough for that
tiny parcel of life. What could I have done? Peggy was
determined. And yet I have always felt that God gave
me a task and I let it slip from my hand.

I know there are many who view a human
foetus as not quite a person. Does it rank with a calf,
I wonder, that it can be slaughtered when it is surplus
to requirement? Is it no better than a chicken, to have
its neck wrung? I have read, Michael, that in the old
Southern states of America, when they were allocating
seats in Congress, a slave was counted as three-fifths
of a person. What fraction of a person is a child in
the womb? It cannot feed itself, but neither can an
infant, neither could old Mr Hollingshead these last
few weeks, waited on by his sour-faced daughter.
Knowledge of life in the womb is lost to us, for the
most part, overlaid by the tumultuous impressions
of the world long before we have words to hold it
by. It is a knowledge that can stay with us only as
metaphor, the strangeness of that state filtered
through images of the familiar and the ordinary.

This is something I have not thought about for
many years. The truth is, Michael, I do remember
being in the womb. And I remember my own birth.

I didn't always know this to be a memory. It came
to me in childhood as a dream from which I would
wake fretful and crying. This was after my mother's
death, because it was my father, I remember, would
comfort me. It was a dream, he would say, holding

me in the dark, just a dream. But it would visit me
again in the same form, which made it seem more
than a dream. I would be walking on a country road
and ahead in a field, where two roads crossed, I would
see a pile of hay gathered – a pale dome-shaped hump
that rose from the dark earth. And as I looked, I found
myself within the haystack (each time I dreamt this it
was the same) and the hump had become a hovel in
which an old woman lived. She would give me my tea
by the fireplace, and it would be time for me to leave,
but there was no door or window. 'How am I to get
home?' I would ask, and the crone would push me
into the hearth and up into the chimney. 'Like thissss,'
she would say, lengthening the word into a hiss, as
she thrust me up into the chimney. And then again,
as I fell back toward the hearth, 'Like thissss,' and
again, 'like thissss.'

When I was fourteen I told this dream to another
boy and he sniggered, and I saw a meaning in it that
I had not thought of, a false meaning, and for many
years the dream became shameful to me. I was an
adult, and a priest already, before I knew it to be a
memory of my last hours in my mother's womb.

But why do I tell you this? Because I know I was
my own self before birth, as I shall be after death
when I have shed this body and must answer for my
sins at the throne of Heaven. And Peggy's child was
its own self when she had it flushed out and tossed
in the hospital furnace.

I believe it was a mortal blow to her father, poor
Uncle Dennis. Peggy had phoned him from London

to say that she had found a job in a music shop and
would not be coming home. And that was hard
enough on him. But it was more than a year before
he learned of the pregnancy.

That was a trying year for me, Michael, knowing
about it all but saying nothing. Your mother wrote
to me the following spring to ask what I thought of
Kieran's plan to spend the summer in London with
Dan Sheahan. Kieran would work in Peggy's shop
until his medical course began, and he would be closer
to his violin teacher. But what sort of a young man
was Dan Sheahan, your mother wanted to know.

I was inclined to think well of Dan, though he
had some growing up to do. He had been willing to
shoulder the responsibility of the child and would
have married Peggy if she'd let him. But your mother
knew nothing of the child. And if I had told her of it,
and of my suspicion that Dan and Peggy now lived
together in a state of mortal and premeditated sin,
perhaps she would have kept Kieran at home until
he could find decent university accommodation. But
I chose to reassure her and calm her anxieties. What
danger could Dan and Peggy be, after all, to Kieran,
a decent strong-willed young man who knew his own
mind?

And now I blame myself for that as well, for saying
nothing, for keeping Peggy's secrets. I have always
been prone to sins of omission.

I was, in any case, in my own spiritual muddle
after a year in London, struggling with the
responsibilities of parish work. I felt I had fallen from

grace. When I said Mass, it terrified me to hold the
host in my hand – to know the dreadful power of
it and my own unworthiness.

It was you I thought about, Michael – I imagine
it will surprise you to know that – the friend I might
have had if circumstances had been different. If I had
worked in a shop like Peggy I could have taken off
when I felt like it and caught the bus down to
Cheltenham. Or later, the train to Brighton when
you had begun at the art college there (Moira's
letters kept me informed of all your movements,
all her hopes and fears for you). If I had knocked
on your door without my black suit and my Roman
collar, you might have taken me out for a drink and
my loneliness would have been assuaged. But this is
foolish. It was foolish to long for it then, and even
more foolish now.

You see, there's so much I have to tell you that
I hadn't even thought of when I began this letter.
And now I find the letter has become a friend and
I am reluctant to let it go. I have more to say, but
not a great deal more.

OCTOBER 1984 LONDON

Michael had found the move to Brighton a bit of a shock. Anticipating his father's disapproval, he'd left it until it was almost too late to apply. He'd scrabbled to find accommodation and had ended up renting an attic room in a house where none of the other lodgers were students, and his landlord fussed over him in a way that he tried not to find creepy.

His photography teacher, TJ, had punk hair and wore leather trousers and spoke in a nasal London accent. He used words like integrity and commitment, which made Michael feel inadequate without quite knowing why. *Better to be incompetent than inauthentic* – that was the kind of thing TJ liked to say. You were supposed to *put yourself on the line*, you had to *make yourself part of the story*, which you were anyway, he said, whether you wanted to be or not. Michael tried to hold these ideas in his head, but when he looked through the lens of his camera he found that all the words blurred and there were just shapes and gestures and patterns of light and shade.

A couple of months earlier, in the envelope with his offer of a place, he had received instructions on a summer project. He was to put together a portfolio of pictures with the title *Working*. Since he was working full time for his father by then, having finished his foundation course, he took his camera with him to the building site. He pointed his lens upward at the fibrous undersides of scaffold planks and the cracks of dusty light that ran between them. He caught roof timbers open to the sky, half-built staircases, window frames rising above the brickwork of unfinished walls. Perspective complicated by unroofed gables became interesting to him, and ladders sloping at different angles. And he liked it when a pattern of lines was broken by the blurred limb of a carpenter sawing the end off a joist, or the haunches of a hod-carrier rising in silhouette. He saw in his own pictures a kind of abstraction that gave him pleasure.

He'd watch the light fall across a fresh expanse of floor-boards. Soon enough there would be three cramped bed-rooms, a landing you could barely manoeuvre a wardrobe through, curtains and carpets and knick-knacks and all the claustrophobic clutter of family life. But for now everything was indefinite, and every angle offered a long view.

His turn to present his project came one afternoon in the second week of term when the sun burned through the broken blinds of the studio. TJ allowed the other students a few minutes to mumble nice things about the work, before laying into it. He pointed out the dehumanizing tendency of the compositional style – the construction workers held at a distance as though a close encounter with a fully real-ized individual would be too threatening to the dominant bourgeois aesthetic. He observed the fetishizing of tools and the voyeuristic focus on musculature, which had the effect of objectifying the human figures both economically and sexually. The photographs were anachronistic in their endorsement of the picturesque, he said, but thoroughly

contemporary in celebrating the Thatcherite boom in the
non-unionized sector. He was reminded of those before-
and-after pictures you seeing hanging in wine bars showing
how the old pub had been gutted and tarted up.

Michael hated his fellow students for their obedient
laughter. To have his name linked with Thatcher's so
early in the course felt like a terrible injustice. He wanted
to protest, but could only stand awkwardly, blinking and
sweating in the afternoon sun, while TJ, posturing in his
leather trousers and too old for his spiked hair, turned
chuckling to the next portfolio.

Rhys Morgan had spent his summer touring decommissioned coal mines in South Wales. He had found a
nightwatchman guarding a locked gate, a cleaner pulling an
old strike poster from a chain-link fence, cards in the
window of a job centre and the face of a middle-aged
man reflected beside them in the glass. Michael liked the
pictures well enough. But TJ's response was orgasmic.
He loved what he called the subversive problematizing
of *Working*, both as title and as concept – the laid-off
mineworkers in marginal employment, working and yet
not working – the system that sacrifices communities to
the god of the market, working and yet not working. These
images, he said, were alive with internal tension, and spoke
with the authentic voice of Rhys Morgan's people.

Michael happened to know that Rhys Morgan's people
sold second-hand cars in Newport. It made him feel better,
this knowledge, because it showed him the limits of TJ's
understanding. Even if it remained a private joke, Michael
felt somehow vindicated by it.

Last to go was a girl called Chrissie Hamilton. Chrissie

had been to California for the summer and had taken pictures of prostitutes on Hollywood Boulevard. Michael watched TJ making up his mind whether to like the pictures or not. On the one hand, Chrissie's real name was Christabel, and her ragged tights couldn't disguise the fact that she came from privilege. How else had she managed to get to California? On the other hand, she was a girl, and not bad looking, and she'd taken pictures of prostitutes – the fact that she was a girl probably made that authentic rather than creepy. Michael made a private bet with himself that Chrissie would get the full fawning treatment. When it came to it, TJ sat on the fence, pronouncing the pictures 'promising'.

It would be a good story to tell Kieran, Michael thought. He was on the train, looking forward to a weekend in London. He had missed Kieran – for these first few weeks of term in Brighton and, before that, for the whole of the summer. The house, in spite of its regular allocation of sisters and parents and casual visitors, had seemed under-populated. There had been times when Michael had registered an absence, a clearing at the edge of his vision, before remembering that it was Kieran who wasn't there – not sounding off at the dinner table, not muttering in his sleep at midnight.

At London Bridge he stepped out onto the platform with his bag swinging on his shoulder and felt the energy of the city rising up through the paving and into his feet. A noise cut through the echoing blur of voices – just outside the exit, sitting on the pavement was an old man playing a violin, and a hat in front of him where his legs should have been.

Kieran had sent him directions, with a map drawn on a piece of file paper and labelled in his scrawling handwriting. He'd drawn the Thames with wavy edges. A fish peered up out of the water with a speech bubble coming out of its mouth and the words *Stop mooching about and do something!* – one of their father's lines. Every time Michael looked at it, it made him smile.

The flat had its own entrance off the street at the bottom of a flight of steps. Kieran was there to let him in, happy to see him, ready to abandon work. While he filled the kettle and cleared his anatomy textbooks off the table, Michael told him how Kath's boyfriend had got himself thrown out of the house.

'Dad walked into her room and there they were on the bed . . .'

'Kath and Jason?'

'No, she split up with Jason. This was Alastair. So there they were on the bed . . .'

'Snogging?'

'What do *you* think? So Dad threw a fit, and Kath said, *Why don't you knock, you horrible man?* And Dad said, *I will not have no-go areas in my own house.* And he marches Alastair along the corridor saying all kinds of mad things like *Go behind my back and you'll find you've bitten off more than you can chew.* I heard most of this from the bathroom. They were halfway down the stairs when I came out, but Dad was still making these pronouncements – *I'm not ready to throw my daughter to the wolves* and *In this house it takes more than two to tango.* It was incredible.'

'Using the word,' Kieran said, putting on his pundit voice, 'in the . . . technical sense of . . . tediously predictable.'

'So next morning at breakfast, Kath's sulking and Dad's making a big show of ignoring it and Mam's fussing about something or other, and right out of the blue Emily raises her hand – you know the way she does – and announces that she's decided she's going to be a lesbian. And she doesn't say it like it's anything significant. Just, you know, I'm dropping geography and I'm thinking about science A-levels and I'm going to be a lesbian.'

'They must have gone through the roof.'

'Not really. They didn't know what to say at first, except to behave as though she'd used a naughty word without knowing what it meant. There was a lot of tutting and snorting, and Mam tried to change the subject, but Emily just kept going. She'd given it a lot of thought, and she'd read an article saying that lesbians don't have to wear special clothes anymore, and you could get all the same kinds of jobs as everyone else, including even running for Parliament, but her main reason was that lesbians didn't have to have sex with men but could stick to having sex with other women.'

'*Stick* to having sex? Did she really say that?'

'Could I have made it up?'

Kieran handed Michael a mug of tea and showed him the rest of the flat. The main bedroom had a mattress on the floor with sheets and blankets strewn across it. There was a jumble of bras and knickers lying on a chair. Michael thought of Peggy having sex with Dan. He wondered what it was like for Kieran, sleeping next door, whether they made noises while they were doing it. More of her clothes were bursting from the wardrobe. There was a view up through shrubs to a high wall where sparrows perched. The boys stood while a train rumbled past, scattering the sparrows and making the room vibrate like a second-class cabin on the Cork ferry.

Kieran told Michael about Dan's band. Dan had been teaching him some Irish tunes, helping him get a feel for the style of the music. 'It's different. The way you hold the bow is different. You don't have to worry about vibrato. You can let the neck of the violin sag a bit. It's looser somehow. Or maybe it's just that I'm looser when I'm doing it, because I don't have to be perfect all the time.' He took some bacon out of the fridge and talked about Otto, his violin teacher, who was concerned that Dan's influence might corrupt the purity of his technique. He raised his head, preparing to do the voice – the strangled vowels, the explosive consonants. 'There is a place, of course, for gypsy melodies. And even the ballerina must be allowed, as it were, to let her hair down in the discotheque. Nevertheless . . .'

Sitting by the table with his mug in his hand, Michael nearly choked on his tea, coughing a brown spray onto the rush matting.

Kieran was laughing too. 'Sometimes he's such a dick-head.' He pulled an unwashed frying pan from the pile, squirted some washing-up liquid at it and put it under the tap. There was a little burst of soap bubbles. 'And Salema's no help.'

'Salema!'

'Well . . . you know how serious she is about music.'

He was still facing the sink, but Michael caught the

awkwardness in his voice. 'Salema's in London, then?' he asked him.

'Of course she's in London.' Kieran looked round, suddenly defensive. 'She's at the Royal College, you knew that.'

'But I didn't know you two were still . . .'

'Still what? We're friends, that's all. We've only ever been friends.' The flow from the tap caught the pan's underside at just the right angle to send a jet of water down his trousers. Cursing, he took a step away from the sink with the frying pan dripping soapy water onto the floor.

'I didn't know you were still in contact, was all I was going to say.'

Kieran took a tea towel from the back of a chair. 'You don't like her. Fine. You don't have to make such a thing about it.' He spoke through clenched teeth, rubbing at his trousers with the tea towel.

'I never said I didn't like her. When did I ever say I didn't like her?'

Standing with the tea towel in one hand and the wet pan in the other, Kieran let out a slow breath. After a moment, he said, 'Do you have any idea how difficult it is to find an accompanist who's really skilful and just gets it right without you having to explain everything? I don't think you ever really appreciated what a brilliant musician Salema is.'

'I used to like her more than you did, even when you were going out, or whatever it is you were doing. And how am I making a thing about it, anyway?'

'You just are.'

'I like her. All right? And I know she's brilliant. And obviously you should play together.'

Kieran stood for a moment, saying nothing. Then he

dried the frying pan with the tea towel, and put it on the cooker.

'Really, Kier,' Michael said, 'I wasn't criticizing.'

'All right, if you say so.' Kieran peeled off four rashers of bacon and laid them side by side in the pan. Then he said, 'We were sort of going out, I suppose. We're sort of going out now. But it gets complicated because she's a bit screwed up about physical stuff.'

'Screwed up how?'

'Sort of intense. We're not sleeping together, but apart from that . . .' He struck a match and lit the gas. 'I just wish I knew from one week to the next what's allowed and what isn't, that's all.'

'So . . . what's allowed this week?'

Kieran laughed. 'Not much.'

Michael sat listening to the bacon fat spitting in the pan. There was a change in the quality of the light, a warmer glow across the surfaces below the window that prompted him to pull out his camera and start fiddling with the shutter speed.

Kieran had opened a tin of beans and put some bread in the toaster. 'The thing is,' he said, 'I don't blame her about the Irish music. I'm not surprised she doesn't get it. It's not just about the music . . . I mean I love the music, but it's not just about that. There's the whole cultural part of it. Do you have any idea what we've done to the Irish over the centuries?'

'Who's we?'

'You know what I mean – *us, them*, the *English*. Do you know how far back it goes?' He scraped the beans out into a saucepan and turned the gas up high.

'Too long.'

'Whenever some medieval king got bored or needed to prove himself he went and bashed up the Irish. Then Queen Elizabeth had a go. She hated the Irish for being Catholics because she was frightened of Catholics. And Cromwell hated them even more because he was a Puritan. And then there was the so-called Glorious Revolution, which some books still call the Bloodless Revolution because it was only Irish people who got slaughtered.'

Michael looked at him through the viewfinder. 'Not forgetting the Potato Famine.'

'Exactly. And do you have any idea what was done to them after the Easter Rising?'

Michael lowered the camera. 'Them?'

'All right, *us*. Do you know how many Irish people were hanged and tortured and had their houses burned . . . *Our* houses, I mean.'

Michael raised his hand, like Emily at the breakfast table. 'Our houses as English landlords, do you mean, or our houses as Irish tenants?'

'Both!' Kieran glared at him. Behind him the toast popped up and the beans began to bubble in the pan. 'Am I being boring?'

'No, you're not actually. It's just that I know most of this already.'

'Yes, sorry.' He began buttering the toast. 'But I bet you don't know any Gaelic.'

'Don't rub it in. I feel bad enough already about hardly knowing any Latin, and getting a D in French.'

'Yes, but you know acres of Latin and French even so, just by knowing English.'

'So . . . ?'

Kieran took a deep breath. 'OK. Look at it this way. How long was India part of the British Empire?'

'A few hundred years?'

'If that. And how many words are in the English language that came from India, words we use all the time like bungalow and pyjamas?'

Michael shrugged and turned to take a picture of Dan's pipes lying on the couch.

'There are hundreds of them. And how many English words came from Gaelic?'

'I've no idea.'

'About two. Galore's one.'

'Like Pussy Galore?'

'Exactly.' Kieran poured the beans out, sharing them between the two plates.

'Or baked beans galore.'

'Or whiskey galore. Which is a better example, actually, because whiskey's the other one. It means water of life. Whiskey and galore, and that's it for Gaelic words in English.'

'That can't be it.'

'I'm telling you. But from India we got jungle and pundit and juggernaut and bangle and shampoo . . .'

'Shampoo, are you sure?'

'Curry, of course, and chutney.'

'Well, if you're counting those, you've got to put boiled cabbage down on the Gaelic list.'

'Very funny.'

'What does it prove, anyway, that we've got all these Indian words?'

'It's just an example of the total lack of respect the English have had for the Irish. Or even basic interest. I mean when it comes to language Salema's Indian relatives would be far more at home in England than us Irish.'

Kieran put the two plates of bacon and beans on the table and sat down.

Michael was staring at him, open-mouthed. 'Do you have any idea what a ridiculous statement that was – what you just said?'

Kieran's face opened in a grin. 'I suppose it was a bit over the top, wasn't it,' he said, picking up his knife and fork.

Michael took the picture – the cutlery hovering over the bacon and beans, the thin light coming down from the street, a blur of musical instruments in the background, and the grin, which was pure, authentic Kieran.

When they walked into the auditorium at the college, Salema was hunched over the keyboard of the concert grand. What always took Michael by surprise when he watched her at the piano was that element in her playing that seemed spontaneous, visceral even. Now, after a gap of months, he was quite undefended against it. Her poise, her focus, her capacity for stillness she carried with her everywhere, but this fierce physical energy came through only when she played.

The texture of the music thinned to open chords and a rising run of notes as distinct as bells. Her hands settled on the keyboard as though they had just that moment discovered that those particular keys were there to be played. She rolled towards the sound, arms and shoulders easing downward, head sideways to catch the shifting hum of it. Then up again – elbows first, and wrists – the fingers at last lifted and withdrawn. The stillness when the sound stopped seemed to bristle, as though the music had reached out beyond itself.

Kieran didn't find her easy and Michael could sympathize. But it must make up for a lot, he thought, that she could do this.

Salema looked round and blinked. She noticed Kieran and Michael, frowned at first as though their presence were an intrusion, or as though she didn't know who they were. Then she smiled. 'Hello, you two,' she said.

'Hi, Sal,' Kieran said. 'Ready for some Irish music?'

Salema pulled a face. 'If we have to.'

'We'll practise the Mahler tomorrow, I promise.'

She tilted her head and looked at him earnestly. 'After Mass?'

'All right, after Mass.' He said it with a kind of bravado to cover his embarrassment, but his sideways glance at Michael gave him away. Not being bothered with all that stuff was one of the things about leaving home that they'd both looked forward to.

In the back room of the Grapes, the musicians sat along two sides of a table. Dan was at one end with his uillean pipes, Kieran was next to him, then a couple of accordions, a tin whistle, and an older man with a belly so big he could rest his fiddle on it while he played. Peggy sat at the end with the goatskin drum she called a bodhran. Her hair was short and dyed in purple streaks.

From across the room, where he sat with Salema, Michael watched Kieran's struggle to cope without written music, and the pleasure he took in the challenge of it. It was an unforgiving discipline, everyone but the drummer committed to this relentless melodic exploration and only the piper's drones allowed an accompanying role. For the fiddlers the demands were more obviously physical than for the others, the bowing arm acting out the leaps and dives of the tune. Michael was struck with the way Kieran had thrown himself into this, as he threw himself into everything he did. It occurred to him that it wasn't Kieran's talent that was impressive. It was his certainty that what-ever he was doing right now was the thing to do. It was a quality that drew people to him, that enabled him to claim Dan and Peggy as his friends, just as he had claimed Salema, casually, with his mind on something else, before Michael could stir himself to act.

He felt the touch of Salema's hand, and the warmth of her breath at his ear. 'Kieran thinks I don't approve,' she said. 'He thinks I'm afraid his technique will slip.'

Michael turned to face her. 'And are you?'

'I suppose I am, yes. It has already, actually, even though he gets angry when I say so. And then there's this whole Irish thing.'

'What about it?'

'I don't really understand it and I don't understand why he cares so much. I know the Catholics want Northern Ireland to be part of the Irish Republic, and in a way, I sup-pose, you only have to look at a map to see that they're right. But the Protestants want it to go on being British and there are twice as many Protestants as Catholics, so I

suppose, in a way, what they want counts twice as much.'
She took a thoughtful sip of shandy. 'My mother talks
sometimes about the partition of India, which happened
when she was a child, and Pakistan was for Muslims, except
her family were Muslims but they were on the Indian side
of the border, so they stayed as Indians. Except it's not the
same at all because hardly any of them wanted the British
to stay, but the Protestants want the British to stay. Do you
see what I'm saying?'

'Yes.'

'Do you?'

'No, not really.'

She sighed. 'Neither do I. I suppose the main thing for
me is that I don't like Dan. It's Dan who'll corrupt him, not
the music.'

The tune was coming to a ragged conclusion. People
around them put their cigarettes in their mouths and their
drinks on the tables to applaud the band. The musicians
were joking with each other.

Salema turned to look at Michael as though she had
something urgent to say. 'I've been reading Father Hopkins.'

'Who?'

'Gerard Manley Hopkins.'

'Oh, the poet.'

'He had such a sense of the immanence of the divine.'

From the musicians' table Peggy was watching him with
a half-smile as though she could see how pushed and pulled
he felt.

'Hopkins thinks the Blessed Virgin is like the air we
breathe,' Salema said, 'Worldmothering air, he calls her.
Isn't that beautiful?'

Dan was coming towards them on his way to the gents.

Salema had her eyes closed. She inhaled slowly, preparing to recite. 'She plays in grace her part about man's beating heart, laying, like air's fine flood, the deathdance in his blood.' Then her eyes were on Michael's. 'I pray for that every night, that the Blessed Virgin will lay the deathdance in Kieran's blood.'

'I'm not sure I get it,' Michael said. 'Could you say it again?'

Dan's hand was resting on the back of her chair. 'She's praying, Michael, that your brother will get laid by the Virgin Mary.'

Straightening her back, Salema directed her reply into the smoke-filled space above the table. 'Trust you to spoil even the loveliest poetry.'

'Trust a priest to fill your head with nonsense.' Dan spoke carelessly, as if the whole thing was a joke. 'It's life that dances in Kieran's blood, sweetheart, not death, and it would in yours too if you stopped injecting ice-water into your veins.'

When he had moved on, Salema gripped Michael's arm, as though to steady herself. After a moment she said, 'Can I ask you a question?'

'Of course.'

'Why do people dislike me?'

'Who?'

'Dan, for a start.'

'Maybe only because you dislike *him*.'

'And other people?'

'I suppose they might feel judged. They can't live up to your standards.'

She looked puzzled. 'That's what people think? That I imagine I'm better than them?'

Michael shrugged. 'I couldn't say.'

'Do you think that?'

'Sometimes.'

She seemed lost in thought for a moment. Her eyes flooded with tears. She wiped them away impatiently but they kept coming. 'That's strange, actually, because I think I'm worse than most people, a lot worse. There are people who find it easy to be good. You, for example.'

'Me!'

'It's effortless for you. It's as easy as breathing.'

'I don't think I'm a particularly good person. I don't know why you say that.' He found it unsettling to discover, after all this time, that she thought this of him.

'There's a way men like Dan look at me that makes me wish I was ugly.'

He thought about how swollen and blotchy most girls looked when they cried, and how amazing it was that it just made Salema's eyes look brighter and the skin around her eyes more luminous.

'You look at me that way too sometimes, Michael.'

'So why don't you wear a bag over your head?' It stung him to be lumped in with Dan. He stared at the table, angry and baffled. He heard the small noises she made in her throat as she wept.

After a while the noises stopped. She blew into a tissue and sniffed. 'Will you do something for me, Michael?'

'It depends what it is.'

She said nothing for moment, so he looked up at her.

'You're bound to like me less and less the longer you

know me. But will you promise that you'll try to go on liking me?'

'All right. I don't see why I should like you less and less.'

'But you'll promise.'

'Yes, I do. I promise.'

'Thank you.' She rested her hand on his and for a moment they sat without speaking. Then with a damp smile she stood up. 'I'd better go and wash my face. I'll be back in a minute.' She walked towards the corner of the bar where the toilets were, dropping her eyes to the floor as Dan passed her coming the other way.

When the band started up again, Michael leant forward to listen. There was a desperate joy in the tune to which a hidden part of him responded. It seemed to float him out beyond the walls of the pub, out of the close air that smelt of beer and warm bodies and cigarette smoke, into the fields by the river beyond the Kilross cattle market.

He woke, and wondered if his head was in the wrong place, because there was a wall instead of the room, and an unfamiliar openness on the other side of him, and a rectangle of grey light where the wardrobe should be, and he realized he wasn't in Brighton but in Kieran's flat.

A pale figure stood in the doorway. 'Did I wake you, Michael?'

'No.'

It was Peggy. Her T-shirt floated in the shadowy space between the hall and the kitchen. She took a step into the grainy half light and her face was visible and her purple-streaked hair. Her legs were bare from the knees down. She stood on the sides of her feet, the toes curling up towards each other, and she hugged herself for warmth.

'I did wake you, didn't I. I'm sorry. Go back to sleep.'

'That's OK. What time is it?'

'About half-past six.'

'Are you all right?'

'Dan never came home.'

Michael sat up, pulling the duvet around his shoulders, and sliding his feet out onto the floor. 'Do you think something's happened to him?'

'Apart from the usual, you mean?'

There were footsteps on the pavement. Peggy moved to the window and lifted the edge of the curtain to look up into the street. A car went past and something heavier, a dustcart or a delivery van, that made the dishes rattle on the draining board.

She let the curtain drop. 'It doesn't matter really,' she said. 'It's not his fault I can't love him. He did his best to make an honest woman of me, as Fergal is fond of pointing out, but I'm not sure I have the makings of an honest woman.'

'You mean he wanted to marry you?'

'Sure, he offered to when I was pregnant . . .' She shrugged as though such an offer wasn't to be taken seriously, or as though the subject was no longer interesting to her. 'Is there room for two under that quilt? I'm freezing to death.'

'Yes, of course.'

He lifted the bedding. She took a few quick steps and slid in under the duvet, pulling the edge of it round her like a shawl, and tucking her feet up.

'You're warm as toast,' she said. A shiver ran through her as she settled against him.

'So why did you move in with him, if you don't love him?'

'A girl's got to live.' There was silence and then the rattle of a train heading towards London Bridge. 'It isn't about sex, really, us living together, if that's what you're thinking. We used to have more sex back in Kilross, even with my father watching my every move. Dan would climb in my bedroom window half drunk or pull his car into a field on the way home from a dance. And sometimes I wanted it and sometimes I couldn't be bothered to fight him off. It's not as though I had many options. Getting pregnant was the end of it for me, though – that wasn't what I'd imagined for my life.' She sighed. He felt the weight of her head on his shoulder as she relaxed against him. 'But then I found myself in London not knowing anyone and with no money for rent. I'm not making it sound any better, am I? I'm sure you think I'm a terrible person.'

'No, I don't.' He wondered if now would be a good time to kiss her. He wanted to, but he wasn't sure if it was just because she was there, and he wondered if she'd let him for the same reason. And then he thought how amazing it would be to have someone as warm and funny as Peggy in bed with you every night, someone you could talk to and have sex with even if you weren't madly in love with her. And he made a movement with his head, sliding his face towards hers.

But she had begun talking again. 'I have plans, actually, to move out. I'm going into business.'

'What kind of business?'

'I've been thinking about this for a long time.' He felt the energy in her body, the shifting angle of her shoulders, the intake of breath. 'When Johnny Logan won the Eurovision Song Contest for Ireland with "What's Another Year", I was only fourteen, but old enough to know it was shite. Now suddenly Irish music means something – traditional music or rock music or any kind of music we feel like making. And it's not just Ireland. There's bands from all over the world doing amazing things most people have never heard before – all kinds of fusions and borrowings. We sell some of this stuff in the shop. But only because Nora knows where to find it. It's all haphazard. Nobody's marketing it.'

'Who's Nora?'

'Nora's the boss.'

'Is she Irish too?'

'No, but her dad was Nigerian and her mother's Jewish, which is almost as good.' She laughed, turning to look at him, and he saw the animation in her face. 'Did you know, Michael, they've finally worked out how to put compact-disc players in cars?'

Michael shrugged. 'I know nothing about cars.'

'Well, for heaven's sake, neither do I, but I know about music and I know how to sell things. And there's this new Discman that Sony's bringing out. Nora thinks we should go into business together. It's just the right time to do it with everything changing.'

'It sounds like a great idea.'

'Worldly women, that's what Nora thinks we should

call ourselves, because we'd be distributing music from all over the world. And because we are, of course.'

Michael laughed, catching Peggy's excitement. 'You're always so positive and . . .'

'And what?

'I don't know. Enterprising, I suppose.'

'And so are you.'

'I'm not enterprising at all.'

'Leaving home? Going to art college?'

'My teacher, TJ, thinks my photographs are bourgeois.'

'How can a photograph be bourgeois?'

'I don't know. It's hard to explain. I took pictures on Dad's building site and TJ said I was celebrating the free market. There was one of Darren, Dad's labourer, going up a ladder with a hod full of bricks and TJ talked about it as though it was gay porn.'

Peggy's eyes opened in delight. 'That's hilarious.'

'Not at the time, it wasn't. I should take pictures of ugly homeless people, except TJ would think I was patronizing them.'

'You should take pictures of Buckingham Palace, so you should, and if he complains tell him from me that a cat can look at a king.'

Kieran came in from the hall in his dressing gown. He yawned and scratched his head. 'What am I missing?'

'Your brother's been cheering me up.'

'That's good.' He walked to the window and drew the curtain back.

'You're up early,' Peggy said.

'So are you.' Kieran looked at the two of them huddled

on the couch with the duvet wrapped around them. 'Or not – it's hard to tell.'

'I was cold.'

'And Michael took you in, just to keep you from the foggy foggy dew.'

'You be nice, or I shan't cook you breakfast.'

'I haven't time, actually. I promised to meet Salema.'

'A cup of tea, then.' Peggy slipped out from under the duvet. 'I'll put the kettle on while you're dressing.'

'No, really. I'll be off in a minute.'

'You're never fasting!'

Kieran smiled self-consciously.

'You're going to Mass again?' Peggy laughed. 'Jesus, Kieran, it's becoming a religion with you.'

'It's just something Salema likes to do. I'm meeting her at the university chaplaincy. Then we're going to do a few hours' practice.'

'So you'll go to Mass,' Michael said, 'and take Communion and all that, even though you don't believe in it?'

Kieran looked through the window up at the street. 'It's not like home,' he said, 'if that's what you're thinking.' He turned to face Michael. 'It's not Father Riley, for God's sake. The sermons at the chaplaincy are really intelligent. They're about ideas, and the right way to live.'

'But I thought we'd given all that up.'

'The stupid part of it, yes. But just because our experience of it wasn't very good, it doesn't mean there's nothing there. I mean, you wouldn't not believe in molecular physics just because you'd had stupid teachers who didn't understand it themselves. And just because your parents smacked you when you couldn't recite E equals MC squared or something. You wouldn't say, oh it must be all nonsense, then – because nuclear physics is bigger than them, it's something outside them that goes on being true whether they get it or not.'

'But E *does* equal MC squared. We've got the bombs to prove it, and the nuclear reactors.'

'And we've got the churches and the cathedrals to prove that God exists, and all the great masses of Byrd and Mozart, and Bach's oratorios, and they're a lot better than bombs and reactors.'

'But you're being illogical. It's not about taking sides between science and religion.' Michael was annoyed with himself for choosing nuclear weapons.

'No, *you're* being illogical, because if God doesn't exist, if Christianity is a huge elaborate fiction, then that's the end of all that music. We might as well make a big pile of the stuff and set fire to it.'

'But we can go on enjoying it.'

'No, because it would be a lie.' Kieran stood staring at Michael and then at the wall.

'Come on, boys,' Peggy said. 'For God's sake, let's not fight about religion.'

'I've got to get dressed, anyway, or I'll be late.' Kieran sighed heavily but didn't move.

Michael felt bad for him. It was obviously all about Salema, this new interest in religion. There was no need to show him up.

'Well, as it happens,' Peggy said, 'we're going to Mass too, Michael and me.'

Michael looked at her in surprise. 'We are?'

'At Saint Sebastian's.'

'Fergal's church?'

'What do you think? I keep meaning to go. He seems awful lonely. And he'd be excited to see you, I know he would.'

'OK, but *I'm* not fasting.'

'Nor me. I'm excommunicated, didn't you know? Fergal was horribly stern about it. He said, I hope you realize you're putting yourself out of communion with Mother Church.'

'So why go and see him?'

'Because he's still my cousin.'

'All right, then,' Kieran said, 'have fun.' And he went off to get dressed.

Fergal's church stood between a newsagents and a betting shop – a pre-war brick building with a steep roof. On a slab above the door was a statue of St Sebastian in a loincloth, his concrete chest stained with the rust from half a dozen arrows.

They were late. An old man in the lobby greeted them with a wink and a sideways nod and pointed with bent fingers to a doorway in the corner behind them, through which they could see a staircase spiralling upward to a gallery.

'Go on, Michael,' Peggy whispered, 'I'm right behind you.'

On the steps Michael caught the stink of incense and the creaking of pews and a voice reading the Gospel – a passage from Luke that he recognized, about a friend knocking on the door and asking for bread.

It was disconcerting to be in a church again and to find it all so instantly familiar. He turned a corner and saw above him a high timbered ceiling. The voice reading, though more breathy and enfeebled than he'd known it, was Fergal's.

Just short of the top step Michael tripped. He landed on one knee, stumbling against the balustrade, and the hollow thud of his elbow hitting the wooden panelling echoed back from the chancel. As he got to his feet he saw faces down in the nave turned towards him.

Standing in the pulpit Fergal had paused in his reading and was searching for his place in the text. He coughed a couple of times, waited while his breathing became steady, and began again. 'And to him who knocks it shall be opened.'

Michael heard a titter from the pews below and a gasp of suppressed laughter. Behind him Peggy snorted. There were shushing noises. More heads turned.

Fergal's head was down. It seemed for a moment that he might be about to throw up, then he turned away to cough into his hand a dozen times or more, his shoulders rocking with the effort.

Peggy clutched Michael's arm. 'Poor Fergal. Is he OK?'

A woman standing nearby leaned towards them. 'It was a summer cold,' she said, 'and then a cough that he couldn't shift. Father Gerard urged him to take more time off, but he insisted he was well. Poor Father Noonan. It sounds like bronchitis he has now, wouldn't you say?'

He did look ill, Michael thought. His eye sockets were deeper and his cheekbones more prominent than when they'd last met.

Fergal had begun reading again. His voice was thin and had a rasping edge to it. 'But if one of you asks his father for a loaf, will he hand him a stone? Or for a fish, will he for a fish hand him a serpent? Or if he asks for an egg, will he hand him a scorpion? Therefore, if you, evil as you are, know how to give good gifts to your children, how much more will your heavenly Father give the Good Spirit to those who ask him! This is the Gospel of the Lord.'

There was more fervour in the response, *Praise to you, Lord Jesus Christ*, than Michael was used to, perhaps because the people were relieved for their young priest that he'd made it this far through the Mass.

They were settling into the pews down in the nave, rearranging handbags and missals. Those without seats took the chance to change position or rest their shoulders against the walls. The woman who thought Fergal had bronchitis was telling her children to bunch up and signalling to Michael and Peggy to sit down beside her.

Breathing heavily, Fergal began his homily. 'Last weekend a fishing trawler was intercepted off the coast of County Kerry. You will have heard about it on the news, no doubt. The security forces found seven tons of arms and explosives – a delivery for the Provisional IRA, bought and paid for.' He looked around the congregation. 'A fishing trawler! What father, asked for a fish, would hand his child a snake?' He paused, gripping the rail of the pulpit to fight the impulse to cough. 'Some of you in this congregation were born in Ireland like me, or were born to Irish parents.

Many of you, I know, are of Irish ancestry. You will have grown up, as I did, knowing of the Great Hunger when the potato crop failed and one quarter of our people died for want of food, or died of fever and sickness, or boarded ships bound for America. *An Gorta Mór*, we call it in Gaelic. And all the while, grain and livestock were loaded at Irish ports and exported to England, and nothing could be done.'

There were murmurs of response from the pews.

'The people asked for bread and the English Parliament handed them a stone. We remember, and we are right to remember. Almighty God created us with the gift of memory. And history is a gift we hand on to our children. But if we remember only to harbour bitterness and to excuse our own wrongdoing, what good is that? Is it not a scorpion given in place of an egg?' Fergal's voice had risen in volume and begun to shake. He broke off, lifting his hand to his chest, pressing it against the embroidered fabric of his chasuble. He stood with his eyes shut, breathing through his nose.

There was coughing now from elsewhere in the church, not like the bronchial hacking that threatened to break out again at any moment from the pulpit, but a wilful throat-clearing.

'I agree with Father, of course,' the woman said, 'but he shouldn't talk politics, not in church. We don't come to Mass to hear politics spoken.'

Halfway up the church, an elderly man had stood and was pushing his way towards the aisle. As he turned, Michael saw his gaunt face and the look of defiance in his eyes.

Fergal was flustered. He had begun talking of the

famine in Ethiopia but seemed to have lost confidence in the thread of his argument. Then he was leaving the pulpit, breathing heavily as he came down the steps. It wasn't clear whether he had finished his homily or abandoned it.

An electronic organ throbbed into life, prompting a drone of words from the congregation. For a moment Fergal was free to settle into his seat by the altar and close his eyes. The acolytes, two teenage girls, sat on either side of him with their candles on the floor. There was a clanking noise. A middle-aged man, whose surplice was trimmed with lace, was crossing the chancel towards Fergal, swinging the thurible by its brass chain. A small boy with the incense boat in his hand trotted to keep up. The man placed himself in front of the priest and lifted the lid of the thurible, releasing a cloud of smoke. The small boy was holding up the brass boat so that the priest could spoon more incense onto the smouldering charcoal. But Fergal had turned his head towards the wall and was waving them away. While he struggled to control his coughing, a small procession moved into view below the gallery, carrying the wafers and the wine and a basket of money. Fergal stirred himself to stand behind the altar to pray over the offerings.

Kneeling with the others in the gallery, Michael watched him do the business with the bread, speaking the words of transubstantiation, holding the host between the thumb and index finger of each hand and eating it over the chalice so as not to lose a crumb. It gave Michael a queasy feeling to be present at the consecration after this gap of time, after the months of sullen resistance, the strategic Sunday morning absences, the battle for the privilege of going to Mass when it suited him so that he could walk straight past the door and wander the streets for an hour, after the grunts and the vagueness about which hymns had been sung, who had read the epistle, what the sermon had been about, until even his mother had left him alone to lapse – to be no better than a heathen if that was what he wanted, God have mercy on him.

Having dealt with the bread, Fergal had turned his attention to the wine. The chalice glinted in the light as he raised it in front of him. His voice was barely audible. 'When supper was ended, he took the cup. Again he gave you thanks and praise, gave the cup to his disciples, and said, *Take this, all of you, and drink from it. This is the cup . . .*' He paused to fight back a bronchial spasm. '*The cup of my blood, the blood of the new and everlasting . . .*' There was the first syllable of the word *covenant* and then nothing but coughing. He turned his head to the side, lowering the chalice away from him to protect its contents from the insult of saliva and sputum. It teetered, too close to the edge of the altar. One of the acolytes moved to catch it as it tipped, tilting it towards the congregation, before settling it on its base. Wine slopped from the rim, a scarlet wave that began at once to darken as it soaked into the altar cloth. There was a gasp from the pews near the front, and a sudden focusing of attention. The chalice was stable, with most of the wine still safely inside it. The girl had taken the priest's napkin and begun dabbing at the stain. The server who carried the thurible was suddenly beside her, yanking her arm upwards with his free hand, as though something more than protocol had been offended.

'The bastard!' Peggy hissed. 'What's eating *him*, do you suppose?'

The girl, white-faced with pain or anger, had pulled away, and withdrew now to the side of the chancel, nursing her shoulder. Fergal, meanwhile, had sunk into his seat and was bent sideways over its Gothic armrest.

The sacristy door swung open. An elderly priest hurried towards the chancel, straightening his chasuble. 'Let us proclaim the mystery of faith,' he said, as though to reassure everyone that the miracle of transubstantiation had indeed occurred, in spite of the spillage and confusion.

The woman standing beside Michael touched his arm. 'It's Father Gerard come at last,' she said. 'It will be all right now.'

Father Gerard had a hand on Fergal's shoulder and had bent down to speak. Fergal nodded, stood unsteadily and made his way down towards the sacristy. Behind him the words of the Eucharist continued. 'Father, we celebrate the memory of Christ your son . . .'

'Let's go,' Peggy said. Michael followed her to the spiral staircase and out into the street.

As they turned up the side of the church, Fergal came out of the sacristy. He looked chilled, though it was a mild day and the sun was shining. Michael called to him and he turned with a startled look that became an anguished smile.

'You were at Mass?'

'Didn't you see us?' Michael said.

'I did not.' Fergal shook his head despondently. 'What a disaster!'

'Not at all,' Peggy said, 'you did great.'

'But to knock over the chalice.'

'So what if you did, Fergal? Do you think God cares?'

'It's a while yet, I hope, Peggy, before I have to meet God face to face. Meanwhile I have Father Gerard to answer to.'

Michael laughed at that, which made Fergal laugh too until his laughter turned to coughing.

Peggy squeezed his arm. 'You're not well. You should be in, in the warm.'

They walked with him towards the priests' house.

'And they didn't like my homily.'

'I liked it,' Michael said. 'To hell with them.'

'And it was only one of them didn't like it,' Peggy said.

'Only one of them walked out, at least. I've bored them half to death often enough, but I've never had them walking out before.'

'Well, there you are, then. You're obviously getting better at it.'

The housekeeper met them at the kitchen door. She had the kettle on and instructions from Father Gerard to poach Fergal an egg and put him to bed with a hot toddy. She lit the gas fire in the parlour, sat Fergal down with a blanket over his knees and prepared his breakfast.

While he ate, Peggy made them laugh with tales of the peculiar people who came into the shop. So Michael described how Emily had outed herself at the breakfast table, but it seemed to him that Fergal was missing the point of the story – that it was funny – being more interested in his mother's feelings. Hadn't it caused her a great deal of anxiety? And what about Emily, struggling at her age with such weighty questions? Too soon the housekeeper came in to bundle Father Fergal off to bed. And

Michael left the house with a feeling that he had missed a chance to connect.

Peggy had gone back to the flat to see if Dan was home yet, so Michael went in search of Salema and his brother. There was a noticeboard in the entrance to the college where students could sign up to book practice cells. He found Salema's name and went to find the room. Music seeped out into the corridor – a clarinettist playing scales, long notes on a French horn.

He expected to hear Kieran's violin as he approached Salema's cell, but heard only the piano. It was like nothing he'd ever heard her play. Consisting of discordant and apparently random clusters of notes, it lurched from one percussive burst to the next in a jerky and accelerating rhythm, fading towards silence as Michael opened the door.

Kieran was sitting on the piano stool, lying back against the keyboard with his eyes closed and a strange look on his face, as though he had been struck by a moment of wild musical beauty while watching someone accidentally stepping on his violin; a look of ecstatic disturbance, accompanied by a groan that hovered similarly between pleasure and pain. Salema sat facing him, her legs straddling his. She wore white ankle socks. Hanging from the toes of one foot, a shoe as light as a slipper seemed still to be resonating to the final chord. The other shoe lay on the floor where it had fallen. Her hair was pushed to one side, and her blouse was open so that from behind Michael had a view of her neck and the curve of one beautifully sculpted shoulder. A silver medallion, the size of a small coin, had been flung sideways on its delicate silver chain. She was not otherwise exposed, though her skirt was bunched up around her on the seat. She settled now against Kieran with a long audible exhalation.

Michael saw the violin, which he hadn't noticed before, resting on the piano keyboard within reach of Kieran's left hand, and the bow on the floor by his right foot.

Michael was motionless for a second or two, long enough for Salema to begin turning her head towards him, and for Kieran to open his eyes and meet his stare with a dazed expression. A noise came out of Michael's throat that might have been the start of an apology but became something else – an *I'm* that lengthened into a hum of awkwardness and distress. Then he stepped back into the corridor and pulled the door shut. He had no reason to be shocked, no right to be upset. What he felt, neverthe-less, was a sensation so intense that noise and movement were essential, and the growling hum was still growing in his throat when he reached the hallway and, taking hold of the handrail, swung recklessly down the stairs.

† The Church of St Ursula and the Virgin Martyrs

Wednesday 19 February 2003

President Bush announced today that America and its allies are called once again to defend the peace against an aggressive tyrant. He was making a speech in Georgia in a place called Kennesaw and there was a great deal of clapping and cheering. He means us to think of Hitler, of course. But it made me curious about Kennesaw, where a man is applauded for standing language on its head. I just looked it up and I see that the town is considered a grand place to raise a family and has a law, enacted only twenty years ago, requiring every household to maintain a firearm. They mean to have peace in the town of Kennesaw even if it kills them.

The sheep farmers in our part of County Wicklow had shotguns to discourage the rabbits. I would hear rumours in my childhood of old IRA men with handguns hidden about the house. But arming the populace has not been a priority in the Republic of Ireland. We've seen bloodshed enough, God knows. Even Hitler could not tempt us into war. For some it is a matter of shame that we remained neutral in the struggle against fascism, but the Irish Free State had become truly free only two years before the

German army marched into Poland. My grandparents'
generation remembered the Troubles well enough.
Perhaps they'd had more than they could stomach
of fighting tyranny and of fighting each other over the
fighting of tyranny.

Standing up to tyrants seems to be back in fashion,
anyhow, and the hard men are impatient to get on
with it.

I have my own impatience to deal with, having
so much to do in preparation for my departure.
I mentioned that I have asked permission of the
bishop to leave the parish for a time, and he has
reluctantly agreed. I did not tell you that I have
been less than straightforward in making my request.
I am certainly at a point of spiritual crisis, that much
is true. And I do indeed intend to withdraw from
the world as I have known it and dedicate myself,
for a period of uncertain length, to the contemplation
of what lies ahead – death, judgement, the hope of
eternal salvation after my sins have been purged.
The past, what parts of it trouble me most, I hope
to leave behind me in this letter.

My first year at St Sebastian's was not easy.
You came once to Mass, I remember. Peggy had been
before, though I had argued fiercely with her. But
to see you there, Michael, when I knew you were
studying in Brighton, was a surprise and a delight
to me. A humiliation also, as it turned out. And
afterwards I talked too much and asked you nothing
about your art course or your new life in Brighton.

I was sick, of course. Pneumonia, the doctor

thought it was, exacerbated by fatigue. He prescribed antibiotics and rest and plenty of fluids. He was concerned that I was not eating regularly. He talked about stress. I was confined to the presbytery for a week. Then I was sent to a seminary in northern Spain for a period of study and retreat. Father Gerard thought I needed a break from parish work. He also thought the climate would do me good. He probably imagined a hot dry landscape of vineyards and olive trees. I arrived in Castile at the beginning of November and was met by bitter squalling rain. I'd have been better off back home in County Wicklow.

Nevertheless I look back on my Castilian month as a blessed time. I walked in the garden of innocence. I devoted my spare hours to a study of Saint Teresa of Avila, a Castilian herself. I loved Teresa for her doubt and confusion, for her struggle with her own wilfulness. She became a nun but lived a frivolous and self-indulgent life, as nuns often did in those times. Eventually she would summon the Carmelite order to a more stringent standard, and open new convents in which the nuns went barefoot. For challenging the establishment she would be pursued by the Inquisition, denounced by the Papal Nuncio for her restless disobedience.

But first she had visions in which Our Lord came to her. Her confessor told her these were diabolically inspired, and that she must dismiss this impostor Jesus with an obscene gesture known as el hico or the fig. Jesus seemed not to be discouraged by this rudeness,

but commended her for obeying her confessor.
She knew then that the priest was mistaken. I felt
challenged by that element in Teresa's goodness that
was both courageous and pragmatic. I took to heart
her advice on eating well, that there's a time for
partridge and a time for penance, and resolved that
once I was back in London I would take proper care
of my own physical needs, so that I could better
attend to the spiritual needs of my parishioners.

I was unwell throughout this time. I had bouts
of fever and delirium. But I was awake and praying
in my cell when Teresa appeared to me. I thought
at first she was a nurse sent because I was sick, but
there was a glow to her, a translucence that was not
of this world. She seemed more alive than I was and
yet the wall against which she stood remained visible.
She spoke to me, promising that I would meet a
violent death bearing witness to the Faith. She
offered it as a gift and I received it as one.

Soon enough I would suspect this vision, as
Teresa's confessor had suspected hers. It was an
invitation to spiritual pride – pride that would
shortly lead, though I did not know it then, to a
fall of equal magnitude.

A long while later, a kindly confessor suggested
to me that it was, perhaps, the memory of my father
and an unconscious eagerness to emulate him that
prompted this illusion.

Before returning to London I was given
permission to travel through Santiago de Compostela,
two hundred miles to the west, and from there

another thirty miles to the very north-west tip of
Spain to visit my Aunt Consuelo, the only member
of my mother's family still living.

Consuelo had written to me earlier in the year.
Her letter had come with a birthday card so it would
have been June. Until then I had scarcely remembered
her existence. She told me in the letter that she had
been unable to visit when my mother died because
she was in prison for demonstrating against Franco.
It was the first time I knew that it was from both
sides of the family that I had inherited an interest
in politics.

I am nearly done with this story, Michael, but
I won't finish it tonight. Tomorrow I will be working
on something for the parish newsletter and preparing
my last homily.

I hear on the news that the Archbishop of
Canterbury has joined Cardinal Murphy-O'Connor
in urging the government to step back from the brink
of war. Thank God for such men. Someone from
Christian Aid has spoken of the humanitarian disaster
that will surely follow for the suffering people of Iraq.
Tony Blair, who is known to be sympathetic to the
Church, is on his way to Rome. I wonder will the
Holy Father, even now at the eleventh hour, knock
some sense into him.

OCTOBER 1984 BRIGHTON

When the joint came round for the third time, Michael said, 'Too much like Communion,' and put it to Rhys Morgan's mouth, intoning, 'The spliff of Christ.' The others fell against each other, helpless with the hilarity of it, except for Chrissie who nodded and said, 'Wow!' making a big round shape of her black-lipsticked lips and wrapping her arms around his neck.

Then someone changed the tape, and they were listening to the cool, breathy voice of Nena singing 'Neunundneunzig Luftballons'. There was the moody, explorative opening and then the bass guitar kicked in, and Chrissie started jerking to the rhythm. 'This is so great. Don't you think it's great? Much better than the English version. The English version is lame. Ninety-nine red balloons – what's that? Only the Germans really get the existential threat of nuclear war.'

Rhys, slumped beside them on the couch, belched and said, 'That's bollocks, that is.'

'It's not bollocks, Rhys. They get it because they live with the Berlin Wall. It's part of their reality.'

'It's bollocks, and the song's bollocks too, in German or bloody English. Even the Welsh version's bollocks.'

'There is no Welsh version,' Andy Cochran said, without raising his head from the carpet.

'How would you know, you Scottish git? And World War Three's never going to start in Berlin, I'll tell you that for nothing.'

'Where's it going to start, then, Rhys?' Michael asked him.

'Most likely possibilities, all right?' And Rhys began counting them off, starting with his thumb, which made Michael think it was going to be a long list.

Chrissie was stifling a yawn, so maybe the same thought had occurred to her.

'First, South Africa, because when the blacks get themselves organized to overthrow apartheid it's going to be a bloodbath, and serve us all right. Second . . .' – he moved to his index finger – 'Afghanistan, because that's where Russia and America are actually fighting, not in bloody Berlin.'

'The Americans aren't fighting in Afghanistan.'

'Shows how much you know. Who do you think's behind the mujahedin, then? And third, Newport.'

'Newport?'

Rhys grinned. 'Well, that's an outside bet, that one. But if I put money on it and it comes in I'll make a killing, won't I.'

'Put a sock in it, you Welsh moron,' Andy Cochran said, and the others started laughing again.

Chrissie murmured in Michael's ear, 'Let's go somewhere we can dance.'

'It's nearly midnight.'

'So?'

'So nothing'll be open.'

'We'll find a party somewhere. There are Tories all over town. We can crash one of theirs.' She giggled. 'A Tory party. That's funny, actually.' She stood up, pulling a long strand of black hair off her face. 'I'll have to get my shoes from my room.' She shared the house with three or four other girls. 'You can come if you like.'

Michael followed her up the stairs. She stumbled near the top and crawled onto the landing, giggling feebly. Rolling onto her back, she raised her hands up for him to pull her to her feet. She led him into the room. There were two girls tangled up on the far side of the bed. They seemed to be asleep.

'Who are they?' Michael asked her, whispering so as not to wake them.

'Not sure. Friends of Polly's.'

'So why aren't they in Polly's room?'

'Because Polly's in Polly's room? With some bloke?'

She sat on the bed and crossed her legs, first one way then the other, to put her shoes on, taking two or three swipes at each foot. Then she opened a drawer in the bedside table and took out a plastic bag. She put her hand in and came out with two pills – small and round like pink aspirins.

'What are they?' Michael said. 'Drugs?'

'Of course they're drugs.'

'What do they do?'

'They make you happy.'

'Like speed?'

'Not speedy – happy.'

'Like LSD?'

'No, nothing like LSD. You don't hallucinate, or any-thing. You just see what's there, only better – what's always been there, but you weren't looking. You see how lovely everything is.'

'It's not dangerous, then.'

'It's fun, that's all. I got them from this guy in San Francisco.' She looked up at him without quite focusing, put her hand on his chest and found the way into the pocket of his shirt. 'Here,' she said, letting go of them, 'we'll take them later.'

'When, later?'

'We'll know,' she said, nodding at the wisdom of her words, 'when it's the right time.'

'When we're surrounded by Young Conservatives, you mean?'

'They're not that bad, Conservatives, not when you consider the alternative.' She stood up, frowned, and sat down again with a bump.

One of the girls groaned and shifted on the bed.

'You know,' Chrissie said, 'I feel dizzy.' She lay down on the pillow, lifting one of her feet off the floor. 'Wake me when it's time to leave.'

'When will that be?'

Chrissie didn't answer. Michael was about to ask again, but she had started snoring. He looked at the three sleeping girls, two of them curled up together, and Chrissie with her skirt bunched up and her legs flung haphazardly across the bed. She was tanned and her limbs were strong from swimming or playing tennis. It was five days since he had walked in on Kieran and Salema, and to stand here while Chrissie slept made him feel like a creep all over again. He left the bedroom, shutting the door behind him, and stood in the sitting-room doorway for a minute, listening to Rhys and

Andy trading insults, waiting to feel some connection. Then he let himself out into the street.

The house Michael lived in stood at the blind end of a cul-de-sac a few streets back from the sea front. Something pale was moving in the shadows near the house – a curtain, perhaps, billowing out through an open window. As he approached he saw that it wasn't a curtain, but a dress. He thought of Katherine. He'd had a letter from her saying that home was hell and she'd try to come for the weekend, if that was OK. He had a twinge of anxiety, thinking she must have been waiting for him. Friday, she'd said. But surely she hadn't meant Friday morning at half-past midnight.

It wasn't Katherine. He saw the black hair and the dark complexion, the stiff doll-like posture. Even in her misery – and her misery was unmistakable to him as he cut across the street towards her – there was a formality in the way she stood, legs straight, feet together, holding herself against the cold.

Her eyes flared up as he approached, as though he might be about to attack her, then settled again into a kind of blankness, which was the only sign that she had recognized him.

'What are you doing here?'

The question seemed to puzzle her.

'What's going on? Is Kieran with you?'

'I couldn't stay in London after what happened. I went home, but the taxman was there.'

'Your stepfather? Isn't that where he lives?'

'He's off work. He fell through the garage roof and broke his ankle.'

'So you couldn't stay?'

'He watches me all the time.' The thought of it brought some life back into her face. 'He sits in the living room reading or listening to Radio Four and he watches me. It makes me sick.'

Michael stood for a moment wondering what to say. He knew about parents who bullied and interfered and made you feel guilty even when you'd done nothing wrong. But the crimes of the taxman were beyond his experience. 'You'd better come inside. We have to be quiet or we'll disturb the landlord, and then he'll drag us into his lair, and we'll have to admire whatever painting he's working on at the moment.'

He unlocked the front door and led her into the hall. She followed him in near darkness up three flights of creaking stairs and into his room. Circling the cramped space, he switched on the bedside lamp and the work lamp on the desk, angling each of them towards the wall. 'Are you cold? I can put the electric fire on. Would you like a cup of tea or something?'

Salema sat on the upright chair by the desk with her arms across her stomach and nodded indiscriminately at his questions until the nodding became a rocking motion.

Not sure how to calm her, Michael put some water in the kettle and plugged it in. He was pleased she had come to him, and felt bad for being pleased because it meant she hadn't gone to Kieran. He took a jumper out of a drawer. 'You can put this on if you like,' he said, handing it to her.

She was wearing the same silver chain he had seen in the music cell. The small oval medallion swung against her and away as she rocked.

'It's pretty, that thing.'

'It's Cecilia, patron saint of music.'

'Can I see?'

Salema leant forward and held it out towards him.

Squatting in front of her, he put his hand under hers to steady the medallion.

'She's playing the organ, which is anachronistic, actually. They didn't have organs in second-century Rome. But anyway . . .' She shivered and pulled her hand away.

'Put the jumper on.'

She stirred herself to pull it down over her head and push her arms into the sleeves.

'So what are you planning to do?'

'I don't know.'

'What happened between you and Kieran?'

'You saw what happened.' She bent forward, putting her hands to her face. 'I'm so ashamed.'

He sat facing her on the edge of the bed. 'There's nothing to be ashamed of. People have sex all the time.'

'It was nothing, then – is that what you think?' The question was barely audible, muttered through her hands into her lap. 'I suppose that's why you ran away, because it was nothing.'

He didn't know how to answer without revealing himself. *I was jealous*, he might have said. *I've always been jealous. I thought I'd got over you, but then I saw you, like that, with Kieran and I felt shut out.* But all he said was, 'I was embarrassed.'

'Embarrassed. That doesn't matter much, does it, not in the long run. That's just about how you look in front of other people. Imagine being embarrassed in front of God.

You can't because it doesn't make any sense.' She jerked her head from side to side. 'Why can't I be normal with people?'

'It probably gets easier with practice.'

She raised her head in a flash of anger. 'I don't mean that.'

He regretted his clumsiness, that he was still talking about sex when she wasn't.

'I mean,' she said with careful emphasis, 'just being with people in a normal way. Talking about things ordinary people talk about. It's not that I don't want to. But it's as though everyone's speaking German and I'm working out the grammar, trying to hold the verb in my head until it's time to say it, and hoping I'll remember what it's supposed to agree with.'

'You're not like that with me.'

She peered at him, searching his face for the truth. The desperation in her eyes scared him.

Then she looked at the floor again. 'With music it's different. It's not that it makes me happy, exactly. But when I play the piano my mind goes to some other place. When I stop, it comes back and brings everything with it.'

Michael wondered what he was going to do with her.

She'd started rocking again. 'I just want it to stop hurting.'

'Let me give you something that will help.'

She looked up, waiting for him to explain.

'Something to make you happy.' He reached in his shirt pocket for Chrissie's pills.

'What is it?'

'Just something to make you feel better.'

'Will it help me sleep?'

He shrugged. 'Probably, if you're tired.'

'It's not a tranquillizer? My mother takes Valium. It just makes her dopey, so she doesn't have to face the pointless-ness of her life.'

'It's not a tranquillizer.' He remembered what Chrissie had said. 'It makes you see how lovely everything is.' He held the pills towards her.

'Is that good?'

'To see the beauty of things? I think so.'

'It's what you do when you take pictures, I suppose.'

He got up off the bed. 'I never made tea.'

'There are two of them,' Salema said. 'Two pills.'

'Yes.'

'One each.'

'Exactly.'

'So we'll take them together.'

'Of course.'

She put her hand out and he placed one on her open palm.

She picked it up and angled it towards the light. 'What does e stand for?'

'Some trade name, I suppose.'

She took a deep breath, opened her mouth and rested the pill on the tip of her tongue. It sat there for a moment, pale against the darker pink. She closed her eyes and swallowed. 'Now you,' she said.

He took his, and they sat for a moment looking at each other, waiting to feel something.

'I thought at first you might be Katherine,' he said,

'when I saw you outside. She's coming for the weekend, and I thought you were her and she was early.'

'That's nice, that she wants to visit you.'

'Things are crazy at home, as usual. You know how mad my parents are.'

'I like your parents.'

She spoke wistfully, and he felt bad for complaining.

He took two mugs, put a teabag in each and poured the water. 'They're all in a state because Eileen's back. She got married last summer, and Mam and Emily went to Manchester on the coach because Dad refused to have anything to do with it. Now Eileen seems to be having some kind of emotional meltdown. She'd been home for a week, anyway, when Harold showed up wanting her back. So now they're both there. Harold's in our old room, mine and Kieran's, and Eileen's in with the girls.' He put a mug of tea on the desk for Salema. 'Sorry, I'm out of milk. Apparently Mam wakes them in the middle of the night, Harold and Eileen, to give them marriage-guidance counselling and say the rosary. She does her best thinking in the middle of the night, she says – or her worst, depending on your point of view. So now Dad's awake, and he decides he might as well get on with some odd jobs like hammering down the loose floorboards. And it's three o'clock in the morning and everyone's getting hysterical.' Michael laughed. 'So Kath wants a weekend in Brighton, and I can't blame her.'

They sat for a while, listening to the timbers shifting in the old house. The wind crept in under the roof and set the air stirring in the chimney.

He felt restless suddenly. 'Do you want to go for a walk?'

'Yes,' she said, getting up.

'We'll have to be quiet on the stairs, so as not to wake Abbott.'

'Your landlord? Has he stopped painting, then, do you think?'

'He never stops painting. He paints in his sleep.'

'What are his paintings like?'

'A lot of cats. A lot of swirly acrylics.'

'I love cats.'

'I didn't know that.'

'Not to live with, maybe. But I like to know they're out there in the dark, doing their catty things.'

They left the lights on and the two mugs of tea hardly touched on the desk, and the opaque patches of air where the light from the desk lamp mingled with the steam.

By the time they reached the street they were holding hands. There was a fresh inland breeze but no noise of traffic to obscure the murmur of the waves. At the sea-front near the Palace Pier they turned westward, strolling under the street lights past the pale facades of the hotels and apartment buildings where random windows glowed. Michael pulled Salema towards him and she huddled under his arm. He felt how slight she was. The wind could take her, he thought, and she'd go fluttering above the buildings and up over the town towards the railway station, and he'd follow. Or they'd vault the cast-iron balustrade and drift down over the surf. He told her this and she smiled and they stopped to look at the sea. Nearly a month he'd been in Brighton and he'd never looked at the sea before, not really. Even in the darkness with a few stars and the street lights softening everything and a haze over the moon, its colours were deep enough to drown you. He told her this too, and they laughed because drowning you was exactly what the sea could do. It was cold so they started walking again. He slid his hand along the wooden rail, feeling its polished grain. It didn't matter that Salema was Kieran's girlfriend, because he loved Kieran too.

They passed the Grand Hotel and he drew her down the long flight of steps into the shadow of the sea wall and onto the shingle. They stumbled in the darkness over the ridges of the beach and laughed, tasting the sharpness of the air in their mouths. Even their stumbling felt easy like a move in a dance. When they reached the edge of the water, they skirted it, skipping sideways as the waves rushed towards them, and wandering back again in pursuit. They separated and came together, enjoying each other's warmth, and the freshness of the space around them. They admired the stars and the open spaces between the stars. There was a tingling vividness to the feel of the shingle under their shoes.

A wave chased them and Salema laughed, breathless with the excitement. 'Elation,' she said.

'What about it?'

'It's what *e* stands for.'

'Oh, yes, of course. Or elixir.'

'The secret of immortality. Or Elysium, where the brave and the virtuous go after death.'

'Or euphoria.'

'Yes, ee-you-phoria.' She clapped her hands. 'Oh, I know . . .' She turned to him with shining eyes. 'Epiphany. That's what it stands for. It came to me just like that.'

'As epiphanies often do. In fact it was e-stounding.'

She gurgled with delight. 'Eee-licious.'

'Eeeee-wonderful.'

She pulled a face, pretending to be indignant. 'Now you're being silly.'

'Now *I'm* being silly? What about all your e-words? What about e-licious?'

'E-licious is all right. E-licious is within the rules.'

He looked at her with delight. 'There are rules?'

'E-licious comes from de-licious. But you can't just stick an *e* in front of any old word and expect it to mean something.'

'This woman goes to collect her husband's gravestone, and it says on it – Lord, he was thin. And she says to the mason, you've missed out the e. So the mason says . . .'

'I love jokes.'

'So the mason says – By gum, so I 'ave, missus. Come back in 'alf an hour. So she comes back, and it says on the gravestone – *Ee* Lord, he was thin!'

'I'm not worried about death.'

Michael was laughing. Salema wasn't laughing because she'd started talking about something else. And Michael saw how wonderful this was, that she didn't feel the need to laugh. Laughing at each other's jokes was superfluous when there was this deep flow of connection between them.

'You're right not to worry,' he said. 'Death's nothing to worry about.'

'When we die we just have to put up with purgatory for a while . . .'

'For a few hundred thousand years in my case . . .'

'And a few hundred million in mine, which is still

nothing compared with eternity – just a blink of God's eye. And then we'll be in bliss. It will be like floating out on that ocean forever.'

It was one of the things he loved her for, that you never knew what she might say. It was so often something no one else would think of saying.

She smiled. 'And I'll see my father . . .'

'Who art in heaven.'

'Unless I get there first and he's still in purgatory and I have to intercede on his behalf . . .'

Michael looked at her in surprise. 'But he was a good man, your father.'

'Or in hell, and I can only watch him, way down below, suffering torment.'

'But he was a saint.'

'Yes, he was a saint.' Salema nodded her head solemnly, as though repeating an article of faith. 'He kept our secret until he died and took it to the next world with him, and never confessed it, not even on his deathbed, not even when the priest came to administer the last sacrament, and I was scared, because I knew he was going to die, although everyone pretended he wasn't, and my mother pulled me out onto the landing, and I was crying, and the priest closed the door.'

'Your secret.'

'Yes.'

'Opus Dei, you mean?'

'No, not Opus Dei. A much bigger secret than that.'

The water rolled in towards them, floundered onto the beach and scurried back between the pebbles. And the moon was so vast and lovely that Michael was dizzy with the sight of it and had to look down to steady himself. He closed his eyes and opened them on the black pebbles at his feet. Something in what Salema had said was troubling him. 'So how do you know?' he asked her.

'How do I know what?' She had gone ahead of him and was standing among cast-iron columns that rose up out of the shingle like the ruins of a temple – all that survived of the landward end of the West Pier.

'After the priest had closed the door, how do you know that your father kept your secret?' The catwalk shut out a line of stars as he approached. It swung out towards the abandoned concert hall, a dark shape hovering over the water.

'I've just remembered I was here before,' Salema said, 'as a child. We'd been to Mass in someone's house. I remember the smell of furniture polish and incense, the brass candlesticks in the sunlight, the murmur of Latin – *In nomine patris et filii et spiritus sancti*. And then later, standing in the wind on the pier, looking down through the railings at the sea.'

'This pier? Not the other one, the Palace Pier?' He waved a hand eastward along the beach.

'This one, I'm sure.'

'They shut this one down in 1970 – I read that some-where – because it wasn't safe.'

'So I was four years old.'

'And how old were you when he died?'

'Nine.' She picked her way across the shingle with her arms out as though balancing on a tightrope.

'How do you know, Salema, that your father kept your secret?'

Taking hold of a pillar, she leaned out from it and swung around and they were suddenly face to face. 'Because when the priest came out of my father's room he didn't strike me dead.'

Michael had never noticed how huge her pupils were – wells of darkness big enough to swim in.

The sound was so sudden and so loud that it pushed against his abdomen, squeezing his lungs. It had physical bulk. He thought he was drowning, but when he opened his eyes the sea was still there at his feet where he'd left it. A spatter of fragments stung his head and shoulders. Salema was cowering at the base of the column. A web of dust and grit had settled on her hair like a veil, and the air tasted of chalk. After a while there were other sounds, voices and car alarms. Someone had cried out, louder than the others.

'Was that you?' He meant was it her voice he had heard. But she had begun to whimper and he understood that the screaming had come from somewhere else. It mingled now with the other distant voices.

He squatted beside her, put his arms round her waist, and lifted her to her feet. 'Are you OK?'

'Did I do that?'

'It was an explosion. Somewhere over there, I think. Look.'

Back along the shore, where the pale rendered frontages peered over the balustrade towards the beach, a dark sliver of sky had cut down into the roofline. A siren sounded.

'I'm cold,' Salema said.

'Yes, me too. We should go back.'

'Back?'

'To my place. That should still be all right.'

'What will we do there?'

'Get warm.'

'Can we go to sleep?'

'Yes. Good idea.'

'I'm tired.'

He took her hand and led her back the way they'd come, stumbling over the shingle towards the noise, finding the stone steps up the sea wall. With a hissing that was louder now than the surf, water burst from severed pipes and cascaded through the wreckage. There was a crowd blocking the road, and Michael thought all the vagrants of the town had gathered to watch, until he saw that they were hotel guests, some wrapped in blankets, some half dressed, dragged from their beds. A blue light flashed on and off through the dust. The police car was abandoned in the street with its doors open.

Someone asked Michael was it a gas leak did he think – an elderly man wearing black trousers with the braces dangling. His belly sagged and his chest was covered in grey hair. 'There are people dead in there,' he said, 'people dying in the rubble,' and he shuffled away. There was blood on his feet.

A younger man was saying to whoever would listen that it was never gas did this, it was the Libyans or the IRA.

Michael could hear a woman shouting for help. Another ran past with her mink coat flapping and a nightie underneath. Everything was dislocated and misplaced. The hotel was like a wedding cake elaborately iced with a piece hacked from it, black innards of masonry and timber spilling into the road.

Michael felt everything coming at him – the noise and the disorder – touching him more abrasively than it should, as though he'd lost a layer of skin. Salema clung to his side, shaking, and some of the shaking was his. He put both arms round her and pushed through the crowd. They headed along the front. People passed them, running towards the commotion. Lights had come on in upper windows. People craned from bedrooms, or hurried out of front doors and hotel lobbies in their dressing gowns. A police car lurched out of a side street. The headlights washed over them and away and for a moment the street was blue, everything coming and going with a sickening pulse. At last the sea was audible again and they turned their backs on it and walked inland.

It was hot in Michael's room. They had left the fire on. Michael emptied the tea from the mugs, rinsed them under the cold tap and filled them with water. Moving like sleepwalkers they kicked their shoes off and brushed the worst of the grit from each other's hair. They took it in turns to use the bathroom, which was on the floor below. They talked incoherently about what had happened, repeating themselves, echoing each other. They felt like lost children. They felt a hundred years old. They lay down on the narrow bed in their clothes and slept.

In his dream he was in the kitchen at home. The roof had fallen on top of him. His mother was weeping and saying the rosary. His father, up among the tangle of timbers, was hammering nails, still trying to fix the slates.

Then he was awake and someone was thumping on his door. Standing up, he was caught out by the tilt of the floor-boards and stepped sideways to recover his balance.

As soon as he opened the door, Kieran walked in. 'You know about the bombing?'

'Yes, I saw it.'

Kieran was still moving, looking around Michael's room, though his eyes didn't settle long enough to take any-thing in. 'It was on the news. Two people dead, two missing, two in intensive care . . .'

'Is that all?'

'What the hell do you mean by that?'

Struggling to frame an answer, Michael felt sluggish and stupid. His head was pounding. 'Sorry,' he said. 'I saw the place after the bomb went off. I just thought . . .'

Kieran slumped onto a chair. He looked exhausted. 'Dan skipped a session last night. He never came home.'

'Dan can take care of himself.'

'Christ, I'm not worried about Dan.'

Michael was missing something. He didn't know why his brother was here. He felt his heart racing and won-dered where Salema was. In the bathroom, perhaps. She'd brought a canvas bag with her, but he couldn't see it. And here was Kieran – in pursuit, of course. 'Kieran,' he said. 'Last night . . .'

'You know it was the IRA?'

'Was it? Somebody said the IRA or Libya.'

'It was the IRA. The Provos, Peggy calls them. Dan calls

them the boys. There are people dead. There were bedrooms collapsing on top of each other, people asleep . . .'
He stopped as though he had run out of steam. '*The boys*.
What does it mean, do you think, that he calls them the
boys?'

Michael shrugged. 'It's what people call them.'

'But what does it mean?'

'That they identify with them, I suppose. Or just that
they grew up hearing them called that, knowing they were
part of the family whether they liked them or not. Are you
OK, Kier? You look terrible.'

'I haven't been sleeping. Salema's buggered off. She
can't handle the sex thing.'

'I know.'

'It wasn't even my idea.'

'I could see that.'

'You walking in didn't help.'

'You could have locked the door.'

'We could have gone somewhere private, but it's all
about high drama for her. Like her religion – all self-
punishment and hysteria. I mean, guilt is one thing, but
she goes on sometimes as though she's going to be struck
down by a thunderbolt or something.'

'Last night . . .' It was floating back into Michael's
mind, something she'd said on the beach just before the
bomb went off. It was hard to get hold of. It was too
long ago. Whatever it was they'd taken had opened everything up. It was as though they had walked naked in the
garden naming everything, weightless and unafraid. Now,
with the dull weight of day settling on him, he could

hardly imagine such courage. 'Before the explosion . . .' he said.

'Did it wake you up?'

'I was awake already.'

'When it came on the news this morning I felt sick. I'd been up half the night, and then I heard Peggy moving about.'

'Do you think something terrible happened to Salema as a kid?'

'Well, obviously. Her father died, for a start.'

'But before that.'

'How the hell should I know?' He stood up from his chair and went to the window. 'Peggy was anxious about Dan. He hadn't come home yet.'

'He's stayed out all night before, hasn't he?'

'But he's never missed a session before. The music was his thing more than anyone's.'

Michael shrugged. 'Dan leads a mysterious life.'

'That's what I'm afraid of. Do you know what the IRA spokesman said?'

'They've got a spokesman?'

Kieran was pulling a piece of file paper from his pocket. 'I wrote it down. *Today we were unlucky, but remember we only have to be lucky once, you will have to be lucky always.*'

'Why were they unlucky?'

'How the hell do I know? There is no reason. That's why they call it luck.'

'But it doesn't make any sense. They killed people. They destroyed the hotel.'

'Are you deliberately trying to be dense?'

'I thought you said . . .'

'They didn't get Margaret Thatcher, that's all it means.'

'But they got two other people – you said two? And more missing . . . ?'

'Forget all that. The point is the words. I've heard them before. That's why I wrote them down. Dan was saying the same thing last week, almost exactly.'

'Saying what?'

'We only have to be lucky once. They have to be lucky all the time.'

'So?'

'What do you mean, so? Don't you get it?'

'They only have to kill her once, I get it – then she'll be dead.'

'Not the idea – the words. Dan used the same words.' Kieran made a visible effort to control himself. 'He'd just finished singing one of his interminable bloody songs about some Irish boy on his way to be hanged . . .'

'Sold out for English silver and martyred for the cause . . . I thought you liked all that stuff.'

'The music, yes.'

'And the politics.'

'All right, yes, the politics too. I want a united Ireland and British soldiers out of there, but not like this – murdering people in their sleep. This is who I've been living with, that's what I keep thinking – this is who I'm playing music and drinking with.'

'The first time I ever met Dan he was going on about Bobby Sands, winning the by-election in Fermanagh, God bless him, even as he starved himself to death in Long Kesh, and the hundred thousand who showed up for his funeral.'

'Yes, but this is different. This is a lot more than talk. Because he was here, wasn't he?'

'Who?' Michael looked around vaguely. 'What are you talking about?'

'Not in this room. I mean in Brighton. Dan was in Brighton.'

'How do you know?'

'Dan, or Dan's friends. Face it, Mike. He's one of *the boys*. He knew what they were thinking, what they were going to say. And if he knew what they were thinking, he knew what they were planning.'

'I don't believe it.'

'Don't, then, it doesn't make it any less true.' Kieran crossed the room from one window to the other and stared down into the garden. Somewhere below in the building a phone was ringing. 'Let's get out of here, for God's sake. I can't stay cooped up like this.' Pausing by the desk, he rested his palms against the sloping ceiling as though to push it away.

Michael ducked to retrieve a shoe from the under the bed and felt the blood pounding in his temples. 'I need a pee,' he said.

Kieran made for the door. 'All right.' He gave the door-frame a couple of slaps. 'I'll wait for you outside.'

Michael listened to him racketing downwards, taking the stairs in leaps. He looked around for Salema's bag, or anything else of hers. He wondered if he'd find her in the bathroom, but there was only her silver chain, dangling from the shelf above the basin. She must have taken it off to wash and forgotten it. He gathered it up and slipped it into his trouser pocket.

Abbott was standing at the foot of the stairs. 'That wasn't you just left, then, making all that noise.'

'No, that was my brother. Sorry.'

'He won't be staying long, I hope. As you know, we're really not set up for overnight guests.'

'No, he's not staying.'

'I caught your dusky mistress creeping out. Enchanting, of course. Nevertheless . . .'

'She won't be back either, I don't think.' As he said it, he realized it was true. Whatever delicate balance had existed in his dealings with Salema and Kieran, and with Salema herself, was irrevocably fractured.

'She walks in beauty like the night of cloudless climes and starry skies.'

'She just turned up. She's actually my brother's girl-friend.'

'Ah.' Abbott's eyes lit up. 'And you're a shoulder to cry on. And now *he's* here.'

'Yes, but not because of that.'

'Alarums and excursions!'

'He's waiting for me outside.' The front door was open but Kieran was out of sight.

'And that was your sister on the phone to say she can't come for the weekend after all. The plot thickens.'

'I didn't know till yesterday that she was even thinking about it.'

'You are naughty, Michael, even so. I don't like being taken advantage of. I can't have your entire family squatting in my attic.'

'Sorry. Did she give a reason?'

'The bomb, of course. Your mother has put her foot

down.' Frowning anxiously, Abbott touched Michael's arm. 'You do know about the bomb?'

In the street everything seemed grey and flat as though he was looking at the world through smog. He caught up with Kieran at the corner by the antiques shop. He was staring at a violin that was propped up on an oak dresser with a big price tag round its neck.

'Thinking of trading up?'

'Nah. Got nothing to trade with. I gave mine away.'

'You did what?'

'I gave it away.'

'Who to?'

'I don't know. Someone.'

'You must know. You don't just give a violin away to anyone.'

'I gave it to a busker, all right? I left the flat with it this morning. I was going to bring it with me. But there's this old man with no legs who sits in London Bridge Station.'

'Yes, I've seen him.'

'He plays this cracked old violin that looks as though he used it in the war to hit Germans over the head.' Kieran managed a feeble snort of laughter, but the pain didn't leave his face. 'Anyway, I gave it to him.'

'That's mad!'

'All right, so it's mad. But what difference does it make? I can't play it anyway. Not well enough to make it worthwhile. That's why I was going to bring it, to show you how bad it is. I've been getting worse for months. But this week it all fell apart. I can't remember now whether I'm supposed to play with vibrato or not, what angle to hold the violin, what the bow should feel like in my hand. Nothing feels natural anymore. My brain gets in the way. I tell my fingers to move and nothing happens. Otto's furious. He didn't raise his voice or anything. He just went white.'

'Otto's a dickhead.'

'Yes, Otto's a dickhead, but I can't play "Mary Had a Little Lamb" without getting in a tangle, so who's the bigger dickhead?'

'So give up the Irish music and start practising again.'

'It's not about practising. Fucking Christ, haven't you been listening?' Kieran pulled himself from the window and started walking.

Michael followed half a pace behind. They were heading downhill towards the sea.

'The more I practise the worse it gets. It's as though I'm on a tightrope and I've only just noticed. I never knew there was all this space underneath me, and now I can't *not* know. It's not even about music anymore. Who cares if I can play the violin or not? That's just a symptom.'

'Of what?'

'Of everything. I keep thinking, what's any of it for? I'd never stopped to ask, and now I can't stop asking. Music was just another series of tests, another set of exams to pass. Why did I apply to university? Do I want to be a doctor? I should because I can – is that it? All your life you've just done what you want, and I've done what everyone else wants.'

'That's absolutely not true – not the bit about me, anyway.'

'It is true.'

'How would you know? There were loads of things I would have liked to do, that I wish now I had done, that

I didn't do, probably, just because everyone else *did* want me to.'

'That doesn't make any sense.'

They'd reached the front. Kieran crossed the road as though the traffic had better keep out of his way. Michael followed more cautiously, feeling the weight of his limbs, the hangover pulsing behind his eyes. They stood side by side looking down towards the sea. The railing was damp from mist or overnight rain. A wave surged towards them, tumbled over onto the beach and pulled back, uncovering a glistening ribbon of shingle.

'I know it sounds pathetic,' Kieran said, 'and I know it's nothing anyone did to me, but you've no idea what it is to be buggered up by what everyone else calls success.'

Michael tried to get his head around this unlikely proposition. 'At least you get to keep the certificates.'

Kieran made a sound that was a single outward breath of laughter, and his mouth buckled into something like a smile.

They watched in silence while another wave spilt itself.

'Kier,' Michael said. 'About Salema . . .'

'What about her?'

'When you see her next, you should give her this.' He pulled the silver chain from his pocket.

Kieran looked at it. 'Where did you get it?'

'She was here last night. She left it in the bathroom.'

'Salema was here? With you?'

'She just turned up.'

Kieran took the chain and let it slither from one hand into the other. As its significance sunk in, the bafflement in his face gave way to anger. 'You know I've been in a state about her all week – you do realize that. I've hardly slept. And you've seen her and talked to her and you didn't think to tell me? Fuck!'

'I've hardly had a chance.'

'She came to complain about me, I suppose – how I've screwed up her life.'

'It wasn't that kind of conversation. It was . . .'

'What?'

'I don't know. Deeper than that.'

'About how *deeply* I've screwed up her life.'

'She didn't say anything about you, I don't think. Not really.'

'Oh, great! Absolutely fucking incredible!' Kieran made a few turns, as though he wanted to be elsewhere but couldn't decide which direction would get him there. Then he set off towards the town.

Michael hurried after him. 'She talked about her childhood. She talked about being ashamed.'

'It's not much of an achievement, if you really want to know – getting deep with Salema. Getting shallow with her is the hard part.'

'This was different.'

'Exactly. Being different is what she specializes in.'

Michael wanted to break through this brittle surface and make things right. 'Why don't we get some coffee? I need to clear my head.'

'I've got to get back to London.'

'Please, Kier.'

'I've got things to do. I've got to find somewhere to live.'

'What's wrong with Dan and Peggy's place?'

'I can't stay there now, can I?'

It scared Michael to see his brother in this mood. He thought about him giving his violin to the busker. 'Don't do anything impetuous, Kier – something stupid you'll regret later.'

'Good advice, Mike. You might have mentioned it eighteen years ago.'

Michael could think of nothing else to say. He matched Kieran's pace, striding just behind him, with the wind chasing him from the sea and the gulls circling. After a while it felt pointless. He slowed down, but Kieran kept walking. He stopped and watched until his brother became a blur, bobbing among the early-morning crowds.

FEBRUARY 2003 CHELTENHAM

They stand on the roof of the family property, in the lead-lined gulley between the parapet and the slates. There are solar panels of various kinds on the slope beside them and, bolted to the parapet walls, an array of miniature wind-generators. These are what Michael has come to see – following Kieran up the ladders and along the scaffolding.

'I wouldn't call them prototypes,' Kieran explains. 'It's about education rather than research. We know how to make them already. But at some point we'll probably have to build forests of the things, so it would be great if people could begin to feel enthusiastic about them.' Some of the generators are like propellers, with fibreglass blades. The more eccentric ones have been knocked together out of ceiling fans or bicycle wheels with plastic paddles twisted into shape among the spokes. One, with canvas sails stretched on a wooden frame, looks like a picture-book windmill.

There are other things to say while they have some time alone, now that Peggy is hearing all about Katherine's boyfriend problems, and Trinity has wandered off around the house, which she has decided is nicer on the whole than prison, for all its weirdness. There are dangerous topics to be broached. But for now it's enough to admire these crude machines, which are beginning to hum and creak as the air blows through them. The long view across the valley encourages silence. The church tower and the tiled roofs around it are suddenly pink in the light of the setting sun. The breeze animates the distant foliage so that the land rising towards the hill seems to shiver.

The roof is the last stage of Kieran's tour. The house has undergone a transformation since Michael saw it last. The rooms and passageways are bright with new purpose. The dining room is full of computers. In the drawing room, where Kieran and Salema used to practise and Mam served tea to nuns, the standard lamps, the bulging armchairs, the sideboards with their job-lot ornaments have disappeared. The walls are white. Shorn of their moth-eaten carpets, the boards breathe. The old pub piano, with its brass fittings and curlicues, is gone. The framed prints and religious icons have been replaced with posters and collages on climate change, alternative energy sources, public-transport systems. There are trestle tables and folding chairs. This is the intellectual heart of Kieran's environmental retreat centre.

Out through the French windows, where the grass grows thin around the beech trees, a colony of improvised structures has sprung up. One that gleams in rectangles of metallic white and silver has been constructed out of old fridges and washing machines. It has concave porthole windows and rubber-sealed doorways. Another uses waxed juice boxes laid like brickwork. There's a Parthenon of cardboard tubes from a carpet store, and walls of polystyrene blocks that bear the ghostly imprints of printers and television sets and DVD players, all of this under a roof tiled with the kind of moulded plastic envelopes in which ink cartridges and computer components are sold. Inside the translucent walls of this temple to packaging, sounds from outside are muffled.

There's an electronics workshop in the basement, and benches stocked with tools. The scullery has been converted into a domestic laboratory where Kieran's students make cleaning materials out of vinegar and baking soda and alcohol and different kinds of soap.

On the exterior walls, the guttering deviates in unexpected directions to fill water tubs and cisterns. The flush box in the downstairs toilet is fed with rainwater, the overflow piped away towards a series of kitchen sinks beside the vegetable garden.

Kieran has plans to disconnect the house from the mains sewage system. He grows lyrical on the biochemistry of sewage treatment. He envisages a series of reed beds and filtered ponds, if he can fit the whole thing along the lower edge of the garden where the brook runs. He'd begin ideally with a cesspit, but would settle for a septic tank – the effluent, odourless and sterile but still heavy with minerals, seeping into wetland streams of reed and rush and sedge, from which would spill water hospitable to frogs, and a fishpond teeming with carp and gudgeon ready for the pan. Hearing this, Trinity stalks off towards the compost boxes, promising in a loud voice never to eat fish in this house for the rest of her life.

Already Kieran has reduced the property's demands on the National Grid. In selected bedrooms, the lights flicker on and off according to the intensity of the sun or the strength of the wind.

Standing now beside the parapet wall, Michael studies

the nearest of the wind generators as its blades turn. Ten feet away, across the hip of the roof, Kieran is fiddling with one of the more sluggish models. A murmur of conversation drifts up from among the fruit trees. From somewhere else comes the sound of a clarinet. A run of notes bubbles up towards them, floating over the ridge tiles and around the chimney stacks.

'She's good, Kieran,' Michael says. 'When did she get so good? She used to puff and squeak.'

'Amazing, isn't it. And she hasn't played for months. She gave up Western music when she started calling herself Yasmin.'

'It's Mozart, isn't it?'

'Yes. The clarinet quintet. I try not to push it. She has to want to play, or what's the point.'

They listen for a minute. Then Michael asks, 'Do you ever miss it?'

'What?'

'The violin.'

'It was just something I could do. Like Latin. It was never going to be my life. You always reach a point when you have to decide – is this going to be a career or a hobby.'

'Or nothing?'

Kieran dismisses the quibble with a shrug. 'I've always had to put everything I've got into whatever I'm doing. There's a doctor in town who gives piano recitals in his spare time. He'll never be as good a pianist as he might have been and he's probably not as good a doctor as he ought to be.'

'But isn't that what they used to call being a well-rounded person?'

'I don't want to be well rounded.'

'No, you want to be spiky and abrasive.'

'Of course. Because that's the only way to get traction, the only way anything ever gets done.'

'And what about Trinity?'

'It'll be different for her. I hope everything's different for her. She's really not like me.' The moment the words have come out of his mouth, Kieran shifts awkwardly, as though aware of their unintended implications. He stares out across the valley.

Michael feels the weight of what has to be dragged to the surface. 'She's quite a lot like you, actually,' he says.

Kieran is watching him, anticipating an ambush.

'Trinity said something over the weekend . . .'

'What did she say?'

'Something that made me wonder if . . . things are OK with us.'

There's a new stiffness in Kieran's posture. 'Do *you* think things are OK?'

'We get stuck. We talk and it seems OK and then we get snagged on something. Don't you think that's true?'

'I've hardly seen you for fifteen years. It's hard to generalize.'

'Right there, for example, in what you just said . . .'

There's the thrumming and creaking of the wind-generators, and the voices in the garden and Trinity playing Mozart.

'It makes me wonder, Kier . . . Do you ever feel you'd like to talk about what happened when we were students?'

'Not particularly.'

'Why not?'

238

'Because it's a can of worms.'

'OK. Here's one thing. You probably don't want to talk about this . . .'

'So let's not.'

'But I do, so just shut up for a minute. Trinity said something in passing about the timing of her birth.' He sees Kieran's face harden but he presses on. 'According to her, you and Salema were arguing and you made some reference to Salema's eleven-month pregnancy.'

'When was this?'

'Before she was born, I assume.'

'Not that. The argument, the reference.'

'Is that important?'

Kieran scowls. 'Because it sounds as though I was making a joke, wouldn't you think?'

It makes Michael's chest feel tight with anxiety to push this conversation forward. But his brother is being obtuse and it helps to be irritated by this. 'Look, Kieran, this is a mathematical point with biological ramifications, and you were always better than me at both of those, but let's assume you were counting backwards from September 1985. Eleven months would get you to October, which must have been about the time I walked in on you two in Salema's practice room.'

'The weekend before they blew up the Grand Hotel.'

'Right. So I have to assume you've thought the rest of it through in terms of dates and opportunities, and ruled out, from your own point of view, December. Also November, I suppose, and maybe January. And you find yourself questioning your role in all this. Am I right, or did Trinity make up this eleven-month thing out of her own head?'

'Don't be a smartarse.'

'I'll stop being a smartarse when you stop being a dick-head.'

'It's none of your fucking business.'

'It is, in the most literal sense, my fucking business if there's some story, some imagined scenario floating around that Trinity's got hold of that somehow involves me.'

There's a murderous look on Kieran's face. 'Is that what she said?'

'Not exactly. And I realize I might have got the wrong end of the stick. But I want you to know that if there's a mystery here, I can shed absolutely no light on it.'

'Is that what you want to tell me – that you've got nothing to tell me?'

'Exactly. Nothing. Absolutely.'

'And that's supposed to . . . what? – make me feel better?'

'I certainly hope so.'

Kieran has turned away and stands now reaching out towards the bicycle wheel, letting the plastic blades in their slow revolutions flip, flip, flip against his palm. Michael waits, uncertain what to say. When he makes a noise as though to begin, Kieran cuts him off. 'Didn't it occur to you . . . if you'd stopped to think for a minute . . . did it never occur to you that if it had to be somebody, I might have preferred it to be you?' When he turns his eyes are wet with tears.

Michael feels weightless. The wind has blown into him, filling him up, lifting him off the roof – or the house has disappeared from under his feet. It's just the two of them and the gaping sky.

'No,' he says. He speaks carefully, repeating Kieran's phrase. 'No, that had not occurred to me.'

After a moment Kieran looks back at the view. 'Do you remember,' he says, 'when we were kids, I used to walk in my sleep, and you'd steer me back to bed. Sometimes I wouldn't wake up and you'd tell me in the morning – you'd found me on the landing, or trying to open the wardrobe.'

Michael smiles, thinking about it. 'Yes.'

'You were good at that – at being my older brother.'

'Seven minutes older.'

'Even so.'

The sun has lost its lower edge in cloud. The colour seeps out above the hill.

Kieran lets out a sigh. 'I need a drink.'

'You're her dad, Kier – you know that. She knows it too.'

He's thinking about the way she clung to Kieran earlier when they arrived. Waking on the back seat as the engine stopped, she slipped out of Peggy's car, ran to the steps of the house where Kieran stood, and settled against him, holding tight. This was home for her, after all. And Kieran had no need to divide his attention, because Katherine was there to shed tears over Michael, and to ask Peggy what she'd been up to all these years, and to tell them both that she was finished with her bastard boyfriend and was feeling good about herself for the first time in longer than she could remember. And so it was a while before Trinity had to loosen her grip enough for Kieran to lead them all through the house into the kitchen, where Jack Cartwright greeted Michael with a bright smile of recognition, saying, 'Ah! The wanderer returns,' while he searched his mind for the elusive name.

The sun is setting as they make their way down through the scaffolding. It's not so cold once they're out of the wind. As they approach the ground they see the source of the music – an igloo made entirely of plastic milk bottles, like a clump of frogspawn, and visible through the domed roof, in the light from a torch, the smudged shape of the clarinettist sitting upright on her heels.

'You've found a new home, then,' Michael says.

The music stops. 'Hi, Uncle Mike.'

'Good to see you're getting used to small spaces. You'll find that invaluable in your criminal career.'

'Ha, ha, not very funny.' Trinity lies on her stomach to poke her head out through the doorway. 'Hi, Dad.'

'Hi, Trin.'

'Would you have missed me, Dad, if they'd kept me locked up forever?'

'I'd have visited you without fail at least once a year.'

'And I'd have written you letters about the shocking inefficiency of the prison heating system.'

Peggy comes round the corner of the house with a glass in her hand. 'We're cooking dinner and getting drunk. Not necessarily in that order.'

'Good for you,' Michael says.

'Did you hear this, Michael, about your sister? She was having an extension built, and she came home from work to find her boyfriend having sex with the plumber.'

Kieran gives a sideways nod towards his daughter, lying in the mouth of the igloo. 'I wonder if that story's for general release.'

'I'm not shocked, Dad. Why would I be shocked?'

'Of course not,' Michael says. 'Now you've spent a night in the cells.'

Trinity wriggles out onto the grass with her clarinet in her hand. 'Two nights, practically.' She's changed into cotton dungarees and is wearing a scarf tied like a hair band, the way her mother used to.

'Now you've spent two nights in the cells you know everything there is to know about life.'

She rises effortlessly from the ground. 'Well, I know there are women plumbers, Uncle Mike. I didn't have to be arrested to know that.'

'Is that a joke?'

She has walked off towards the darkness under the beech trees, adjusting her reed.

Michael turns to Kieran. 'Was she making a joke?'

Peggy is laughing. 'She's reverting. It's what people seem to do when they go home. I've just left Katherine giggling in the kitchen. She was stabbing a melon and saying, "So much for the Prince of Light." '

'The boyfriend,' Kieran explains to Michael. 'She's always called him the Prince of Light, right from the start. At some point there must have been a transition from admiration to irony, but I missed it.'

Peggy is taking a turn around the milk-bottle igloo, which is still glowing in the dusk, and the polystyrene temple. 'So this is your vision of the future, Kieran.'

'It's my vision of the present.'

'But the wheels of commerce would grind to a halt if everyone lived like this.'

'The wheels are coming off anyway.'

243

'And you think this is what we'll be reduced to – living under plastic?'

'If we're lucky. Meanwhile, it's not a bad idea to look at what we're chucking into landfill sites.'

'And you make a living at this?'

'Business is booming. Everyone wants to save the planet, haven't you noticed?'

'Not too fast, I hope, or you'll be out of a job.'

Kieran laughs. 'Fat chance.'

'Well . . .' Peggy tilts her glass towards him. 'We should probably think about eating, before Katherine keels over.'

'Yes, right. I'll round up Trin.' Kieran sets off towards the trees, following the sound of the clarinet.

Peggy lifts her glass to Michael's mouth. 'Take a sip,' she says, quietly, just for him to hear.

He tastes the drink. 'A lot of gin and not much tonic.'

'Your sister's post-break-up recipe. You talked to Kieran, then.'

'Yes. How does he seem to you?'

She glances towards the trees. 'On edge, I'd say. How did he react?'

'Surprisingly well, actually. I'll tell you later.'

'Shall I mix you one of these?'

'One of us should be sober.'

'Unless we stay, and drive back in the morning.'

'Can you be late for work?'

'I'm the boss. I can do anything I like.'

He takes her hand and she gives a low gurgle of laughter as he draws her onto the veranda by the French windows where the shadows are deepest. 'So let's stay somewhere else,' he says.

'Where?'

'Anywhere. Somewhere here in town if you like. Just not this house.'

The tiled floor has been cleared and swept. Overhead there are neat patches of sky where the broken panes have been removed but not yet replaced. The wisteria twists so thickly around the wrought-iron columns that it seems to be the only support the canopy needs.

She rests her head against his, and he breathes in the scent of her skin, and she says, 'OK,' so quietly that it's not so much the sound he responds to as the movement of air and the feel of her mouth forming the word. Her arms reach round under his jacket. 'You've been sort of on edge yourself.'

'Yes.'

'But better now?'

'Much better.' He thinks of Irena Lipska and of how important she seemed. And he sees that she was a kind of figment, a self-generated obstacle to trip him up in his running.

By the kitchen door they come across Jack Cartwright looking up at the wall. 'Horrible job!' He does a little dance of distress, wincing and shaking his head from side to side.

Kieran has stopped to ask what's bothering him.

'Look. It's not right.' Jack points up at a piece of improvised guttering – a plastic downpipe running at an angle into a cast-iron hopper head.

'Don't worry about it, Dad, we can talk about it in the morning.'

'But it needs sorting out.'

'First we have to eat.'

'Ah, yes, she's making something lovely for dinner.'

'Kath's a good cook. And Peggy's been helping. You remember Peggy O'Connor? And here's Michael.'

Jack's face lights up as Michael comes towards him. 'Ah! The wanderer!' He smiles with delight. 'She was wondering where you'd got to.'

'Who was wondering, Dad?' Michael asks.

'Your mother.'

Later, when Jack has gone to bed and Trinity has disappeared to phone her friends, Michael, Kieran, Katherine and Peggy sit at the kitchen table, picking at cheese and fruit. To save electricity, or because Katherine likes it, they have eaten by candlelight. There are a couple of empty wine bottles on the table. The conversation has sunk to inebriated banter, when Katherine wrinkles her nose and asks her brothers what they were arguing about on the roof. Kieran glances at Michael, stares into his wine glass and announces that he doesn't know who Trinity's father is. The word *father* comes out with a snort of laughter, as the tension of holding this thought is released, or in recognition of the absurdity of his ignorance.

Only Katherine is surprised. 'Since when?'

'Since forever, more or less.'

'And does Trinity know?'

Kieran looks at Michael again before answering. 'Mike tells me she's beginning to ask questions.'

Katherine's first instinct is to offer comfort, putting an arm round his neck and resting her head on his shoulder. Then other things begin to occur to her. 'You've discussed this with Salema, I suppose.'

Kieran drains his glass. 'According to Salema it was a virgin birth.'

Michael, who has risen from the table to open another bottle, pauses with the corkscrew in his hand.

'And, more to the point,' Kieran says, 'a virginal conception.'

Katherine looks puzzled. 'Isn't that the same thing?'

'Actually not.'

'It's like an *immaculate* conception, then, is it?'

'No, that's a whole other thing. How can you have forgotten, Kath? The nuns must have taught you all this.'

'The nuns in Kilross taught us nothing,' Peggy says. 'They were big on sacred mysteries. And every other kind. Where anyone's baby might have come from wasn't on the syllabus. How about you, Michael?'

'I had Father Kenton. He had his own priorities. I remember one time he told us all about intra-uterine baptism.' Michael pulls the cork out of the bottle and begins filling the glasses.

'Look, it's not that complicated!' There's a note of hysterical levity in Kieran's outrage that resonates around the table. 'Man rogers woman in the normal way. Are you with me so far?'

'I should bloody well hope so,' Peggy says.

'So then . . . child conceived, but by some miraculous intervention not stained with original sin. You haven't forgotten what original sin is, I hope, Kath?'

'An innate tendency to fuck things up?'

'Exactly. Which this child hasn't got, having been *immaculately conceived* so that she'll be a pure vessel for the purposes of becoming, for example, the mother of God.'

Michael raises a hand. 'Are there any other examples?'

'Not that I know of. Now – completely different case . . . Virgin impregnated by Holy Spirit. As well as being divine, the resulting child has been *virginally* conceived, no corporeal rogering having taken place. Got it?'

There are murmurs of assent.

'And here's the amazing bit . . .'

'The other bits aren't amazing?' Peggy asks.

'Not half as amazing as this bit. Woman gives birth and yet remains *virgo intacta*. Hence virgin birth. Divine infant enters the world like sunlight pouring through a window.'

'Yes,' Peggy says, 'that is amazing.'

'And fucking complicated, as it turns out.'

There's a silence as the others take this in, their brows furrowing in the candlelight.

Peggy is first to attempt a question. 'You mean . . . ?'

'Salema and I have always had an intense spiritual bond.'

'You have?'

Kieran looks up, completely serious now. 'Actually, in so far as I know what a spiritual bond might be, I think we have, yes, and we've always had one thing in common – completely unique to us – which is that we're Trinity's parents. It's hard to explain how important that is.' He looks down again into his wine glass, searching for the right words. 'Taking care of Trin is the one really significant thing I've done, ever.'

Katherine nestles against him, making supportive noises.

'It was strange,' Peggy says after a while, 'seeing Salema yesterday. It brought back a lot of things I thought I'd forgotten. I remember one time she drifted into the shop. It can't have been long after you'd moved out of the flat, Kieran. She looked dazed and had dead leaves in her hair, like she'd been sleeping in a park. I assumed it was you she was looking for. But it was Fergal.'

'Fergal? What did she want with Fergal?'

'Sure, I don't know. Father Fergal, she called him, as she always did. She said she had something to confess. I told her she was out of luck, because he'd gone to Spain. She drifted out again. And that was the last I saw of her until your wedding.' She sips her wine. 'Remember the university chapel, Kieran, and the gang of us bursting out into the hall afterwards and down the steps as though we'd been let out from school.'

'Yes, and lunch in that spaghetti place.'

'Where we all made speeches just like a proper grown-up wedding.'

Katherine opens an eye. 'If Salema confessed to Fergal, then Fergal might know who Trinity's father is.'

'Except you'd never get it out of him,' Michael says. 'He'd never break the seal of the confessional.'

For a while nobody speaks. They drink. The candles flicker. Katherine begins to snore gently. Under the table, Peggy moves her hand on Michael's leg. It's time to go.

† The Church of St Ursula and the Virgin Martyrs

Saturday 22 February 2003

We had had a week of storms, high seas that
threatened to inundate the houses near the harbour.
The wind had howled through the night, making the
shutters rattle, and my sleep had been fitful at best.
Feeling restless, I had been up that morning and,
against Consuelo's advice, had struggled out to walk
through the town, but the blustery wind and the cold
had driven me indoors, and then I had felt feverish
again and had gone to bed.

It was midday. The sky had remained dark but
the sun shone with a strange light. Consuelo had gone
to her work at the library, leaving me in the care of
her elderly neighbour. I was in bed, dozing with my
breviary fallen from my hand, when the old woman
knocked on my door and told me that a person had
come who said she was my cousin.

I must explain something to you, Michael, that I'm
afraid will shock you. My feelings for Peggy were in
those years more complicated than anyone knew, with
the exception of my confessor. During that summer
in Kilross when I met you for the first time, I began to
experience feelings for Peggy that I knew to be wrong.
I was studying for the priesthood. We were cousins.

But I was in love with her. I wrestled with physical desire and all its attendant humiliations. At night, the knowledge that she was asleep in the room next to mine often kept me awake. I wish I could say that I always resisted the temptation, during that hot summer, to entertain sinful fantasies, and worse.

My first foolish thought, when the old woman said that Peggy had come to see me, was that she had heard that I was still sick and wanted to take care of me. Then, more rationally, I guessed she must be in serious trouble herself to have travelled all the way from London. My momentary hope – I blush to admit to you, Michael – was that she had nurtured a passion for me as intense as mine for her and was here to declare herself at last. Since ordination I had struggled to put all such thoughts from my mind, and had succeeded in remaining celibate in the most complete sense. It distressed me that I could give way so easily to such a deluded wish.

When the door opened it was not Peggy at all, but a young woman dressed in black, and veiled with a mantilla. I judged her to be young, though I could not see her face. But when she crossed the room towards me she walked with a shuffling gait, favouring one leg. Reaching the foot of the bed she fell to her knees and began the familiar words of the sacrament of confession – Father, forgive me for I have sinned. By this time I had thrown the quilt aside, and was sitting up with my legs over the side of the bed. I reached a hand towards her, meaning to encourage her to stand up. I had recognized her voice by now, of course.

She had a bottle of olive oil – a local brand I
recognized from Consuelo's kitchen. Before I could
forestall her, before I had guessed what she had in
mind, she was pouring oil from the bottle onto my
feet, and telling me that she had come like Mary
Magdalene as a penitent sinner. Her hand was dark
against my foot as she spread the oil over my instep
and toward my toes. I stood and, stumbling from her
grasp, hurried away across the room, leaving a smear
of oil on the floorboards.

Lifting the mantilla from her face, she pleaded
with me not to reject her entirely. She may have been
crying, because her face was wet, but I don't think
so because her hair was wet also from the rain and
dripped water onto the floor where she knelt. She said
she had claimed to be my cousin for fear of being
turned away. There were seven demons, she said, that
must be cast out of her. I asked what demons they
were and she began listing her sins, as she imagined
them – pride in her musicianship, envy of you,
Michael, for your ease in the world, the lust that
had risen up between herself and Kieran threatening
their immortal souls, anger at her stepfather for being
so much less than she wanted him to be. Sloth she
mentioned also – her sloth in neglecting the growing
disorder of her life. I don't remember that she had
anything to say about gluttony or avarice. Perhaps
I interrupted her. I know I wanted her to stop. But
avarice and gluttony were unlikely sins for Salema,
anyhow, and her inventiveness in self-condemnation,
considerable though it was, would have been

challenged, I suspect, by the attempt to claim those
sins as her own. I remembered her from our few
earlier encounters as an unworldly child, not given
much to eating. And she was now bone-thin. Her
dress, which was torn and stained, hung from her.
And there was an odour that she had brought with
her into the room as though she had gone unwashed
for days.

'Let me find you some food,' I said. Or perhaps
I asked her first to get up off her knees. She looked
worn out. Perhaps I said something else altogether –
I can't remember. Her appearance was so unexpected
and her behaviour so outlandish that I would have
thought her a product of my delirium if I was not so
cold in the draught from the open door with my feet
naked on the oak boards and nothing on me but my
pyjamas.

When I had induced her to sit, she said that
Peggy had told her where I could be found, and that
hearing that my aunt's town was so close to Santiago
de Compostela she had taken it as a sign. She had
read of people walking the pilgrim's path to Santiago.
And so she had come on foot in search of absolution.
I asked her had she walked in those flimsy shoes, and
she looked at me, I remember, uncomprehendingly,
and I wondered if she had brought anything with her
at all other than the clothes she wore. There was a
canvas bag she had dropped in the doorway, but no
sign that she had equipped herself with hiking boots
or warm clothing. She pulled her shoes off and I saw
they were shredded from the rough path, and the

socks underneath them were all holes, and I saw the
cause of her limping.

I asked her where she had been sleeping, how
she had managed for food. She told me she had spent
time in a convent a few days back along the road.

I found myself sitting beside her on the bed.
She had moved and I had moved and there it was.
The door was closed, so I suppose I must have closed
it. And I had taken a blanket from the bed and put it
around her shoulders. She took my hand and said I
must bless her. 'Of course,' I said. 'But what if I am
damned already,' she asked me, 'and my father is
saved, having told his story first?' The question
revealed, I remember, a childish notion of judgement
in its suggestion that the dead might tell tales against
each other. 'God would know,' I said, 'God has always
known what is in your heart.' And I reminded her
that we are assured of Heavenly grace if we confess
our sins freely with a firm purpose of amendment.
Her eyes moved disconcertingly all this time as
though we were not alone in the room and the words
we spoke were only part of what she heard.

'But there's a deeper sin,' she said, 'a sin I took
from my father.'

'Of course,' I said, 'the sin we are all born with,
since Adam fell, since our universal mother plucked
the fruit of the tree of knowledge.'

She had my right hand still in hers and moved it
now into her lap, gripping it with surprising strength.
When she pulled at her dress I thought at first she
was in pain or meant to scratch herself, but knew

otherwise when she lifted the hem and placed my hand between her legs. 'Here,' she said, 'you must bless me here and take away my sin.'

What overcame me that I was unable to stop her even then? Surely to God, though I was weakened in my body by my illness, and in my mind also, I could still have held her off, if my will had not failed me.

I need not describe what followed.

If Salema had found me dressed in my soutane with its thirty-three buttons, one for each year of our Blessed Saviour's life, if I had that morning put my belt around my waist, praying, as I had been taught to pray – Bind me, O Lord, with the cincture of purity and extinguish within me unwanted passions so that I may experience the virtue of continence and chastity – these encumbrances would surely have saved us. Saved me, I should say, for the greater sin was mine. What was for her a venial slip, excused further by her confusion and distress, was and remains a mortal stain on my soul.

As it was, it was over almost before I knew it had begun. At the moment of crisis, it came to me that this was God's will. It was as though the Holy Spirit whispered a blessing on me and enfolded me in His wings. I know of course that I was mistaken absolutely and I report it now not to excuse myself but to show how cunning are the wiles of the devil, because it was surely the devil who urged me on. Ever since Peggy had allowed her unborn child to be killed in her womb I had blamed myself for not fighting more fiercely for its life. Not a day passed when I did not

pray for the poor mite. And now – this was my
momentary thought – I would be a channel of divine
creation, allowing, if it were God's will, another child
to fill the place of Peggy's in the world. And then, too
late, I came to my senses, and Salema was lying across
me with her thumb in her mouth. I was struck with
the incongruity of it. She had been an instrument of
corruption and now looked suddenly like a child.

I lifted her from me onto the bed and let her sleep.
I dressed quickly and walked to the harbour. I tried to
pray but felt utterly cut off from the presence of God.
Below me the sea reared up and smashed itself against
the harbour walls and I could see no purpose in it but
chaos only and destruction.

When I returned to the house and opened the
door to my bedroom, Salema was awake. She had
woken that instant, I think, disturbed by the creaking
of the staircase or by the church bell which was
striking the hour. It was three o'clock and I thought of
St Peter denying Jesus as the cock crew. She stood up
from the bed and yawned, covering her mouth with
the back of her hand. Such politeness, I thought, in the
midst of such degradation. She looked at me as though
it took her a moment to bring me into focus. Then she
smiled. 'Thank you, Father,' she said, 'for letting me
rest.' It was as though she had taken all her agitation,
all her guilt and shame, and handed them to me. She
picked up her bag in the doorway.

I asked her would she be all right. Though I felt
responsible for her safety, I wanted her gone. She told
me she would return to the convent, that there was a

bus, and she searched in her bag and pulled out a timetable. The sight of it in her hand, and her so untroubled, made me angry. She had thrown my life into utter disorder, but she had a timetable. It was useful to me, this anger, because it allowed me to shut the door on her.

That was early December. I didn't hear of her again until January when I was back in London. Kieran came and told me that he and Salema were engaged and would I marry them. I knew at once that this would be impossible. Naturally he was surprised at my unwillingness. I urged him to wait. 'Why hurry,' I asked him, 'young as you both are and you with years of college ahead of you?' Kieran said he had already given up medical school and was looking for work. And besides, Salema was pregnant. He thought it was rotten luck, he told me, given that they had been together only once. I realized that the child could as easily be mine as his. He had come to me as a priest, had laid himself open to me. Dear God, I should have torn the collar from my shirt and gone on my knees before him. But I said nothing.

I heard later from Peggy that the wedding went ahead, that you were there as best man, and your sisters, but not your parents because your mother was too angry. When the child was born, I knew from the date that it must be mine. Not long after, Kieran and Salema moved out of London, Peggy lost touch with them and I heard nothing more. I felt like someone who thoughtlessly pulls a thread and watches the whole garment come unravelled.

I have told you almost everything. I read in this
morning's paper that our Prime Minister has been
urged by the Holy Father to pause and reconsider
and his reply is that only Saddam Hussein can stop
this war. And so our elected leaders wash their
hands and abdicate the power we have entrusted to
them. They favour a spring invasion, in spite of the
summer heat. This morning I confirmed my travel
arrangements. I will be flying first to Madrid and from
there to Lebanon. A bus will take me from Lebanon
to Baghdad. I have no idea what will become of me
when the bombs begin to drop. I doubt that my
presence there, and the presence of others like me,
will sway minds made up on other grounds. But
we will at least assert the equal value of every life.
If Iraqi lives are cheap then let mine be also. And
for as long as I am spared, there will be work to do
among the wreckage. I haven't your skills, Michael,
or your father's skills, but I can carry stones.

Do I hope, by doing this, to win redemption in
spite of everything? Have I made a selfish calculation?
I have wrestled with this question. I have kept up a
lie for eighteen years, but that is nothing compared to
the cunning twists of the human heart. Only God can
see through the layers of deception and self-deception
to the very bottom.

Certainly I hope to make amends. But this is not
martyrdom I am courting. I have not been picked out
for persecution because of my virtue. Though I wear
the vestments of a priest, and I hear confessions, and
I am entrusted with the mystery of the Blessed

Sacrament, I am not therefore better, but worse than my fellow men, who lead decent lives without the trappings of a higher calling. If I die, my death will be ordinary – crushed under falling concrete, bleeding from shrapnel, or struck like my father by stray fire from a machine gun.

I have one comfort, that there is a child living in the world, a joy to her parents. I have her name now from Peggy. In wishing my sin undone I cannot wish anything for Trinity but life in abundance.

God bless you, Michael. Know that I felt always a special affection for you, a love indeed that I hope will register as credit when I am called to render my account. Forgive me for being so much less than I set myself up to be, and for burdening you at last with this knowledge, which you must do with as you think best.

Your loving friend,
Fergal

MARCH 2003 KILROSS

The Cartwright children are gathered in the churchyard for the inurnment of their mother's ashes. They stand by their grandparents' grave near the church wall. Some of the older parishioners have stayed after Mass to show their respects to Moira Doyle, whose parents used to make their suits and dresses, and who left for England forty-five years ago. It's a cold blustery morning and the dampness blows against the mourners in soft gusts of rain. Away down the slope towards the parish hall, the dark shapes of the gravestones recede into mist.

Of his older siblings Michael has vivid memories, discrete moments of illumination which seem to speak directly from their pre-conscious selves to his. He has shared with them the unguarded intimacy of childhood. But he meets them now as sympathetic strangers.

Christopher, an architect, has just developed a fresh interest in churches having been commissioned to design one. He stands at the graveside between his teenage daughters, who have been fighting. Eileen, who teaches German, has her latest husband in tow and an accumulation of children. Matt, who struggles as a freelance journalist, is wearing a green tie with shamrocks on it, the only one he could buy in Kilross on a Sunday morning. Emily, for some reason, is in a pink hat. She's come with her partner, Binh, a Vietnamese choreographer. Binh's English is limited. Emily is learning Vietnamese. They speak meanwhile, when speech is necessary, in halting French. They seem perfectly suited. Katherine has taken charge of Jack, who looks obediently solemn. Trinity, subdued by the sadness of the event, huddles close to her father.

Michael is sad too, though his sadness competes with other feelings. Peggy, who knows all this without having to ask, squeezes his arm and touches his head with hers. The sadness is for his mother and for the parts of his life about which there is no longer anything to be done.

The priest, having finished the scripted part of the service, has begun the Litany of the Virgin – 'Holy Mary, mother of God' – and the Cartwright children join in the responses, though there isn't a practising Catholic among them – 'Virgin of virgins' – *pray for us* – 'Mother of Christ' – *pray for us* – 'Mother of divine grace' – *pray for us* –

Michael misses her not so much for what she was in his life as for the possibility of what she might have been. He regrets the conversations they didn't have – about his childhood, about her growing up in this place, and her experience of England as a stranger which he would have understood. His vision blurs and he feels as though he might topple forward. Tightening her hold on his arm, Peggy raises her mouth to his ear to ask if he's OK. He nods and reaches for her hand.

'Virgin most faithful' – *pray for us* – 'Mirror of justice' – *pray for us* – 'Seat of wisdom' – *pray for us* – 'Cause of our joy' –

He thinks about the unexpected turn things have taken

since he landed in London. With the travel website launched, he has been asked to take over as managing editor of the Rootless enterprise. There are plans for a book of photographs. He has signed a one-year lease on his flat. He has mastered all the routes by bus and tube to Pimlico where Peggy lives. After years on the move, he brims with excitement at the knowledge that such a life is available to him.

'Mystical rose' – *pray for us* – 'Tower of ivory' – *pray for us* –

The British and American leaders are meeting in the Azores, while their armies gather. In a televised interview, the Vice-President has asserted that the troops will be greeted as liberators, his mouth twisting in that odd lop-sided smile.

'Health of the sick' – *pray for us* – 'Refuge of sinners' – *pray for us* – 'Comforter of the afflicted' –

And any day now Michael will open Fergal's letter, which came last week with a cryptic note telling him to read it only in the event of war. The day it arrived, Peggy took him to Fergal's parish, where the housekeeper told them that Father Noonan was on retreat in Spain. Fearing for his old friend's health, Michael has written to him, care of his Aunt Consuelo, and waits for a reply. It seems likely that war will arrive sooner. Either way, he expects bad news.

The mist has evaporated. The sun has broken through the clouds. Jack Cartwright is patting Katherine's arm absentmindedly as though he isn't sure why she has begun to sob. Eileen too is weeping, and Trinity with Kieran's arm around her. Michael feels Peggy's hand tightening in his, for her own comfort now. A lump rises in his throat at these ritual words, planted too deeply in his mind ever to be fully rooted out.

The priest gives the blessing and the gathering begins to break up with murmurs of conversation and scattered bursts of laughter as the tension eases.

Michael and Peggy will join the rest of the family for an hour or two, but plan to spend the afternoon alone. Peggy has promised to show him Kilross as she knew it – the corner where the convent school wall was easy to climb and hidden by trees, the secret places along the riverbank, the shop where cigarettes could be bought one at a time from an open packet behind the counter. And they'll wander towards the cattle market, where the smell of livestock will linger in the empty pens, and out along the lane that was once the high road to Cork, and they'll talk about journeys taken and journeys still to come.

picador.com

blog
videos
interviews
extracts